DARK REBEL'S MYSTERY

THE CHILDREN OF THE GODS
BOOK NINETY-TWO

I. T. LUCAS

Dark Rebel's Mystery is a work of fiction! Names, characters, places, and incidents are products of the author's imagination or are used fictitiously and are not to be construed as real. Any similarity to actual persons, organizations, and/or events is purely coincidental.

Copyright © 2025 by I. T. Lucas

All rights reserved.

No part of this book may be reproduced in any form or by any electronic or mechanical means, including information storage and retrieval systems, without written permission from the author, except for the use of brief quotations in a book review.

Published by Evening Star Press, LLC.

EveningStarPress.com

ISBN: 978-1-962067-66-9

1

KYRA

Kyra lay flat on her stomach, peering through night-vision binoculars at the compound below. Even without the military-grade equipment, her enhanced vision would have given her a clear view of the guards patrolling the perimeter, but she'd learned to hide her extraordinary abilities, including keeping the truth from her closest friends and allies.

Kurds were highly superstitious, and the most rational and educated among them had no problem believing in evil spirits, or Jinns as they were called in these parts. If they realized how strong she really was or how good her night vision was, they might start fearing her. Already, Kyra had earned the reputation of being invisible to the Malak al-Maut based on how many times she'd narrowly escaped death.

"Six guards on rotation," she whispered. "Two at

the main gate, two patrolling the eastern wall, and two more on the western side."

Soran, her second-in-command, shifted silently beside her. "The intel was good then. Matches what our source said."

She nodded, studying the way the guards moved. These weren't the usual poorly disciplined conscripts that her team typically encountered. Something about how they patrolled the ground, alert and silent, tugged at her memory, but like most things from her past, the thought slipped away before she could grasp it.

They must have important prisoners in there for an elite unit to be guarding the place, and none of the people she'd come to rescue qualified as such.

Who else was being held in this facility?

Or maybe she had it all wrong, and the special unit wasn't there to guard prisoners but a high-up commander from the Islamic Revolutionary Guard.

Funny how the oppressors called themselves revolutionaries. The inversion of truth was not only ironic but also infuriating.

The amber pendant that was hidden beneath her shirt pulsed, warm and insistent, pointing her in the direction of the eastern wing of the compound. She'd found it years ago, or perhaps it had found her, and she often wondered if its guiding power came from the stone itself or from something inside her that the stone merely amplified.

It was just one more mystery in a life full of them.

"The prisoners are being held in the eastern building," she said without explaining how she knew that. Her team had learned to trust her intuition and not ask too many questions. "We'll need to create a diversion on the other side."

Soran touched her arm, a gesture that would have earned anyone else a swift takedown, but he'd fought beside her for over fifteen years and earned the right to such familiarity.

"The usual?" he asked.

She shook her head. "No explosives this time. Too many civilians in the surrounding buildings. We need to do this clean and quiet."

Soran's lips formed a tight line, but he nodded.

Explosives would have made things much easier and faster, but they were fighting to free the people from oppression, not deliver them faster to their Maker. Still, she would be risking her team by sending them to potentially interact with an elite fighting force without providing proper distraction.

Behind them, the rest of her twelve-person team waited for instructions. They were all hardened and loyal fighters. They'd followed her on countless missions like this one, freeing political prisoners, rescuing women from honor killings, and striking back against those who thought they could break their people's spirit.

She shifted to face them. "Hamid, Zara—you're on diversion duty, as we discussed. Simulate a perimeter breach on the western wall and try to make it look amateurish; I want them to think that it's just some local teens causing mischief. Soran will lead teams two and three through the eastern approach."

Out of habit, her fingers moved along with her words in the hand signals they had developed over the many years of working together, showing each team their exact route and timing.

"What about you?" Zara asked, though she likely knew the answer.

"I'm going over the roof." Kyra had already spotted her route—a drainage pipe that looked sturdy enough to support her weight, though anyone else would have probably considered it too risky.

Soran frowned. "Alone?"

"I'm stealthier on my own."

It was true. Kyra could easily scale walls and leap between buildings while others struggled to keep up. Her body simply did things that should not have been possible, and she'd learned to hide it as best she could.

She checked her watch. "Thirty minutes until shift change. That's our window. Get into position and wait for my signal."

As her team moved out silently, she watched until they disappeared into the shadows before turning back to study the compound. The pendant's warmth had settled into a steady pulse, confirming they were in the right place. Somewhere in that building were people who needed their help.

Her hand went to the scarf covering her hair—black, to blend with the shadows. She never went anywhere without her head covered, but it wasn't because of religious conviction. She didn't want her face to be seen and remembered, and when on a mission, she covered her mouth and nose with it, leaving only her eyes exposed. The fewer people who knew what she looked like, the better.

Kyra waited until Hamid and Zara were in position before moving down the ridge. The drainpipe was precisely where she needed it to be, and her enhanced vision picked out every handhold on her planned route. As always, her body seemed to know exactly what to do, moving with a fluid grace and power that felt as natural as breathing.

She shouldn't be that strong or that agile. Not even the youngest and fittest men in her team could match the kinds of feats that she found easy.

That was another odd thing about her. She just didn't age. In the past twenty years, not a single wrinkle had appeared on her face, and despite her long days in the sun and the hard life she was leading, her skin was just as smooth and as taut today as it had been in her youth.

The only possible explanation was that she'd been experimented on in that asylum she'd escaped from nearly two and a half decades ago, and she'd been changed into something that wasn't quite human.

Kyra shook her head. Now wasn't the time to ponder questions for which there were no answers, at least none that were available to her.

The first sign of the disturbance her people had caused was subtle—just enough movement at the western wall to draw attention away from where the rest of the team was about to infiltrate.

Two of the guards immediately moved to investigate while the others maintained their positions. Professional, disciplined, and familiar, but very surprising to find in these parts. An outpost in the middle of nowhere didn't justify elite forces.

She pushed the thought aside and began her ascent. The pipe held her weight easily as she climbed, her movements quick and silent.

Hamid and Zara escalated their diversion—voices arguing, the sound of a bottle breaking, enough to demand a response but not enough to trigger a full alert.

The roof was empty, just as their surveillance had suggested.

Kyra moved across it in a low crouch, using the ventilation units for cover. Her pendant grew warmer as she approached the eastern side of the building. The prisoners were close, she could almost feel them, their fear and hope mixing with her anticipation of the fight to come. Through her earpiece, she heard Soran's team reporting that they were in position.

Reaching the edge of the roof, she peered down. There were two guards below, their attention divided between keeping their eyes on their patrol route and the disturbance on the other side.

She could disable them both before they raised an alarm.

Her hands closed around the hilts of the two combat daggers sheathed at her waist, and as she pulled them out, she appreciated their solid weight and how good they felt in her palms.

Did she need to kill these men, though?

After her many years in the resistance, she should be inured to death and killing, and she was well aware that her sympathies might be misplaced, but she still couldn't bring herself to kill when she could achieve her objectives without ending lives.

She could just as easily incapacitate them.

Sheathing the daggers, Kyra measured the distance, calculated the trajectory, and then simply let her body fall.

The landing was silent, her feet and leg muscles absorbing the impact that should have shattered them. Before either guard could react, she had them both in sleeper holds, and they slumped unconscious seconds later.

"Eastern entrance clear," she whispered into her com. "Move in."

As she worked the electronic lock, Soran's team emerged from the shadows. Disabling security systems was another oddity of hers. Somehow, she knew how to crack them almost instinctively. It was as if she'd been trained to become an operative, and maybe she had. She had no idea what she had done before finding herself in the mental asylum, which in reality served to brainwash rebellious young women into obeying the regime and their parents' dictums.

Inside, her pendant led them straight to the interrogation room where the new prisoners were held—six political activists who'd dared to speak against the regime. Their eyes widened at the sight of her team, and their hope warred with disbelief.

"We're here to help," she told them. "Can you walk?"

They could, though one limped severely. She gestured for Zara to support him as they began to move toward the exit.

Everything was going smoothly.

Too smoothly.

Kyra's instincts screamed a warning seconds before the alarm sounded.

"We've got company," Soran said. "Four hostiles approaching from the west."

She pushed the prisoners toward the exit, where the rest of her team waited. "Get them out. I'll handle this."

"Kyra—" Soran started to protest.

"Go!"

He knew better than to argue. As the others retreated with the prisoners, Kyra turned to face their pursuers. Four men in tactical gear rounded the corner, weapons raised.

Elite forces, given their uniforms, but she could handle them.

She had done it before.

Time seemed to slow as they spotted her. Kyra's body moved without conscious thought, crossing the distance between them in the blink of an eye. The first man's eyes widened in shock just before her knife connected with his throat. The second managed to squeeze off a shot that she somehow knew would miss before it even left the barrel.

She moved through them like a ghost, her strikes precise and lethal. When it was over, she stood among the bodies, breathing heavily, not just from exertion but from the strange euphoria of combat.

The killing was never easy, and she would pay the price later in nightmares and in missing pieces of her soul, but for now, it felt good to be alive while her enemies lay in pools of their own blood.

As she followed her team's exit route, the

pendant's warmth faded to a comfortable glow, telling her the mission was complete.

Kyra caught up to the others at their fallback position. The prisoners had already been loaded into the vehicles, and Soran nodded as she joined him at the cabin.

"Did you get them all?" he asked.

"Of course." She touched her pendant through her shirt.

It had led them true again, but tonight's mission left her unsettled, and it wasn't just about the dead bodies she'd left behind.

Those guards had been better trained and more coordinated than usual. If she hadn't been there, her team would have failed the extraction and probably ended up dead.

2

SYSSI

Syssi burst into Kian's office, her heart still pounding from that horrible dream that had felt more like a vision. She needed to tell him what she'd seen, but more than that, she needed the comfort of his arms around her and his solid presence to ground her.

He was her rock, and right now, she needed an anchor.

The sight of him at his desk steadied her somewhat, but it wasn't enough to disperse the horror she'd seen, especially since the office was steeped in darkness and Kian's face was illuminated only by the soft glow of his laptop screen.

"Syssi?" He got up and strode toward her. "What's wrong?"

"I had a dream or a vision. I'm not sure what it was, but I saw Kyra again. Or rather, for the first time. She didn't have a scarf on, and I heard her name spoken, so I knew it was her without a doubt."

He wrapped his arm around her and led her to the couch. "What did you see?"

Syssi opened her mouth to speak, but then another vision washed over her, hijacking her mind without warning.

"Syssi?" She heard Kian say her name as if it was coming through a tunnel.

She latched on to the sound like a lifeline, pulling herself out of the vision that was trying to show her what she'd managed to avoid seeing the first time around.

Clutching on to Kian's arm, she forced her eyes to open. "Oh, dear Fates. The poor woman. We have to help her."

"What did you see?" he repeated, sounding alarmed and impatient.

Syssi's throat was so dry that talking was difficult. "I need coffee."

To anyone else, that declaration would have sounded strange in light of the frazzled state she'd arrived in, but her mate knew it was exactly what she needed to calm down.

"Of course." Kian lifted her into his arms and walked with her to the family room.

How did he know that she didn't want to be left alone, even for the few minutes it would take him to prepare the coffee?

Syssi wound her arms around Kian's neck and held on tight. "I can walk, you know."

"I know." He dipped his head and kissed the top of her head. "But I enjoy carrying you and holding you close. Any objections?"

She managed a smile. "None at all."

Once he'd seated her on the couch, he walked over to her cappuccino station. "I've seen you work this machine a thousand times before. I should be able to figure out how to work it."

She chuckled. "It does everything automatically, and it's connected to the water supply, but you need to put in the coffee beans and the milk."

"Got it."

The familiar sounds of grinding and thumping soothed Syssi's frayed nerves, helping her relax enough to organize her thoughts. The image of Kyra chained to that metal bed was burned into her memory—the woman's face so similar to Jasmine's that there had been no mistaking her identity, unless her mind had superimposed Kyra's face on that of a stranger to play tricks on her.

That wasn't likely, though.

After a lifetime of visions, Syssi knew the difference between normal dreams and those that were trying to convey a message, and this one had been loaded with meaning.

The problem was deciphering it. The call for help was obvious, but once again, the clues about how to proceed were missing.

"Here." Kian set the two cappuccinos he'd made on the coffee table and sat beside her. "I hope I didn't mess it up too badly, but it's definitely not up to your standards." He pointed to the frothed milk. "I tried to make a heart, but it didn't come out right."

It was funny how worried he looked, but his concern wasn't entirely unwarranted. Syssi wasn't obsessive about many things, but she was very particular about her coffee and how she liked it.

"I'm sure it's great." She lifted the cup and took a sip. "It's perfect," she said, and it wasn't a lie. It might not have been as aesthetically pleasing as the cups she made, but he'd gotten the taste and temperature perfect, which wasn't easy even with the automation.

She kept the cup cradled between her palms as she folded her legs under her robe to keep them warm.

"That's a relief." Kian pretended to wipe sweat from his forehead. "It means a lot to get a compliment from the master."

She laughed. "You did well, my faithful apprentice."

Smiling, he dipped his head. "Ready to tell me what you saw?"

Syssi nodded. "Kyra was in a cell, and she was chained to a metal bed by her wrists, but not her ankles. Except, she was so heavily drugged that I don't know why they bothered to chain her."

He frowned. "How do you know she was drugged?"

"I'm getting there." Syssi took another sip, hoping the warmth of the coffee would bolster her courage. "At first, when the dream started, I didn't know that she was drugged and assumed she was asleep." Syssi closed her eyes. "She was young, no older than Jasmine is now, and the resemblance between them was striking."

"The vision must have been from the past," Kian said. "Unless..."

She arched a brow. "Unless what?"

"Unless it was just a dream rather than a vision, and your mind put Jasmine in that cell."

Syssi shook her head. "No. It was definitely a vision. It had that quality—that sense of watching something real unfold before my mind's eye." She took a shaky breath. "The differences can be subtle, but I have enough experience with visions to recognize the particular feeling I get when the universe is trying to tell me something."

Kian nodded. "I don't doubt that. What else did you see?"

The coffee suddenly tasted sour in her mouth. "There was..." Syssi swallowed hard. "There was a man." The words felt like broken glass in her throat. "He entered the cell wearing a doctor's coat, but instead of checking on Kyra, he sat on the bed beside her and started touching her inappropriately." Her hands tightened around the coffee cup.

"Kyra didn't fight him. That is why I think that she was drugged. She just lay there and let him pull down her pants." She swallowed. "Along with her underwear." Syssi's voice cracked. "I forced myself to wake up when he mounted her. I couldn't watch what happened next."

Kian's expression darkened, but then he attempted a weak smile. "Are you certain it wasn't consensual? Some people enjoy playing kinky games—"

"Don't." Syssi lifted a hand to stop him. She and Kian enjoyed slightly spicy activity from time to time, but what she'd seen in the vision hadn't been about fun and games. "This wasn't play, Kian. And just to make sure that I did not have any misconceptions about what I'd seen in the dream, there was the second vision that barreled into me while I was in your office."

His smile faded. "Did he say anything to her?"

Closing her eyes, Syssi forced herself to recall what she'd witnessed. "Yes. He said a few words. I think it was in Farsi, but I'm not sure."

"Did she respond?"

Syssi shook her head. "She just stared at him with glazed-over eyes. There wasn't any panic in her expression or even revulsion, and yet I knew it wasn't consensual. Something was done to her."

"Tell me about the room—the cell. Any details that can help us identify the place."

It was easier to focus on the practical aspects of

the scene rather than the emotional impact. "At first glance, I thought it was a prison cell. There were bars on the small square window, and the bed was one of those old metal-frame types you see in movies about prisons or asylums. The paint on the walls was peeling, and the linoleum floor was coming up in patches. Everything looked run-down. When the scumbag entered wearing a doctor's coat, I realized it must be a hospital of some sort."

"Do you think you can draw the room?" Kian asked.

"I can try."

He rose to his feet. "I'll get your tablet from the bedroom."

Syssi nodded despite dreading him leaving her alone even for a minute. She focused on the cappuccino, which was indeed excellent, taking small sips and savoring the taste until Kian returned with her tablet in hand.

"Here," he handed it to her. "It's a good idea to sketch what you saw while the images are still fresh in your mind."

"What good will that do?" Syssi took the tablet and detached the stylus. "It happened a long time ago in another country. I doubt it will help us find Kyra."

"Someone who escaped the regime might have been detained in the same place and recognize the institution," Kian said. "Especially if it was used to house rebels and brainwash them to abandon their rebellion in favor of blindly following the regime. Remember the story about the Iranian girl who took off her clothes in the middle of the street?"

Syssi nodded. "She was accosted by the modesty police because her headscarf wasn't covering every strand of her hair. After they tore her hoodie, she just snapped and took everything off except her sports bra, panties, and socks. I was terrified for her. I thought they were going to hang her like they did other women who dared to rebel or take her eye out. I was so glad that they just put her in a mental institution." She shivered. "I feel so sorry for these women and so proud of them at the same time. They are fighting an impossible fight."

Syssi opened the sketching application and started outlining the room, the window, the door, the floor, and the bed. Her artistic talent wasn't good enough to provide a realistic representation of what she'd seen, but perhaps she could give the drawing to someone to enhance with her guidance.

"When the story exploded all over the world, everyone was afraid the regime would kill her," Kian said. "But they didn't because of the international pressure. They held her in the mental asylum for a while and later released her."

"Yeah, if that's true. I'll believe it once I see her with my own eyes." Syssi shifted her gaze to him.

"Do you think it might be the same place Kyra was in?"

He shrugged. "It's possible, and since it was made famous, maybe I can get some information about it."

Syssi had a feeling that he was just saying that to give her hope. "I'll try to sketch a portrait of that so-called physician. It will probably not be good enough to identify him, but maybe Tim can enhance my sketch with my input. Those former Iranians you wish to show my sketch to might recognize the pervert if he's a physician who's sold his soul to the devil and is working for the regime."

"Good thinking." Kian lifted his cup and took a long sip. "If anyone recognizes him and knows where we can find him, he might lead us to Kyra, and once we find her, we will avenge her." He gave Syssi a chilling smile. "I would be delighted to rid the world of that vermin. One less demon to walk the Earth and prey on the vulnerable and the defenseless."

Syssi sighed as she opened a fresh file and started sketching the fake doctor. "I sometimes dream of having god-like powers, and I don't mean an Anumatian god. I mean the real master of the universe, so I could wish all the monsters dead and liberate the world from evil."

Kian leaned back and draped his arm around her shoulders. "The master of the universe, if such an entity exists, leaves the governing of the physical world to those living within its boundaries. It is up to us to uphold good and eradicate evil."

"I know. And I'm glad that I don't have such powers." She lifted her eyes off the sketch to the beloved face of her mate. "With immense power comes immense responsibility, and I don't delude myself into thinking that I'm strong enough to shoulder it."

"It's not about strength." Kian's hand tightened on her shoulder. "It requires a level of detachment that you don't have. Be glad for that. The detachment is bought with pieces of your soul."

There was something to that. Empathy was a luxury that warriors often had to go without in order to be able to do their jobs. "Kyra looked to be about Jasmine's age in the vision, so the event I saw must have occurred shortly after she was taken."

"Taken?" Kian's eyebrows rose. "From where?"

"Her home." Syssi set the tablet down. "Kyra didn't just decide one day to leave her husband and daughter, fly back to Iran, walk into that institution, and ask to be chained to a bed."

"She could have gone to visit her family and got caught by the regime for some reason. Maybe her family was up to something."

Syssi shook her head. "If Kyra had left the US voluntarily, she would have told her husband and said goodbye to her daughter. Then she would have found a way to contact her husband once she escaped the asylum and joined the Kurdish resistance. She would have wanted to know if her daughter was alright."

"Unless she was afraid to contact them," Kian suggested. "Perhaps letting them know she was alive would have put them in danger."

"That's another possibility. But what are we supposed to do with this information? The vision showed something that happened over twenty years ago, and Kyra is clearly not in that place anymore. That entire facility might no longer exist."

Kian pointed at the tablet. "Showing your sketches to people who might recognize the facility or the so-called doctor is a long shot, but that's all we can do with what we have." He set his coffee cup on the table. "In your other visions, the ones of Kyra with the resistance—did she look older?"

Syssi shook her head. "It was hard to tell. Her face was always covered with a scarf, and she wore loose clothing."

"Jasmine is going to speak with her father soon," Kian said. "I know that she wants to take Ell-rom with her, but neither of them can thrall, so a Guardian will need to accompany them. Once he gets into Jasmine's father's memories of Kyra, we might learn more."

"Which Guardian are you planning to send?"

"I haven't decided yet. Why?"

She shrugged. "Max should go with them."

Kian arched a brow. "Why Max? He doesn't even like Jasmine. When Amanda tried to play matchmaker between him and Jasmine on the cruise, he made it clear that he wasn't interested. Jasmine reminds him of someone from his past he has bad residual feelings about. Also, I'm quite sure that Jasmine wouldn't be happy about him accompanying her either."

Syssi knew the general gist of that story, but her gut told her that Max was the right guy for the job, even though she couldn't explain why. "Maybe it's time he got over it. He needs to move past his prejudice, and spending time with Jasmine would show him how different she is from that woman who wronged him."

"I still don't think he's a good choice for this little mission," Kian said. "Then again, he has seniority, and I need someone capable to watch over Ell-rom."

"Maybe that's exactly why Max needs to go." Syssi pressed her face against Kian's chest, breathing in his familiar scent. "I trust the Fates, and they are telling me that Max is the right choice. What's the worst that can happen if I'm wrong? Max getting over his phobia of curvy, gorgeous brunettes?"

Kian laughed. "Well, when you put it like that, there is really no good reason for him to decline the mission."

3

KYRA

As the first rays of dawn filtered through the canvas of Kyra's tent, she looked over the medical inventory list, her eyes cataloging the supplies they'd pilfered during last night's mission. Regrettably, antibiotics hadn't been part of the loot.

Six prisoners had been rescued, three of them with old wounds that appeared to be infected, and they didn't have the right stuff to treat them.

They had driven hard all night to get away from their pursuers, taking them on a wild chase until losing them in the mountains. The truth was that the pursuit had been half-hearted, and she was worried that they had been allowed to take the prisoners on purpose, and one or more of them had a tracker and would lead the guards to them.

Sitting beside her, Soran leaned over and

tapped his pen on the list. "We'll need to trade for antibiotics."

"I have a contact in Erbid, but we can't risk sending anyone right now. I also think that we should move the prisoners out as soon as possible. This extraction was too easy."

Soran laughed. "It might have seemed easy to you, but there was nothing easy about it." He pushed to his feet. "I'll get us coffee."

"Thank you." Kyra smiled at him. "You're a lifesaver."

Shortly after he'd left, the tent's entrance rustled and Zara ducked inside. "The wounded have been tended to," she reported. "Hamid treated them as best he could with what we have, but we'll need the supplies to avoid complications. Or we can drive them a few hundred miles away from here and get them to a proper doctor."

"We can't drive them anywhere for at least a week." Kyra's hand unconsciously moved to the amber pendant at her throat, a nervous habit she was trying to overcome.

In moments of frustration, the stone provided comfort—in others, it guided her toward whoever and whatever she was seeking.

Perhaps this time, it could guide her to a stash of antibiotics her team could steal.

They needed so many things, and everything was so hard to come by. The lives of rebels were not easy, but what choice did they have?

To live under oppression was no life at all, and for women, sometimes death was preferable to the suffering they were made to endure under a regime that regarded them as less than human and took sadistic pleasure in trampling them under its filthy feet.

It wasn't only women, though. The men who stood by them and dared to voice opposition often found themselves at the end of a noose in the city square.

With a sigh, Kyra leaned in her chair and looked through the tent's open flap. The camp was coming to life, and she found solace in the sounds of conversations and laughter. Her people were comprised of rebels and rescued prisoners—political activists who had spoken out against the oppression. Some of them had been too traumatized to speak in the first days after their arrival, their eyes haunted by recent terrors, but soon hope rekindled in their hearts, and to hear them laughing and talking freely was the best reward she could hope for.

"Coffee?" Soran entered with a cup.

She took the cup and inhaled the brew. "You are my favorite guy in the world right now."

He chuckled nervously before turning around and walking out of the tent.

Soran had hinted on more than one occasion that he had feelings for her, and she'd had to let him down gently. Her excuse was that as the leader of their group, she couldn't fraternize with any of its members, but the truth was that she just wasn't interested—never had been, as far as she knew.

If she'd ever been with a man, it had to be before she'd lost her memory in the asylum. She didn't get periods like other women did, so she couldn't have children, which would have been her only motivation to get intimate with a guy.

Probably not even then.

The truth was that the very idea repulsed her. Perhaps she'd always been like that, or maybe something had happened to her in that place, as it had for so many of the other women she'd helped escape. There was no doubt in her mind that she hadn't been spared and had been violated like the others, but mercifully, unlike them, she didn't remember it.

There were other things she wished she could remember, though. Like that fragment of a recurring dream flickering at the edges of her consciousness. Golden eyes. A child's face. A beautiful girl that looked a lot like her.

The same golden eyes, the same chestnut-colored hair. It could have been just a memory from her own childhood.

"Kyra?" Soran's voice broke through her reverie.

She blinked, forcing her attention back to the present. "Yes?"

She hadn't noticed that the rest of her team had assembled in the tent, each holding a cup of coffee.

"What's our next move?" he asked.

Intelligence suggested increased military presence in the region, and after talking to the rescued prisoners, she'd learned that the elite team they'd encountered at the compound had arrived along with a high-ranking commander of the Revolutionary Guard.

The only reason for them to be stationed in this remote area was to fight the rebels. That meant that the window for operations was narrowing, and from now on, their missions would be more dangerous, and the stakes would be higher.

"We can't keep running defensive operations forever," Hamid argued, spreading a worn map across the makeshift table. His finger traced mountain passes and strategic points. "We need to strike first and eliminate this new threat."

Zara's hand came down firmly on the map. "We're not an army, Hamid. We're a resistance. We can nip at their heels. That's all."

The debate was familiar. Kyra listened, her mind both present and distant. Something about how the light caught the map, the specific angle of Hamid's finger—it tugged at a memory just beyond her reach. Or was it the amber pendant trying to tell her something once again?

After more than an hour of futile arguing, she called the meeting to an end. When everyone had left, she drank the last remaining drops of coffee in her cup and closed her eyes, finally alone with her thoughts.

Who was she?

Kyra's memories were fractured like broken glass, sharp edges that cut whenever she tried to piece them together. A restlessness settled over her. The dream from the previous night—that child with eyes of gold refused to fade.

"Something troubles you." Soran entered the tent. After fifteen years of fighting together, he could read her better than anyone.

Kyra smiled, but she knew that the smile didn't reach her eyes. "Just thinking."

"Dangerous habit," he teased, but his eyes were serious.

The amber pendant pulsed again, a rhythm matching her heartbeat.

A reminder.

A warning.

But of what?

4

KIAN

Anandur turned to Kian. "Do you want me to check on Toven, boss?"

The god was late, which wasn't typical of him. Normally, he was punctual to a fault.

"No, that's okay." Kian leaned into the comfortable back seat of his SUV. "He must have a good reason for keeping me waiting." And if he didn't, Kian preferred not to hear it in front of his bodyguards.

Sitting next to Anandur in the front of the vehicle, Brundar didn't say a word or even acknowledge the conversation.

Not for the first time, Kian wondered if the Guardian's stoic demeanor was just a veneer hiding turmoil or whether Brundar had managed to attain true inner peace. If he had, then Kian envied him for achieving what he'd been struggling with most of his life. It seemed like a storm had taken up permanent residence in his mind, and it never got tranquil in there.

Well, never was a strong word. He had moments of pure joy with Allegra and Syssi, and occasionally things quieted enough in the clan to allow him to take a deep breath. Kian had learned to cherish those rare moments and collect them like pearls on a string.

When Toven finally arrived, he seemed rushed and annoyed, and as Brundar stepped out to open the back passenger door for him, he thanked him with just a nod of his head.

"Apologies for making you wait." Toven slid into the seat next to Kian. "Bridget stopped me on the way, and I got swept up in the conversation, not noticing the time."

"That's okay." Kian motioned for Anandur to start driving. "I didn't set a specific time for our visit to the dungeon. I only told Max that we are coming over this morning."

"I remember Max," Toven said. "He was instrumental in the Kra-ell rescue and Igor's capture."

"He's a good male," Kian agreed. "I put him in charge of the team guarding the prisoners, but I will have to pull him away next week."

Toven arched a brow. "What's happening next week?"

It was a private matter, and Kian didn't feel comfortable sharing it with Toven. It was up to

Jasmine to choose whom she wanted to confide in about getting her father's memories searched.

"Nothing of great importance," he said. "But since Syssi insists that Max needs to be part of this, I'm not questioning her."

Toven shifted in his seat so he could face him. "Does it have anything to do with Jasmine's trip to her father's hunting cabin?"

"You know about that?" It was a relief not to have to talk in circles.

The god shrugged. "Jasmine's friendship with Margo means that she is also close to Mia and Margo's other friends. Jasmine told them about the trip and that she would need a Guardian to accompany her and Ell-rom. I'm just surprised that you are letting Ell-rom out of the village."

"He's not a prisoner."

"Of course not," Toven said. "But in many ways, Ell-rom is like a kid, and he shouldn't be let out on his own."

Ell-rom was far from helpless, but Toven didn't know about his ability to kill with a mere thought, and Kian wasn't ready to tell him about it.

He wasn't even sure why he was keeping it a secret from members of the council. Perhaps it was because Ell-rom's powers hadn't been tested yet, so he couldn't give the council good information about the limitations of his ability.

Soon, Ell-rom would test his death ray on the pedophile monsters Peter's team had collected, and perhaps then Kian would have enough information to present the news to the council.

"Ell-rom will not be on his own when he travels with Jasmine and Max," Kian said. "But I will probably add one more Guardian to their excursion just to be on the safe side."

Toven nodded. "That's prudent, and I'm sure your mother will appreciate the added security. Morelle and Ell-rom are very important to her."

The god hadn't been updated on the true nature of Morelle's power either, but Kian once again hesitated before revealing it. Morelle seemed embarrassed by it, and she probably didn't want rumors to spread about her ability to draw psychic energy from others.

Kian nodded. "It's a day trip. They aren't even going to stay overnight."

"I see." Toven glanced out the window, and for a moment, neither of them spoke. Then the god turned to him once again. "So, how do you want me to handle these Doomers?"

Kian regarded him with a sardonic smile. "In the most straightforward way possible. Compel the scumbags to tell us all they know and in as much detail as possible. They are just run-of-the-mill Doomers, so you should have no problem bending them to your will."

Toven sighed as if he was bracing for explaining a complicated problem to someone who was not an expert on it. "Compulsion is a precise art, Kian. If they have a shred of intelligence and know how compulsion works, which they do since Navuh uses it on everyone in his compound, they will find ways to avoid answering me unless my questions are precise. The best ones are those that can be answered with a yes or no, but we don't know enough to limit ourselves to confirmations and negations."

"They are drugged, so their resistance and mental acuity is shit, but if you want, we can prepare a list of questions."

The god loosened a relieved breath. "That's an excellent suggestion." He pulled out his phone. "The sequence is also important."

Kian leaned back and crossed his arms over his chest. "What I want is a list of all the politicians and celebrities who Navuh has dirt on. The money he's making from this is just the bonus."

"I doubt the lowlifes can answer that." Toven duplicated Kian's pose. "We will have to catch someone higher up in the chain of command for that type of info."

5

ROB

Rob sat at a back table in the village café, holding his coffee cup between two fingers. His newly acquired immortal strength had already crushed two cups this morning, which resulted in coffee stains on his jeans and ceramic shards on Gertrude's kitchen floor.

After the disastrous morning, he'd changed pants, cleaned the floor, and headed to the café. A paper cup was much more fragile than ceramic, but it was also more flexible, so as long as he paid attention, he had visual cues about the force he was applying.

The transition had left him with enhanced everything—sight, hearing, strength—but apparently not enhanced grace or coordination. He felt like a teenager going through a growth spurt, constantly misjudging what his body was capable of. He hadn't been to the gym yet, though, and he expected to be impressed with his performance.

When Margo walked in, her eyes immediately located him, and she wove between the tables with a smile on her face. "You look good," she said, settling into the chair across from him. "How are you feeling?"

"Like I could bench press a car but might accidentally crush the steering wheel." He managed a wry smile. "How are you?"

"Excellent. Frankie and I are working on an idea for a new Perfect Match adventure. It will be so exciting if our idea gets accepted."

"That's great." He lifted the cup gently and took a sip.

She pouted. "Aren't you going to ask me about it?"

He sighed. "Maybe another time. Right now, we need to talk about how to deal with our parents and Mom's potential to become immortal."

"Did Gertrude talk to Bridget about what we discussed?" Margo asked. "You know, all the aspects of inducing a female Dormant."

He winced. "Yes. In fact, she arranged for Bridget to come and explain it to us." He preferred that his sister be the one to ask the doctor all the relevant questions.

Margo rolled her eyes. "You're immortal now. Maybe it's time to get over this silly squeamishness. Our parents are healthy adults who enjoy sex. At least, I hope they enjoy it."

"No, they don't. We are the product of immaculate conceptions, and our parents have a platonic relationship."

Bridget's throaty laugh made them both jump. "Males and their mothers." The doctor pulled out a chair and joined them, looking amused. "For some reason, daughters seem much more open to the idea of their mothers enjoying a healthy sexual relationship with their fathers, but sons like to pretend that it never happens."

"Is Julian like that?" Margo asked.

"A little bit," Bridget admitted. "He wasn't comfortable with me and Turner, and I understood that." She leaned her elbows on the table and rested her chin on her fist. "So, what did you want to talk to me about?"

Rob's face felt like it was on fire. "Didn't Gertrude explain? I'd rather not repeat the questions."

Bridget's expression turned professional. "She said that you were looking for alternatives to the traditional method of inducing transition for your mother."

"That's right," Margo said. "I don't think our parents will be open to my mother having sex with an immortal to induce her transition."

"I understand." Bridget lifted her hand to wave

Aliya over. "There is another possible option, but I'm not sure it will work."

They waited patiently for the doctor to order a coffee and a pastry.

When Aliya left, Bridget continued. "We can collect and store semen from a willing donor, but venom can't be harvested. The production of venom has to be triggered by arousal, same as semen, but even if harvesting it was an option, which it's not, I'm pretty sure that it has to be injected directly into a receptive body to be viable."

Rob had thought a lot about that since the idea had been floated, and he'd come to the same conclusion. Immortal males weren't snakes, and it was impossible to milk their venom glands. The moment the situation became clinical and the arousal waned, the production of venom stopped.

"So, Mom would still need an immortal to bite her, but she could be artificially inseminated?" Margo asked.

"Yes," Bridget confirmed. "You would need to find an unmated volunteer because mated immortals can't bite anyone other than their mate." She pursed her lips. "Well, that's only true for bonded mates, not for regular couples, but the vast majority of couples in the village are bonded. Finding a bachelor shouldn't be a problem, though. There are plenty of unattached males, and most will gladly assist. The caveat is that the donor would need to self-stimulate until the urge to bite manifests, and some might not be comfortable with that."

"Oh God," Rob muttered. "I really don't want to have this conversation."

Bridget continued as if she hadn't heard him. "Ideally, the same immortal would provide both the bite and the semen donation for artificial insemination. We've never tried to do this that way, but I have a feeling that using the same source for both will increase the chances of success."

"That's sounds doable," Margo said. "It's almost clinical."

"Not really." Bridget paused to thank Aliya for the coffee and Danish she delivered. "The bite itself is quite intimate. It's something your parents would need to discuss whether or not they are comfortable with it."

"I think they would be." Margo looked at Rob. "Right?"

He had no idea. In fact, he was pretty sure that his dad wouldn't be on board with the whole thing.

Rob shrugged. "Maybe, but what I would like to know are the chances of success. I know it hasn't been tried, but can you guesstimate?"

"The chances are definitely lower than with the traditional method," Bridget admitted. "But they are not negligible. Given your mother's age, she will be taking a risk attempting transition, and if she's not in perfect health, her issues have to be resolved first. That being said, we had a woman in her mid-fifties transition with relative ease. Ultimately, it has to be your mother's decision, and I agree with Gertrude that you shouldn't make the decision for her just because you want to save her from having to make difficult choices."

The doctor finished her coffee and put what was left of her Danish back in the paper bag. "I have to go. If you have any more questions for me, don't hesitate to call or text me."

"Thank you, doctor." Rob rose to his feet and offered Bridget his hand. "I appreciate you coming out here to talk to us."

"It was my pleasure." She offered him a bright smile, shook Margo's hand, and strode away on her insanely high heels.

"How can she even walk on those?" Margo murmured. "My toes hurt just from looking at her feet."

"You are immortal now." Rob sat back down. "A lot of things that you thought were difficult or impossible before should be easy with your new and improved physique."

"They are, but squished toes still hurt." Margo took a sip of her coffee, which was probably cold by now. "Maybe we should just tell Mom first. Without Dad. Let her decide if she even wants to consider it."

"Makes sense." Rob ran his fingers through his hair. "But I can't be the one to explain all this to her. That has to be you."

She chuckled. "I'll handle the birds and bees talk, but we need to ensure that she doesn't reveal what we tell her. No one would believe her, but they might think she's insane."

Rob arched a brow. "Might think? Mom is crazy."

"She is complicated," Margo corrected him. "Anyway, we need a compeller or someone who can thrall the memory away if she decides against it. Compulsion will work better because we can let her think about it for a while before deciding, but compellers are more difficult to come by. Thralling the memory of what we tell her means that she will have to decide on the spot, and that's asking a lot, but since almost all immortals can thrall, it will be much easier to get someone to do that."

Rob grimaced. "It's unfair that neither of us can thrall."

Apparently, thralling had to be learned as a teenager when the mind was still malleable. Those who transitioned as adults had a much harder time learning to do it or couldn't do it all.

"Gertrude can thrall Mom," Margo said. "Or Negal. It will not even look suspicious if we invite Mom to lunch with our partners."

"We might have no choice." Rob leaned back in his chair. "Let's see who can compel. Kalugal's too busy being important, Parker's too young for this kind of thing, and Drova..." Rob paused. "Actually,

Drova might work if they let her out of the village, but she's also young."

Margo laughed. "She's a girl. I bet she will have no problem with the subject matter even if she's still a virgin."

"Is she?" Rob asked. "Given the swagger on that girl, that's not likely."

Margo pursed her lips. "I think Drova is full of it and is insecure on the inside."

He wasn't going to argue with her. His sister was a much better judge of character than he was, especially when it came to the female gender. "What about the Clan Mother?" he suggested half-heartedly.

Margo stared at him. "You want to ask the goddess to compel our mother about transition logistics involving biting and artificial insemination?"

He shrugged. "She might surprise you. I think the goddess is full of love and compassion."

"She is, but I would never ask her for such a favor."

"Excuse me." A soft voice came from the next table, and as Rob turned, he saw a female immortal looking at them apologetically. "I couldn't help but overhear your conversation, and there are two more compellers that you might not be aware of. Eleanor and Emmett are both compellers, but they are stationed in Safe Haven. Either would be happy to help, but you might be more comfortable with Eleanor. She used to be human up until not too long ago."

"Eleanor?" Margo straightened. "Did I meet her?"

"She was here for the wedding. A tall, very thin woman with small dark eyes and wavy dark hair."

The unflattering description didn't ring any bells. "What makes you think that she will be willing to help?" Rob asked.

"I know her well." The immortal smiled. "She was my sister-in-law when my first husband was still alive." The female extended her hand. "I'm Vivian, Parker's mom."

Rob felt terrible about discussing Parker within earshot of his mother without knowing who she was. "It's nice to meet you, Vivian, and thank you for the recommendation."

"You are most welcome. You could take your parents to Safe Haven for a spiritual retreat or a paranormal one if she's into those kinds of things. It would provide the perfect cover for talking to your mother privately and for Eleanor to ensure that the conversation stays between you."

"That's a great idea," Margo said. "Mom could use one of those retreats to unwind. She's always so stressed."

6

KIAN

As Kian stepped out of the plush interior of the elevator behind Toven, he was greeted by the slightly moist tang of the stone blocks that composed the walls of the keep underground, the sharp bite of cleaning solution that had been used on the floor, and a lingering, almost palpable scent of despair.

The concrete floor under his boots might have been polished to a shine, but he could almost see the footprints of the evildoers who had been brought here.

Was it his imagination conjuring the foreboding ambiance, or was there something more to it? A warning, perhaps?

He'd walked down this same wide corridor many times before, and it had usually smelled faintly of air freshener and echoed with the hum of fluorescent lights, but even when it had housed

Igor, it hadn't felt so grim. This time, though, the air entering his nostrils contained a residue of darkness from the many vile and twisted individuals the dungeon currently held, humans and immortals alike.

He should be glad that they had captured so many, or at least happy for the young victims they had freed from torture and eventual death, but he felt no satisfaction. It was just a drop in a vast, roiling figurative bucket of depravity, one he wished he could fling into the empty void of outer space so it would never touch Earth again.

A world without predators. Wouldn't that be something?

He chuckled softly at the thought, a faint sound echoing in the wide corridor. One could dream.

It reminded him of what Syssi had confided—her own fantasies about banishing all monsters to where they could never harm another innocent soul.

"What's amusing you?" Toven asked, glancing back to look for what Kian could have possibly found humorous in the keep's dungeon.

"My own imagination," Kian said with a half-smile. "I was fantasizing about ejecting all the monsters off into space. I will never understand how anyone can hurt children for their own sick, twisted pleasure."

Toven's gaze flickered across Kian's face before he nodded in agreement. "I don't care what anyone does in private as long as it is between consenting adults with no one getting seriously injured." He snorted, shaking his head. "Although, to be frank, is a seventeen or an eighteen-year-old really an adult? Their bodies might be sexually mature, but their brains are not. I think the age of consent should be at least twenty-one."

Kian cast him an amused sidelong look. "I agree, but people who are that age will not. I was nineteen when I married my first wife, and I was convinced that I was mature enough to be a husband and a father." The memory still stung nearly two millennia after the fact.

He'd made a mistake, and even though things had worked out in the end, his daughter, his own flesh and blood, had grown up with a stepfather caring for her, and so had his grandchildren and their children and so on. Eventually, the last one of his descendants had died childless, and that was the end of that line.

Toven arched a brow. "I didn't know you were married before. I assume she was a human?"

Kian nodded. "My mother tried to convince me not to do it, but you know how the young are. We think we know everything. Needless to say, it didn't end well."

"I bet." Toven offered him a small, sad smile. "Perhaps you can tell me about it some other time."

They continued down a hallway lined with thick metal doors until they reached the

Guardians' station, which was situated in one of the more spacious converted cells. Plush-looking chairs had replaced the standard-issue cots, and a large console of monitors glowed with the silent feed from security cameras mounted in the occupied cells.

Max, who had been perched on a chair near the monitors, rose to greet them. The Guardian lacked his usual easy smile. "The prisoners are ready for you," he said. "Lightly sedated, as you requested."

"Thank you." Kian settled in one of the chairs, motioning for Toven to join him. "While we are waiting for Anandur and Brundar to arrive with the coffees, I would like to get a look at the Doomers." He tilted his head toward the array of monitors. "Can you tell me who is who?"

"Of course." Max motioned for the Guardian to monitor the screens and move them aside. "We relocated them to the interrogation cell." He tapped the top-left screen, the image flickering with a live feed of a cell, part of which was sectioned by bars. "I debated whether to bring them out one at a time or together but ultimately decided on bringing them both. They're behind bars and sedated. They don't burn as quickly through the new sedative Bridget developed." He turned to Toven. "Do you prefer to separate them for questioning?"

"I don't mind them being together," Toven said, crossing his arms over his chest. "I just need to know their names so I can address them individually. Otherwise, my commands will affect anyone within hearing distance." He turned to Kian. "Do you have your compulsion filtering earpieces with you?"

"I do." Kian patted his pocket. "And the Guardians never leave home without them."

"Good." Toven seemed to relax. "That will make my job easier." He turned to Max. "Please, continue."

Max nodded and pointed at the monitor. "The one with the long beard calls himself Don, and the other one calls himself Nox. Those are the names on their fake documents, too. I didn't press them to reveal their real names. You can probably compel them to give them up."

"That's good." Toven's arms remained folded, and his posture made him look even more imposing than usual. "I find it's best to work with a fresh mind. It might sound counterintuitive, but people are easier to compel when they're not exhausted or flooded with adrenaline from fear or pain, so I'm glad you didn't try to get it out of them by force."

Toven's approach was humanitarian in its own way, but Kian also wished he'd never asked for the god's help and instead got the information out of the vermin the old-fashioned way. Regrettably, Toven's method was more effective than torture.

"Did they give you any trouble?" Kian asked.

Max's lip curled in disgust. "I wish they had so I could have wiped the smirks off their ugly faces. The bastards think they're safe because the clan believes itself too civilized to torture prisoners." He tapped a restless finger against the console. "It was really difficult not to correct their misconception."

"I appreciate your restraint," Toven said.

Kian's stomach tightened. These predators likely believed themselves above whatever moral standards existed in the world, and they had outdated information about the clan.

In the past, captured Doomers had been placed in stasis and spared execution only because of his mother's ban on ending the lives of immortals. But she had changed her stance when it came to those who committed particularly heinous crimes. These monsters wouldn't get another chance, like their slightly less monstrous brethren might have.

"I hear the elevator," Toven said, tilting his head toward the corridor, where the soft ping signaled the arrival of Anandur and Brundar.

"Good." Kian glanced briefly at the monitor feed before rising to his feet. "Let's meet them next to the interrogation cell."

When they intercepted the brothers, Anandur lifted a large bag. "I got us some pastries. I was a little peckish."

"Thank you," Kian said. "We can have them later in the car."

The Guardian's face fell. "Do I have to wait?"

Kian chuckled. "We are going in now, so if you can manage to munch on a croissant and look menacing at the same time, go ahead."

As Max produced his phone and tapped the screen, a mechanical whirr preceded the outward swing of the heavy door, and once it completed, Kian caught a first real look at the Doomers. The two males were sprawled on twin cots behind a barred partition, their postures artificially casual. It was obvious that they were feigning sleep even though they tried to keep their breathing deep and slow.

Did they honestly believe they were fooling anyone?

He could hear their heartbeats galloping like a pair of frightened horses.

Neither of the prisoners spoke as Kian, Toven, Anandur, Brundar, and Max entered the cell. The space was sparse, with several metal chairs facing the bars at a safe distance from them, and on the other side were two low cots. A utilitarian bathroom was located behind a glass block, which offered a modicum of privacy.

Kian settled himself in one of the chairs, a paper cup of coffee cradled between his palms. He took a slow sip, the steam fogging briefly in front of his eyes, and watched the prisoners, waiting to see who would break the silence first. For a long moment, all that could be heard was the soft slurp of coffee and the distant hum of the ventilation system.

Finally, one of them stirred. He sat up with a sneer, curling his lips, trying to look unafraid and to project arrogance. "Hey, Nox, wake up," he drawled. "The big guns are here. They're going to ask us really hard questions, and we'll need to work real hard on not answering them."

The lazy scorn in his tone set Kian's teeth on edge, but he schooled his expression into cool detachment. He noticed Toven shift in his seat, eyes narrowing as he observed the prisoner. On Kian's other side, the three Guardians remained silent.

Kian studied the Doomer with dispassion. The man's bravado was a thin veneer, a poor attempt to mask the fear below the surface. "You seem to be operating under the misconception that no harm will come to you," Kian said, his voice calm, each syllable measured. "It is true that we are not barbarian savages like you, but I believe that those who abuse children deserve a special place in hell, and I'm very capable of delivering it."

Toven might not be happy with him for scaring the prisoners, but Kian was sure the god was powerful enough to compel the two scumbags even though they were terrified.

7

MAX

This wasn't Max's first interrogation of prisoners. He'd done enough of these to know what to expect. He'd been present when Igor and his lieutenants had been captured, and at the time, he'd thought that they were as evil as they came.

He'd been wrong.

The Kra-ell leader and his minions had been bad, murdering the males of several Kra-ell pods and enslaving the females, and they had also severely oppressed everyone living in the Karelian compound, including a community of humans. But even they hadn't stooped so low as to horrifically abuse children as these Doomers and their so-called human clients had.

Guarding the scum and interrogating them felt like wading waist-deep in the murkiest swamp imaginable. A part of him longed for simpler times, a world where justice was swift, and evil was less insidious. He couldn't wait to leave the dungeon and be rid of the rot that clogged his airways.

On Kian's other side, Toven regarded the impudent Doomer with an impassive expression. "Don," he said, enunciating the name, "I believe that's what you call yourself, correct?"

The Doomer, whose posture was still defiant, opened his mouth then quickly snapped it shut, the flicker of fear in his eyes betraying his confusion. Finally, he gave a curt nod, looking like he was about to throw up.

Max stifled a chuckle. The poor fool had no idea what he was up against. Toven's compulsion made it impossible to resist answering direct questions, especially ones that required a simple yes or no. They didn't allow for evasions or clever comebacks, only compliance.

"What is your real name, Don?" Toven asked in the same calm and measured tone.

The prisoner's eyes widened, pupils constricting as he realized that there was no fighting the god. He was forced to give up the truth, and the tension in his jaw spoke volumes. "Do...Dondish," he spat out as though the name itself were a betrayal.

"That's more like it," Toven said, his expression still cool, with just a hint of satisfaction in his eyes. "What's your cellmate's real name?"

"Noxmore," Dondish said, darting an uneasy glance at the other prisoner.

The Doomer who called himself Nox shifted but remained silent.

After all, Toven had addressed the question to Dondish, so Nox couldn't have answered even if he'd wanted to. He was just as susceptible to compulsion as the other dirtbag.

Toven nodded. "Very well, Dondish. I have several questions for you, and you will answer them truthfully and completely."

"Who are you?" Dondish asked, a slight tremor betraying the anger bubbling beneath his forced compliance. His voice sounded raspy like he was choking on his own bitterness.

"Who do you think I am?" Toven countered with a question instead of answering.

The Doomer's lip curled. "An immortal," he said, almost spitting the word. "Like the others. One of the betrayer's descendants."

That was new. Had Navuh spun a new tale about Annani where she was cast as the betrayer? Who had she betrayed? Mortdh? Or had Navuh told his followers that Annani had been responsible for obliterating the gods' assembly?

Max wouldn't be surprised if that was precisely the story Navuh was spinning. He and his followers were experts in inverting the truth, turning victims into oppressors and perpetrators into victims.

It was infuriating, and Max had no doubt that each of the males sitting on his side of the bars was seething with anger.

But Toven kept his outward calm demeanor. "My name is Tom," he said, ignoring the Doomer's sneer. "And you don't need to know who I descend from. What I do need is for you to tell me about the Brotherhood's pedophilia network—how it works, who is involved, and what purpose it serves. Let's start with my first question. Tell me about the network."

Dondish's face contorted with the effort to resist, his features tightening as if he were physically straining against a heavy weight or battling constipation. For an instant Max thought the man might pass out, shit his pants, or start frothing at the mouth. But Toven's compulsion was potent, and the words started pouring out of Dondish like a poison-laced confession.

As the Doomer described the network of corruption the Brotherhood had been building, he sounded furious and terrified at the same time, though Max wasn't sure what he feared more, Toven and Kian or his own leader's wrath.

Listening to every vile detail was like having nails scraped across Max's soul.

He tried to keep his face neutral, but his stomach churned at the things these monsters had done. The way they used vulnerable children, the perverse clients they catered to, the hush money that changed hands—every revelation was an additional layer of filth.

"Interesting," Toven said, his voice as measured and as detached as a physician's diagnosing an injury. He directed his gaze to the other Doomer. "Who benefits most from the intelligence you gather, Nox?"

Noxmore straightened, his cheeks twitching as he tried to fight the compulsion forcing him to speak. "Our leader ensures the information reaches those who can best use it to guide policy," he said, the words sounding by rote as if recited from memory.

"And what are those policies designed to achieve?" Toven asked, leaning forward, his gaze boring into the Doomer like a drill.

Whatever inner struggle Noxmore was waging must have come to a halt because the floodgates opened. With surprising clarity, he described how they used blackmail to influence legislation, promote destructive social policies, redirect resources away from the military and law enforcement, and funnel funding into organizations that sowed further destabilization. He detailed, in almost proud terms, the carefully orchestrated attack on society at its moral and institutional core.

"Destabilization through moral decay," he added, as though reciting a mantra. Perhaps the compulsion was forcing him to volunteer more than was asked, or maybe he took twisted pride in the Brotherhood's clever program. "Create chaos, erode trust in institutions, turn people against each other. When the economic empires fall, wars will erupt all over the globe, accelerating the decline of the world's population. Then, when everything lies in ruin, Earth will be ripe for enslavement by the Brotherhood. We will conquer without having to wage war. All of those who are in power today will grovel at our feet and beg us to step in and save them from their own stupidity."

A tense hush fell, and Max could feel the coiled energy in the room ready to spring. He slanted a glance at Kian, whose fists were clenched so hard that his knuckles had turned white. Kian's jaw muscle twitched, and even though Max couldn't see his eyes from where he sat, he was sure that Kian's eyes were blazing with the same anger that was boiling Max's blood.

They had all assumed that Navuh was busy building a smarter army of Doomers with his new breeding program to achieve that objective, but it turned out they had underestimated him. Policy manipulation and infiltration to strike at the heart of established governments and communities had always been part of his modus operandi, but before, his methods had been less vile and more obvious.

The Doomers' island was one big trap for men of influence, where pictures and videos of them in compromising situations were taken and later used for blackmail. It hadn't been the only tactic he used, though. His army of mercenary immortals had been great at starting regional wars and ensuring victory for Navuh's protégés.

Evidently, though, Navuh had discovered a much simpler, more insidious path to achieving his goals—one that didn't require an army to storm battlefields or mount large-scale attacks, nor did it require luring influential men to the island. He'd found a way to rot and collapse those who thought of themselves as advanced societies from within.

"How long has this operation been going?" Toven asked.

"About six years," Dondish said flatly. His throat bobbed in a hard swallow as if speaking the words tasted bitter. "It started slow, and at first, our leader was not enthusiastic about this operation, but once he realized how effective it was, he gave it his full support."

"Who is in charge of the operation?" Toven pressed.

"Hocken," Noxmore said, the name coming out in a breathy rasp. "It was his idea, and our illustrious leader let him run with it."

Hocken was one of Navuh's adopted sons, and his portrait hung in the gallery in the office building along with those of his brothers, for no other purpose than for every clan member to get acquainted with the faces of their enemies.

The fact that these two knew so much about the operation's history and its originator was surprising. Usually, the Brotherhood compartmentalized its secrets, like various heads of the same Hydra, ensuring that no single underling knew too much. Navuh believed in ruling through division and in never allowing any of his real or adopted sons to gain too much power. By constantly moving them around and reshuffling their duties, he prevented them from building a following or consolidating influence. It was a smart approach, but it had its drawbacks. In the Brotherhood, the left hand often had no idea what the right hand was doing.

Kian leaned toward Toven, his entire body radiating with barely suppressed rage. "I need a list of all the politicians and influencers they're extorting. I also need the names, locations, and contact information of other cells. We'll start with the ones located in the United States, and after we clean house here, we'll move on to Europe."

"That's somewhat ambitious, Kian," Toven said quietly.

"We'll make it a priority." Kian crossed his arms over his chest. "I hate to admit it, but Navuh is a fucking genius. We have to stop him before it's too late, and saving the kids he's ruining for his agenda is just the cherry on top. If we do nothing and let this continue, Navuh will win, and we will find ourselves in another Dark Age, perhaps for good this time."

The admission hung in the air, and for a moment, no one spoke. The only sounds were the thrum of ventilation, the faint hum of overhead lights, and the muffled breathing of everyone present.

They'd come here expecting to chip away at Navuh's forces, to corner some of his lesser agents and discover a few tidbits of intelligence. Instead, they'd unearthed a grand-scale operation, a malignant web of influence that entwined itself into the highest echelons of power. And worst of all, it involved harming children in unimaginably vile ways.

Rage and disgust mingled in Max's gut, and his only solace was the knowledge that Kian was about to unleash the full power of the clan on this twisted web of evil.

8

ROB

Rob found Gertrude in the clinic, looking bored as she usually was during her shifts when no one was there. Her face lit up when she saw him, or rather the steaming cups of coffee in the cardboard tray and paper bag in his hands.

"Just in time." She lifted on her toes and kissed his cheek. "I was getting hungry." She plucked one of the cups from the tray and relieved him of the paper bag.

He followed her and sat down on one of the chairs in the waiting area. "I don't know why you are required to be present at the clinic at all. If anyone needs help, they can call or text you, and you can meet them here."

"We tried that." She removed the lid and took a careful sip from the coffee. "What ended up happening was people showed up at the house instead of going to the clinic. Hildegard and I decided that it was best to just divide shifts between the two of us and spend them at the clinic."

Rob pulled the pastries from the bag and handed Gertrude her favorite chocolate croissant. "You could have just put an announcement on the clan's bulletin board that it was unacceptable, or hung a sign on your front door directing patients to the clinic."

She chuckled. "You forget that most of us are related, and people feel entitled to barge into your home because they tore a ligament in the gym or someone got hurt during a mission. I would never turn them away. Besides, I can read or watch podcasts here the same way I would do at home. The only difference is that I wear scrubs at work."

He leaned over and placed a kiss on her cheek. "You look very sexy in them."

Gertrude rolled her eyes. "You think that I look sexy no matter what I'm wearing."

"Is that a bad thing?"

"No." Her smile softened. "It's amazing. I feel so fortunate to have been gifted with such a wonderful mate."

"Same here." Rob put his coffee down on the side table and, in one swift move, lifted Gertrude onto his lap. "I love this new immortal strength."

"So do I." She looked at him from under her long lashes. "You are getting stronger by the day."

He glanced at the door and then back at his mate. "What say you that we lock the door and duck into one of the treatment rooms?"

Gertrude lifted the cup and pastry she was holding. "I love the idea, but I wouldn't dare. You'll have to be patient, my love, and wait for me to be done with my shift."

That wasn't what he'd wanted to hear, but he'd expected that. Gertrude was dedicated to her work, and she wouldn't lock the door when it was supposed to be open.

Luckily for him, William was very flexible about work hours, and as long as what he assigned was done, he didn't care about the when and where. Although he'd warned Rob about that changing dramatically when a project was deemed urgent. People in William's lab worked around the clock to complete urgent assignments, and these occurred frequently.

"Bummer." He planted a kiss on her forehead. "Bridget came to talk to Margo and me at the café earlier."

"I know. I was waiting for you to bring that up."

"Why did you wait?"

She shrugged. "It's a private matter between you and Margo and your parents."

"You are my mate, and I don't keep anything from you, not unless I'm forced to."

"Margo might not be happy about my involvement."

"Nonsense. Margo loves you."

"I know." Gertrude released a breath. "So, what did Bridget say?"

"She repeated more or less what you said. Semen can be harvested, but venom cannot. She recommended we find an unmated immortal male who would be willing to donate both. She said most would be happy to help, but personally, I doubt it."

"I can ask around," Gertrude offered. "I can do that very discreetly."

"Thank you." It was a huge relief not to have to do the search himself and explain to potential candidates what he needed from them. "You have no idea how much I appreciate your offer. I was dreading having to explain what I needed."

"Anytime." She straightened in his arms and kissed his jaw. "What else did Bridget say?"

"That's it. Then, Margo and I discussed how to present it to our parents while keeping the clan's existence a secret. A lady named Vivian overheard us talking and suggested asking Eleanor from Safe Haven if she would be willing to compel our parents to be silent on the subject. Vivian said that we could arrange a retreat for the six of us together as a family vacation and do it there. That way, we will be able to talk with our mother first and see where she stands on the issue. If she's against the idea, there is no reason to tell our father."

"When are we going?"

He chuckled. "When can you take time off?"

Her face fell. "I'll have to wait for Hildegard to return, and that will only happen once the prisoners in the keep are gone." When he lifted a brow, she shook her head. "I can't tell you about that, so don't ask."

"I'm not. Margo told me that there was a dungeon in the keep, but I was under the impression that it was rarely used to house prisoners and that it didn't even look like a dungeon."

"That's true," Gertrude confirmed. "It is often used as a transition place, I mean when people are not ready to be brought into the village but need a refuge from somewhere else."

"I thought that was the purpose of Safe Haven."

"You are right, but we use the keep a little differently. We also have the mountain cabin that, from time to time, serves that purpose too." She chuckled. "We call it the love cabin because that's where Amanda and Dalhu fell in love. Then they moved to the dungeon, so maybe we should rename it the Love Underground or something like that."

Rob laughed. "That sounds like the name of a kinky club."

She narrowed her eyes at him. "What do you know about kinky clubs?"

"Absolutely nothing." When she arched a brow, he lifted his hands in the air. "I swear. I must have read something somewhere. I really don't remember."

That earned him a suggestive smile. "I have a few books that you might want to read to broaden your education." She cupped his cheek. "Maybe it will help you get over your prudishness."

"I'm not a prude."

Gertrude arched a brow.

"Well, maybe a little."

9

KIAN

Kian was developing a headache, and it was the kind that radiated in slow, pulsing waves behind his temples. It rarely happened, and usually only under intense pressure or after too many sleepless nights.

Today, though, the reason was a crushing sense of failure.

He'd been dealt a check by Navuh, but hopefully, it wasn't a checkmate. Not yet.

The suspicions had started a while ago, but he'd never expected the operations to be so extensive and to have done so much damage in such a short time.

He'd been complacent, secure in his knowledge of the Brotherhood's plans because he had a spy in their midst, but he should have suspected the real reason behind Navuh's decision to send Lokan to

China. He wanted his son away because he suspected him on some level.

Whatever the case was, Kian had allowed it to happen. His arrogance had led him to get outmaneuvered and outsmarted by the enemy he had underestimated and misjudged. He had no one else to blame but himself.

Worse than the setback itself was how stupid Kian felt for accepting the notion that Navuh had been dedicating his resources almost exclusively to building a smarter army and financing it through drugs and prostitution. Lokan had reinforced that belief, but maybe Lokan had been misled or misinformed by his father.

Or perhaps Lokan wasn't as loyal to the clan as Kian had believed.

As he considered each possibility, a dull throb pounded behind his eyes.

None of the options were good. If Lokan was being kept in the dark by his father, it likely meant that Navuh was suspicious of him and that alone was dangerous. Navuh wouldn't hesitate to assassinate his own flesh and blood if he suspected treachery, and if Lokan was being fed disinformation, it was even worse, suggesting that Navuh was aware of Lokan's divided allegiance and was keeping him around just so he could deceive the clan.

The final possibility was the worst of all, and Kian

refused to believe it. There was no way Lokan was knowingly misleading the clan. Kian didn't want to even entertain the thought, but it still lurked at the edges of his mind. Lokan was far from a paragon of virtue, but he was mated to Carol, a clan member, and betraying her people would mean betraying her. He shouldn't be able to bring himself to do that. Besides, Lokan had taken enormous risks to free his mother from Navuh's clutches. Areana had refused to leave Navuh, but that didn't diminish the enormity of risk and effort her son had put into the effort to free her.

Her choice still baffled Kian. Why stay with a man as twisted and ruthless as Navuh?

Love was a strange phenomenon, and the Fates' tapestry of destinies was stranger still. They must have had some inscrutable reason for pairing Areana, a gentle and loving soul, with a tyrant like Navuh. It was as if an angel had been bound to a demon.

Perhaps her influence on Navuh, as insignificant as it seemed to be, was critical. Even if she only managed to smooth down his edges, providing a minuscule nudge away from total darkness, she might have saved countless lives over the years.

Kian had no way of knowing how events would have played out without her presence, but it was possible that she had prevented Navuh's darkest impulses from manifesting.

The real question, however, was what all this

meant for Lokan and what Kian should advise him to do. His gut told him that Lokan ought to flee Navuh and come live in the village with the clan, especially since the intelligence he brought back from the Brotherhood was clearly incomplete—or worse, intentionally manipulated. If Navuh knew what Lokan was up to, then every moment Lokan stayed behind enemy lines was another moment he risked a violent end. Even worse, he was endangering Carol.

There was no easy answer.

If they pulled Lokan out prematurely, would they lose an inside angle on Navuh's machinations? The possibilities swirled in Kian's mind.

He had to face the reality of what these Doomers had revealed. Not too long ago, he would have refused to believe that Navuh could stoop to such depravity, but the discoveries they'd made in Mexico proved how wrong that assumption had been. The Brotherhood's involvement with the cartels, and what they had allowed or even encouraged those monsters to do, was undeniable. But Kian had still been clinging to the hope that these operations had been carried out by rogue elements within the Brotherhood. But now, that delusion was shattered. Navuh knew exactly what was happening, and he had authorized it.

It forced Kian to accept that the clan's archenemy had no moral compass whatsoever, no line he wouldn't cross. If he ever had a soul, he must have sold it or tossed it aside like an outdated garment. Navuh had become a living embodiment of ruthless, rabid ambition. Evil incarnate.

Fates, what do you expect me to do?

The interior voice that often guided him was silent at first, but then a single word rang in his head like a clarion call.

Fight!

The word felt like both a direct command and an echo of his own defiance. Maybe it was the Fates' directive, or perhaps it was his own stubborn will that caused him to refuse to surrender. Either way, the meaning was clear. His only option was to fight, and the way to go about it was not to chase after the endless tentacles but to cut off the head of the Hydra.

Navuh.

The guy's paranoia gave Kian one huge advantage. The Brotherhood was divided, and none of Navuh's adopted sons had managed to gain a substantial following. If he eliminated Navuh, there would be no one to take his place. The Brotherhood would split into many small militias, and those would cause countless headaches around the world, but they wouldn't be able to pull off grand-scale operations without Navuh to direct them and force them to work together.

They wouldn't be able to bring the entire world to its knees.

The problem, as always, was the size of his

army. Counting the Kra-ell alongside the clan still wouldn't be enough to rival the Brotherhood's ever-growing force. And unlike Navuh, Kian had no breeding program to churn out new immortals in vast numbers. The odds tilted heavily against him in a direct confrontation.

The hopeless, grim reality was oppressing.

It's never hopeless, the Fates whispered, or maybe that was just the resilient spark of his inner voice encouraging him to keep strategizing.

Find a way. The words comforted him for a moment, though he wished for something more concrete. Visions. Guidance. Anything beyond a vague directive to fight.

Kill Navuh. It was the only way. But Navuh never left his fortified island, and sending a strike team there with the warriors Kian had was akin to suicide and would achieve nothing. Bombing the island out of existence would be equally catastrophic—countless innocent lives would perish alongside the guilty, and Kian couldn't stomach that. His aunt lived there, Wonder's sister lived there, and so did thousands of abducted humans who had been forced into semi-slavery under Navuh's rule.

Could he sacrifice all those lives to end the monster and save the world?

Logically, sacrificing a few thousand to save billions made sense as a cold, rational calculation, but Kian couldn't treat his own family members as mere numbers.

He was still grappling with these impossible dilemmas when Toven finished extracting the names of blackmailed pedophiles from the two Doomers. Kian hadn't been actively listening, but the few names he'd heard and recognized were enough to turn his stomach.

Every new name added to the sickening pile of corruption they'd discovered, but at least it was knowledge they might be able to use.

Kian rose to his feet and turned to leave.

"Wait!" one of the prisoners called after him, sounding desperate even though he tried not to. "What are you intending to do with us?"

Kian pivoted slowly, hands tucked into his pockets.

"As long as you cooperate and we have need of you, you'll live," he said curtly. "Once your usefulness runs out, I'll grant you a swift and painless death, which is more than you deserve. But if I learn that you lied or tried to withhold information, I'll feed you to a bunch of hungry sharks and watch gleefully as they tear you apart. Then I'll let you regenerate and heal, only to toss you back in again and again. I'm quite vindictive when it comes to those who hurt children."

Both Doomers blanched, realizing that he'd meant every word.

Evidently, they were not as dumb as he had

once believed, and their leader was an evil, fucking brilliant mastermind.

Navuh had outplayed the clan, orchestrating broader societal collapse while misleading Kian and making him believe that the Brotherhood was strapped for cash and dealing in drugs and trafficking to refill its dwindling coffers.

10

MAX

Once the interrogation was over, Max left the cell along with Kian, Toven, Anandur, and Brundar.

The hallway outside the interrogation room was a nothing-special industrial-looking space, with reproductions of fine art adorning the walls in an effort to soften the look, but right now, it was a breath of fresh air despite the lingering lemony scent of the cleaning solution.

"I need a word with you." Kian motioned for Max to walk with him a few paces away.

"Of course, sir." Max followed, hands reflexively going to his belt and the slight weight of his holster.

Something about Kian's body language when he'd made the request troubled Max. Kian was assertive and decisive, even terse, but his expression was slightly hesitant as if he were uncomfortable with whatever it was he needed to talk to him about.

Toven put a hand on Kian's shoulder. "We'll wait for you in the car."

Kian nodded. "This won't take long." His eyes flicked toward Anandur and Brundar, who both inclined their heads silently before following Toven out. The retreat of their footsteps left a soft echo and then silence returned.

Kian leaned against the concrete wall, crossing one leg over the other, and his intense gaze settled on Max. "How do you like this assignment?"

"I like the promotion, but I don't love dealing with the scum of the Earth. That being said, I assure you I will always do my job to the best of my ability, no matter how unpleasant or difficult it is."

Kian's expression softened, and the tightness around his mouth eased. "I wouldn't have expected anything less, but given that you don't love it, I assume you wouldn't mind a short break from this place. I have a special assignment for you next weekend. I can ask Onegus to appoint someone else in charge while you are gone, or you can choose your own temporary replacement."

Max arched an eyebrow. "No problem. May I ask what the assignment is?"

A thousand possibilities flickered through his mind—guarding one of the twins on a trip somewhere? Or maybe Syssi and Kian were going on a vacation and needed additional guards. He studied Kian's face, searching for clues, but his face didn't reveal anything.

Kian crossed his arms over his chest, exhaling softly. "Jasmine is visiting her father in his hunting cabin to ask him about her mother's death... or rather, her disappearance." Kian paused for a heartbeat, letting that detail sink in. "He was never forthcoming with information regarding how her mother died or even where she was buried. We have reason to believe that she is still alive and has joined the Kurdish resistance, but we need confirmation that she isn't dead, and the father seems to know more than he's been willing to reveal so far."

Max didn't know what to think about the revelation, so he merely nodded.

"Jasmine doesn't expect him to answer her questions this time, either," Kian said. "She's planning to ambush him in his cabin because he'll be alone out there, and her stepmother won't be around to interfere. Naturally, Ell-rom plans to accompany her, but neither of them can thrall. I need a strong thraller to get into the father's head while Jasmine is questioning him about her missing mother. I also need someone I trust to watch over both of them, but especially Ell-rom. He thinks that he doesn't need protection because no one knows who he is, but given how important he is to my mother, I don't want to take any chances with him."

Max swallowed. He'd never considered thralling to be his strong suit. He could do it, like any other immortal who'd transitioned in his early teens, but he wasn't remarkable at it. Many of his fellow Guardians were better. He also couldn't help his illogical dislike of Jasmine. It wasn't her fault that she bore a striking resemblance to someone from his past who'd driven a wedge between him and his best friend at the time.

If it were anyone other than Jasmine, he would have welcomed a short babysitting assignment. Leaving the dungeon for a day or two was appealing, and a trip to a remote hunting cabin could be nice. But when he pictured Jasmine, with her stunning face and dark cascading hair, all he could see was that ghost from his past.

"I'm not a particularly strong thraller," he tried, hoping the admission might excuse him from the assignment. "I'm average at best, and if Jasmine's father is resistant—which he probably will be, given their history—I might not be good enough to break through his barriers. Perhaps you should choose someone else."

"It's possible that he'll be difficult," Kian conceded, "and on top of his reluctance to discuss his former wife, he's also Russian. From experience, we know that Russians are typically more suspicious by nature than other nationalities and that skepticism makes them harder to thrall."

Max let out a low breath of relief, ready to

pounce on that angle. "Then I'm certainly not strong enough. Brundar, on the other hand, can break through most people. Maybe he should go. I'll gladly take his place as your bodyguard for that weekend."

Kian gave him a small sympathetic smile. "Normally, I would agree with you," he said, "but there's one more factor I didn't share with you yet." He raked his fingers through his hair. "Syssi insists that you need to be the one accompanying Jasmine and Ell-rom, and I know better than to argue with Syssi's gut feelings."

Max's breath caught in his throat. If Syssi's visions or gut feelings were pointing a finger at him, his assignment wasn't negotiable. "Did Syssi see me in a vision doing something important?" Max asked.

Kian shook his head. "It was simply a gut feeling. But with Syssi, a gut feeling is as good as a prediction. I'm aware of your dislike of Jasmine, but I'm sure you can keep it bottled up for one day. She's happily mated to Ell-rom, so it's not like you are expected to charm her. Polite will do."

Max pressed his lips into a thin line. Kian's request, especially when backed by Syssi's intuition, was more like an edict. Even if Max had confessed to loving his current duties, Kian would still have sent him with Jasmine.

The knowledge that no measure of protest

would change the outcome felt both frustrating and freeing.

At least he knew where he stood.

Besides, there were some obvious upsides to the assignment beyond getting a break from the damn dungeon.

Given that Jasmine was mated to Annani's half-brother, she was considered part of the clan's royal family, and it would be smart of him to work on improving his relationship with her.

This mission provided the perfect opportunity to atone for the way he'd treated Jasmine when they had first met. He'd been unfriendly, and she had been gracious despite his stinky attitude. Perhaps this was his chance to redeem himself.

"I'll do my best to be not only cordial but also friendly," he promised Kian. "The truth is that I don't actually have anything against Jasmine. She seems like a genuinely nice person, and she's obviously talented—an excellent singer. Her resemblance to someone who wronged me a long time ago shouldn't affect how I feel about her and certainly not how I behave around her."

"That's very wise of you." Kian pushed away from the wall. "Especially given that her mate might not appreciate you being rude to the female he adores." He delivered the sentence with a smile, but Max heard the underlying warning loud and clear.

"I'll do my best, sir. I know how much the Clan

Mother cares about her brother and how important his happiness and safety are to her. Which brings me to my next question: am I going to be the only Guardian accompanying them?" He suspected he wouldn't be, but he wanted clarity.

"I'd likely send another Guardian who's a stronger thraller." Kian rolled his shoulders. "Brundar is a good choice, and since I don't have any plans outside the village for the weekend, I don't really need to bother with a replacement bodyguard."

Max silently berated himself. He'd been the one who mentioned Brundar, and now the prospect of spending a weekend with the man loomed in front of him. Brundar was probably the best Guardian on the force, but he had the personality of a block of ice.

"I can suggest a couple more Guardians who are strong thrallers," Max offered, hoping to remedy the situation. Perhaps naming some alternatives could lead to a better fit and possibly lighten the environment.

"Please do," Kian said, stepping closer. He reached out and gave Max a hearty clap on the back, which Max accepted with a nod. The friendly gesture was as much a dismissal as it was encouragement. "Text the names to me when you get a chance."

"Will do, sir."

As Kian turned to head for the exit, Max stayed

put for an extra beat, leaning against the wall himself. Taking one last deep breath, he pushed off from the wall and started toward the Guardians' station.

He reminded himself that loyalty and performance were more important than his personal preferences. If this was what needed to be done because Syssi's intuition pointed at him, then so be it. He would do the best job he could.

11

JASMINE

Evening settled over the village, bringing with it a cold breeze that nipped at Jasmine's skin, but she didn't mind. Walking hand in hand with Ell-rom along the winding path to Kian and Syssi's house, she appreciated how beautiful the village looked in the fading sunlight.

She lifted her chin and breathed in the crisp air. "Sometimes, I still can't believe this is my home now."

Ell-rom squeezed her hand. "I know what you mean. Growing up in the temple, I never imagined a place like this could even exist."

She turned to him. "The gods lived in beautiful cities. Didn't you get to see them? I mean, in videos?"

He shook his head. "The temple didn't have any

screens. Only books. I suspect that the head priestess hid one in her chambers, but Morelle and I only heard of televised events. We never saw one."

"Maybe that was a blessing in disguise," she said, resting her head against his shoulder. "Books force you to imagine and process. Your brain has to work harder than when images are fed to you. Perhaps that's why you and Morelle are so smart."

"Are we?"

"Of course you are." She lifted her face and kissed his cheek. "You have no idea how stupid people can get because you don't interact with the mindless masses, and the ones in your small sphere of family and friends are all intelligent people."

"You forget how much televised content I've been consuming on a daily basis in order to educate myself about your culture," he said as they walked up the steps to Syssi and Kian's front door. "I didn't realize it might be detrimental to my mind."

She chuckled. "You're an adult now, and your mind is not as malleable as it was while you were growing up, but maybe you shouldn't watch as much. Stupid might rub off on you."

He affected a horrified expression. "Promise to wash it off me if it does."

"I promise." Smiling, she leaned over and kissed his cheek.

The silly banter helped ease the knot in her stomach. Syssi had been deliberately vague when she'd called to invite them for coffee, saying only that they needed to brainstorm what they knew about Kyra, but Jasmine had a feeling that there was more to the invitation than rehashing old information.

Taking a deep breath, she pressed the doorbell button.

Okidu opened the door, greeting them with a deep bow. "Good evening, Mistress Jasmine, Master Ell-rom. Please, come in."

"Good evening," Jasmine said, returning his smile.

He led them to the living room, where Kian and Syssi sat on the couch.

They both rose to greet them.

"Just in time," Syssi said. "Okidu baked a chocolate cake, and I warmed up the cappuccino machine so it would be ready as soon as you arrived."

"Wonderful." Jasmine walked into Syssi's embrace and kissed her cheek.

With Kian, she'd learned that shaking hands was as far as he would go. The guy was uncomfortable getting hugs from anyone other than his wife, mother, sisters, and daughter.

"Someone is missing," she said, glancing around. "Where is Allegra?"

"She's at Annani's." Syssi motioned for them to sit down. "She has her grandmother wrapped around her little finger."

"Like everyone else," Kian said with pride in his voice.

After Syssi made everyone cappuccinos and Okidu served his chocolate cake, they all got busy oohing and ahhing at the divine taste of chocolaty goodness. Some small talk ensued, and then Syssi put her cup on the coffee table and looked at Jasmine with so much concern and compassion in her eyes that Jasmine's guts twisted in anticipation.

"I had another vision about your mother," she said. "I didn't summon it or even think about her while falling asleep. It came out of nowhere and hit me over the head like a brick."

Jasmine winced. "That doesn't sound good. What were you shown?"

"Kyra looked about your age in the vision, so what I saw must have happened long ago, close to when she disappeared from your life. She was in some institution. It looked like an asylum."

Jasmine's hand tightened around her coffee cup. "An asylum? Like a mental institution?"

Syssi nodded, looking even more pained. "It looked like a hospital, but the walls were covered in faded, peeling paint, and there were bars on the windows. There was only one bed in the room, the metal kind, and Kyra was chained to it."

The coffee cup started to tremble in Jasmine's hand. She set it down carefully as Ell-rom's arm went around her shoulders. "Chained how?"

"By her wrists, although I don't know why they bothered to chain her. She was drugged out of her mind."

Jasmine's throat started closing up on her as her memories of being drugged and abducted suddenly bubbled to the surface. "Why do you think she was drugged?"

Syssi swallowed audibly, and Jasmine braced for what she was about to say. "A man wearing a doctor's coat entered the room but wasn't there to help her." She met Jasmine's eyes, letting her see the pain and anger there. "Kyra didn't fight him, but it wasn't because she welcomed what he was doing to her."

Jasmine lifted her hand to stop Syssi from saying more but then shook her head. "I'm sorry. Please continue. I need to know."

"I woke up," Syssi said. "I forced myself to wake up because I couldn't stand seeing him violate her. But the vision was relentless, and it followed me to Kian's office."

Jasmine struggled to keep her composure. Her hands trembled in her lap as she pictured her mother chained to the metal bed, drugged and helpless, while that monster in a doctor's coat violated her.

A wave of nausea rolled through her stomach.

She wanted to cry, to scream, to hunt down everyone responsible and make them suffer, but more than anything, she wanted to understand why her mother had been taken and whether she was still alive.

Ell-rom's hand closed over hers, his touch warm and steady, his quiet strength helping to ground her.

"I'm so sorry," Syssi said softly. "I debated whether to share this with you, but you deserve to know the truth."

Jasmine swallowed hard. "No, I'm glad you told me. I wonder if any of it has to do with my father. If he knows."

"You will find out soon enough," Kian said. "The good news is that we know Kyra escaped and joined the resistance. Syssi's visions of her later in life prove that."

Visions were not proof, but everyone said that Syssi was exceptional and that her visions never lied. They could be misleading, though. She'd never seen Kyra's face when she had visions of her in the resistance. What if she was young in those as well, and the scene from the asylum had happened later?

"You should prepare for your conversation with your father," Kian said. "I want us to go over everything we know about Kyra."

Jasmine nodded.

"By the way." Kian put his empty cup down and

reached for the plate with the cake. "I've chosen Max to accompany you and Ell-rom to handle your father's thralling."

Jasmine couldn't suppress her grimace at the mention of Max. The Guardian had made his disdain for her clear from their first meeting, treating her with barely concealed contempt just because she reminded him of someone from his past.

"I know you and Max didn't get along," Syssi said gently, "but I have a strong feeling about this. He needs to be the one to go with you."

Looking into Syssi's earnest face, Jasmine felt her resistance softening. "If you say he needs to come, I won't argue with your impeccable intuition. I'll do my best to show him I'm much nicer than that woman he compared me to."

"That's not your responsibility," Ell-rom said, his voice carrying an edge. "You weren't the one who wronged him, and you don't need to prove anything. Max is the one who needs to work on his attitude." His fingers tightened protectively around hers. "If he steps out of line, I'll handle it."

Warmth bloomed in Jasmine's chest at her mate's protective instinct, but she shook her head. "I appreciate that, my love, but I can handle Max. I've dealt with plenty of people who've prejudged and misjudged me, including bullies." She smiled. "Usually, they come around once they realize how charming and sweet I am." She batted her eyelashes at him.

"You shouldn't have to charm someone who is supposed to do his job and act professionally," Ellrom muttered.

"No, but I choose to be gracious." She squeezed his hand. "It's easier than holding on to anger."

12

KIAN

Kian cleared his throat. "Let's focus on what we know about your mother. The more information you have going in, the better prepared you'll be to get answers from your father. It's best to get everything he knows about her in one go."

Jasmine straightened, looking relieved to shift to practical matters. "Most of what I know is from what Roni has gathered about her. Her original name was Kyra Fazel, and she changed it to Kira Orlova when she married my father in 1989. She came from Iran on a student visa in 1988 but dropped out of university after getting married."

"Do you remember her saying anything about her family?" Syssi asked. "Did she ever mention her mother or father?"

Jasmine shook her head. "I don't remember much. I was very little when she supposedly died."

She closed her eyes for a moment. "The best memory I have of her is her singing to me at night. It was in another language, and I always assumed it was Persian, but now I wonder if it might have been Kurdish."

"We can find recordings of both languages," Syssi suggested. "See which one sounds more familiar."

"That's a good idea," Jasmine agreed. "I can do that tonight. I will search for lullabies in both languages."

Kian nodded. "We also know that there is no record of her being declared dead or her being buried anywhere. The divorce papers she sent from Iran looked legit, with all the proper seals and signatures. It could be a sophisticated forgery, or her signature could have been obtained while she was drugged, and then a notary bribed to authenticate it."

Syssi cut off a small piece of cake with her spoon. "Which means she was either alive to sign them or someone went to a lot of trouble to forge them convincingly, which doesn't make sense. Why bother, right?"

"Why indeed?" Jasmine rubbed her chin. "The divorce papers were an act of kindness, freeing my father to remarry. No one other than my mother should have cared enough to go to all that trouble."

That was a good point, one which Kian hadn't considered before. "I guess we will only find out who did it once we find Kyra, but that's one more indication that she's alive."

Jasmine sighed. "I wish that to be true. Regrettably, the jewelry box that she left behind didn't hold any mysteries other than the tarot cards that were hidden in a secret compartment. The rings and the gold chain were just simple jewelry."

William's team had put the box through an X-ray machine instead of taking it apart, but they hadn't found anything hidden in the lining or additional secret compartments. The one where the tarot had been hidden wasn't even that clever. It was just an empty space at the bottom that was revealed once the partitions were pulled out. Kian wasn't even sure that Kyra had intended to hide them.

"The tarot cards themselves might be significant," he said. "They suggest she had some paranormal awareness. You probably inherited it from her."

Jasmine nodded. "That's one more reason I'm so hopeful she's still alive. Syssi was shown my mother when she asked to be shown Khiann. If my mother can also scry like me, but better, then all the puzzle pieces fall into place. She will help us find Khiann."

There was a long moment of silence as they all contemplated her statement.

"That's what I think as well," Syssi said. "I

remember you saying something about the tarot deck being special?"

"The deck wasn't unique when it was first printed in the nineties. It was quite popular, but it's no longer printed. I've always wondered if she was trying to tell me something with those cards, but I'm coming to the conclusion that she didn't really leave them for me. I think she left those things behind because she had to leave in a rush or against her will. My father got rid of all of her belongings except for that box, probably thinking that I should have something of hers."

"Did your father ever explain to you why there was no grave?" Syssi asked softly. "No memorial of any kind?"

"He didn't say that there was no grave." Jasmine looked like she was on the verge of tears, which made Kian profoundly uncomfortable. "He just refused to talk about her. He could barely look at me because I reminded him so much of her." She drew a shaky breath. "I used to think that it was just grief and that he must have loved her fiercely, but I'm no longer convinced of that. The emotion I mistook for pain could have been anger. It's also possible that he thought he was protecting me by shielding me from the truth."

Kian leaned back against the couch cushions. "Everything is possible, and speculating is good because it provides us with several avenues of investigation. When you ask your father for answers, you will have a larger arsenal of questions."

"I wonder if he knew that she had special abilities," Syssi said. "You should ask him about it."

"I will." Jasmine pulled out her phone. "I should write it all down and memorize it before heading out to the cabin. I will probably be so stressed that I will forget half of what I intended to ask him."

"I can remind you," Ell-rom said.

"Thanks." She cast him a smile.

"You can allow yourself to hope," Syssi said softly. "The visions were clear. Kyra is alive, she's strong, and she's doing important work."

"But she was also hurt." Jasmine's voice cracked.

"She survived," Syssi said quietly. "She escaped and found her way to the resistance."

13

KYRA

Dust rose in small clouds with each movement of Kyra's young fighters. She stood at the center, her body a coiled spring of potential energy in case one of her students got hurt.

They were practicing basic defensive techniques, but sometimes people got overexcited and forgot that this was training and they needed to be careful not to injure one another.

"Your stance is wrong," she called to Malik, a gangly teenager whose enthusiasm outpaced his skills. "Feet wider. Root yourself like a mountain, not a sapling in the wind."

Malik adjusted his movements, awkward but earnest. He had potential—raw, unrefined, but present. These fighters would continue the resistance long after she was gone.

Even if the angel of death never found her,

which given her twenty-some-year experience of effectively eluding him seemed likely, she would have to leave this base and move to another to hide the fact that she wasn't aging.

Kyra was going to miss them.

Some new fighters had been with her for months, others only weeks. Within them, the same fire burned—the desire to fight against oppression, protect their people, and make a difference. It was that fire that drew her to teaching, even though others in the camp were equally capable of providing instruction.

"Remember," she said, her voice carrying across the training ground, "your enemy will always be stronger. More heavily armed. Better equipped." She paused, meeting each student's eyes in turn. "But they are not smarter. They are not more determined. And they do not have our cause. They will run to save their lives while we will keep fighting until our last breath to save our families, our people. We are the shield that keeps them alive."

Kyra demonstrated the movement again, her body flowing from one position to another. The other trainees watched, most with admiration, some with envy, and a few with a twinge of fear. She pretended not to notice the whispers that sometimes followed her—stories of her impossible feats, rumors of her supernatural abilities.

Let them wonder.

Mystery was its own kind of shield.

"Watch how the body moves," she instructed. "It's not about strength. It's about understanding your movement, your breath." She adjusted a young woman's arm position. "Feel the flow of energy through your body. Let it guide you."

The amber pendant at her throat warmed slightly—a familiar sensation she'd learned to interpret as guidance and other times as a warning. Sometimes, she wondered if the stone was sentient in some way, if it had chosen her rather than the other way around. It had been with her since her escape from that place of horror and darkness, though the exact circumstances of finding it were lost in the haze of her fractured memories.

A flicker of movement caught her peripheral vision. It would have been nothing to anyone else—a loose stone, perhaps, or a shift of wind, but Kyra's enhanced senses detected the precise moment a training knife was about to slip from its poorly secured sheath.

She leaped and caught it before it could pierce the foot of the clumsy young fighter, her movements faster than should have been possible.

Her students froze, looking between Kyra and the fallen weapon. She could read the questions in their eyes, the same questions she asked herself daily but never found answers to.

"How did you move that fast?" Malik asked. "And how did you know it was going to fall?"

"Training," she said dismissively. "One day, you'll develop the same ability. Always ensure your equipment is secure and your shoelaces are tied. Small mistakes of negligence can cost you your life." She demonstrated the proper way to fasten the sheath for the umpteenth time, shifting their attention from her impossible speed to the practical lesson.

Rashid, the camp's healer, watched from the edge of the training ground. His lips curled up in a knowing smile, making Kyra's skin prickle. He was too bright not to notice that she never let him treat her wounds, always dismissing them as scratches. More than once, she'd caught him studying her with thoughtful eyes, trying to solve the puzzle she presented.

The training continued as the sun climbed higher, and Kyra kept moving among the young fighters, checking stances and correcting techniques. She loved doing that. Perhaps it filled the void in her chest that craved motherhood.

After all, this was probably as close as she would ever get.

The little girl with eyes that mirrored her own that sometimes appeared in her dreams might be the manifestation of her yearnings, but what if she was real? A sister, perhaps? Was there a family out there somewhere wondering what had happened to her?

The asylum had stolen so many memories, leaving only fragments that made little sense.

"Enough for today," she called as the sun descended. "Practice what you've learned until it becomes as easy as breathing, as automatic as a heartbeat. The better you get, the better chance you have of surviving."

Most of them knew that there was no way out and that they would probably die fighting, but everyone needed hope, a light at the end of the tunnel, and training might make the difference between life and death.

As the students dispersed, wiping sweat from their brows and collecting their equipment, Kyra noticed Rashid pushing off the post he'd been leaning against and then walking toward her.

"Interesting training today." His eyes lingered on a fresh tear in her sleeve—a tear that revealed unmarked skin beneath where a blade should have left a wound hours earlier. She'd been careless, letting her guard down momentarily during a demonstration. The blade had definitely nicked her, she'd felt it, but like always, the wound had healed almost instantly.

"Your healing is remarkable," he said softly.

"I was lucky." She shrugged. "The blade never touched my skin."

But they both knew she was lying. Just as they

both knew about the other wounds that had healed on their own—bullet grazes that disappeared within minutes, knife cuts that sealed themselves but had left a trail of blood stains on her uniform that were difficult to explain.

"One day, you'll tell me what they did to you to make you so resilient. It's not natural."

Kyra turned away, busying herself with collecting the practice targets. "I don't know what you're talking about."

"Right." Rashid stepped closer, lowering his voice. "Why are you lying for the regime dogs? Are you afraid that they will come for you?"

Yes, she was, and it was tempting to share her concerns with someone, but she couldn't.

It was too risky.

Still, for a brief moment Kyra allowed herself to imagine telling him about her enhanced strength and speed, rapid healing, hearing, eyesight, and sense of smell, and how she never seemed to age. About the fragments of memory that haunted her dreams, the child's face that brought tears to her eyes without explanation. About the fear that whatever she was, whatever had been done to her in that asylum, might someday be used against her people.

Instead, she straightened her shoulders and met his gaze. "Let it go, Rashid. Not everything needs a scientific explanation. Sometimes, it's good to accept there are such things as luck and fate."

14

ELL-ROM

Ell-rom looked out the window, turning his face away from Kian and pretending to observe the scenery they were passing by on the way to the keep.

The male was so strong, so capable, so ruthless that he made Ell-rom feel ashamed of his own cowardice. He'd tried to keep his expression schooled, but it was hard to do when his stomach churned with self-loathing, not for the task ahead, but for his fear of it.

Still, there was no hiding his knuckles from Kian, which were white from clasping his hands tightly in his lap to conceal their trembling.

The trip to the keep might be more tolerable if Jasmine was with him, but he didn't want her to see him executing these humans with no more than a thought. She'd seen him do it before, but that was a knee-jerk reaction to the vagabond holding a gun to her head. He hadn't planned to do that, hadn't even been sure that he could, and he'd done it to defend her.

The only other time he'd used his lethal ability had been in the temple back on Anumati, and he hadn't been aware of doing anything other than just wishing the guard dead for tormenting his sister. When the head priestess had confronted him and Morelle about the guard's death the next day, Ell-rom had been shocked, and he hadn't really believed her. Still, from that day forward, he was careful about wishing anyone dead.

Now, he was going to kill in cold blood.

Ell-rom had no idea what it would do to him, and he didn't want Jasmine to be exposed to the aftermath.

"They deserve far worse than what you are about to do to them," Kian said from beside him, his voice sounding just slightly less gruff than usual. "By delivering a swift death, you are showing them a mercy that they wouldn't have gotten from me otherwise."

Ell-rom turned to his nephew. "I know that logically, but going from an acolyte to executioner is not easy. I'm about to deliver death not in the heat of a battle or in the defense of those who can't defend themselves."

"That's the wrong way to think about it," Anandur said from the front of the vehicle. "By killing them, you will be saving countless victims.

With the way our justice system works or rather doesn't, it would have taken far too long to even get these monsters arrested, tried, and sentenced, and in the meantime, they would have been free to continue the devil's work. And even if they eventually ended up behind bars, they would have been back on the streets in no time. Money talks even in the halls of the so-called justice, and those perverts have lots of it."

Ell-rom shook his head. "Are the human judges so easy to bribe?"

"Not all of them," Kian said. "But enough, and since these pedo rings seem to be run by Doomers, they can thrall jury and judges to deliver minimal sentences and then commute them even further." He crossed his arms over his chest. "I don't like taking on the vigilante role, and I would much rather leave the dirty work to the human authorities. But when a government fails to protect its most vulnerable citizens from criminals and terrorists, people need to take matters into their own hands and safeguard their children."

Brundar, who usually didn't show a reaction to anything, nodded in agreement.

Easy for them to talk. They weren't the ones with the finger on the trigger, so to speak.

"I'm not arguing with you about the merit of eliminating these evil humans, but you are not the ones tasked with their execution."

"Let me tell you about something we've

recently encountered in Mexico," Kian said, shifting to face Ell-rom more directly. "We were on a wedding cruise, a grand vacation that included almost every clan member, and none of us expected to do any killing. Then, a group of us on a shore excursion stumbled upon a cartel operation." Kian's jaw tightened. "They slaughtered an entire village, including babies and elders, except for the young women and girls of that village, whom they planned on selling as sex slaves. They did that to teach the locals a lesson so no one would dare oppose them. Then they violated these women who had just witnessed their families being murdered."

Bile rose in Ell-rom's throat. "Why are you telling me this?"

"Because the Guardians who were on that shore excursion, who were there to have fun, tore the monsters apart with their bare hands and fangs." Kian's eyes shone with an inner light, and his fangs elongated. "They had weapons on them, but they chose to do that up close and personal. They tore the evil scum to shreds. It wasn't quick, and it wasn't merciful."

"Talk about an execution," Anandur said. "It was done with extreme prejudice."

The gruesome descriptions should have horrified Ell-rom, and in a way they did, but somehow, they had also eased his stress and lessened his anxiety. At least he would deliver justice with just a thought, not with his hands and fangs.

He wondered if he would have been driven to such savagery if he had witnessed what those Guardians had.

If trained immortal warriors, who had no doubt experienced war and savagery before, had been so enraged by the pain and suffering they'd witnessed, the depth of human evil, then he would have probably reacted the same way and joined them in their savage act of revenge.

"Thank you for telling me this." He gave Kian a weak smile. "I will probably have nightmares because of the images you planted in my head, but I feel a little better about what I'm about to do."

"You are welcome." Kian's fangs started to recede. "Several Guardians have verified the guilt of the humans in the dungeon. You can skip verification if your thralling ability isn't fully developed yet. Perhaps it would be better if you didn't peek into their minds. The things you will see in there will give you much worse nightmares than what I've just shared with you."

Kian's insinuation was a little offensive. His nephew, the clan leader, saw Ell-rom as someone with a weak constitution—a former acolyte who was ill-suited to violence.

Kian wasn't wrong, but he wasn't entirely correct either. Kra-ell priesthood was not merciful, and it wasn't peaceful. It couldn't be. They served a harsh goddess and a warring population. He and his sister had trained in hand-to-hand combat from early childhood. For a Kra-ell, Ell-rom's aversion to killing was a character flaw. But if he wanted to be useful to his sister and her clan, he needed to toughen up.

"I trust the Guardians' judgment," he said, "but I still need to verify the guilt of those humans myself." He hesitated, then asked the question that had been bothering him for days, "Is there a chance that what I see in their minds could be fantasies rather than actual deeds? Imagining such horrors is despicable but does not call for an execution."

"There's a clear difference," Kian said. "As your thralling abilities develop, you'll be able to access deeper layers of consciousness where fantasies are stored. They have a fuzzier quality to them than real memories, so it's not likely that you will see them, and if you do, you'll know the difference. The tricky part can be recent memories of movies or television that can feel quite real. Still, the subject won't be personally present in those memories of what he saw, so you'll be able to tell the difference."

Ell-rom was relieved. His thralling skills were still developing, but since there weren't many humans in the village to practice on, he hadn't made as much progress as he would have liked with that. Still, he was improving.

The SUV fell silent except for the soft hum of

the engine, and Ell-rom watched the barren mountains sliding past. So many of them were scorched by recent fires.

As he thought of the gross incompetence of the authorities and all the bad decisions they had made that led to this disaster, echoes of what Kian had said reverberated in his mind. When the government failed to protect its people, they needed to form their own militias to protect themselves from crime.

Ell-rom chuckled softly. He was thinking like a Kra-ell.

Back home, each tribe had its own guard and its own resources, and for hundreds of thousands of years, they had killed each other off in endless tribal wars. It took a ferocious queen to stop the endless bloodshed.

The wars had ended, but the tribal structures remained intact, and he couldn't say in good conscience that the Kra-ell system was better. The truth was that if even the gods, who'd ruled this galaxy for hundreds of thousands of years, hadn't come up with a perfect system, it likely didn't exist.

15

KIAN

Ell-rom looked a little less frazzled, but perhaps he needed a wider view to understand how crucial his talent might be if it could work from a distance. Kian desperately needed a way to take Navuh out, and Ell-rom's unique ability might be the only tool at his disposal that could achieve that while preventing catastrophic loss of life on the Doomers' island.

On the other hand, Ell-rom was barely hanging in there, and telling him about more crap could potentially break the tentative hold he had on himself. It could also go the other way and force to the surface the steel Kian was sure his uncle possessed.

The problem was that Ell-rom's death-by-thought talent, or death-ray as Jasmine called it, might not work on immortals, in the same way that other immortal paranormal talents didn't.

Still, Ell-rom was half god, half Kra-ell, which made his and his twin sister's talents as unique as their heritage. Perhaps he was capable of killing immortals from afar just by wishing them dead, but Kian couldn't test it on the two they had because he still needed them.

Perhaps once their utility was exhausted, he would let Ell-rom experiment on them.

Then another thought hit Kian. What if he revived some of the Doomers they were keeping in stasis and let Ell-rom practice on them?

Annani would disapprove of that, he was sure, but what if he didn't tell her about it until after it was done?

His mother would be mad, but Kian preferred apologizing to asking for permission and being denied, especially given the stakes involved.

"The humans we captured are disposable," he said. "They are the end users, the perpetrators of the crimes, but they don't know much about the organization and how it is run. The masterminds behind the operation are our enemies, and we captured two in the operation. I would have loved to test your ability on them as well, but I need them for a little longer. Toven and I interrogated them the day after they were brought to the keep, and what we learned was troubling."

Ell-rom released a very un-princely snort. "More troubling than torturing children?"

"Good point, but I guess there is no bottom to

greed, to thirst for power, and to depravity, and in this case, it's all three. During the interrogation, the Doomers revealed that their pedophilia rings aren't just about sick pleasure or money, which I have already suspected. I just didn't realize the extent of the operation. The Brotherhood have always used extortion to influence global politics, but until a few years ago, they did that the old-fashioned way by trapping influential men with evidence of them having sex with paid partners and then threatening them with exposure if they didn't cooperate. But people these days don't care about men who cheat on their wives or even those who crawl naked on all fours with a dog leash around their necks. They do care, however, about those who hurt children." Kian grimaced. "For now, at least. I wonder how long it would take for humans to accept even that as normal. Some countries have recently lowered the age of consent for girls to nine, and I didn't hear widespread condemnation in the media, on campuses, or among the intelligentsia."

Ell-rom's eyes blazed with anger. "That's monstrous. Pure evil."

At the front of the vehicle, Brundar uttered a vicious curse. "I would personally castrate any pervert who thinks that a nine-year-old girl is bride material."

Ell-rom's eyes widened, probably not because of the vehement declaration but because it was more than he'd heard Brundar say since he'd met the guy. "Tell me when and where, and I'll join you."

Kian laughed, clapping Ell-rom on his arm. "There's the steel I knew you were hiding. I just wonder which side of you is responsible, the Kra-ell or the god."

"The one with moral clarity," Ell-rom hissed between his elongated fangs. "Is that the Doomers' doing?"

Kian shrugged. "I don't think even the Doomers would do such a thing. They don't benefit from it, and as much as I despise them and everything they stand for, the third-world countries that perpetrate ever-worsening abuse of their female populations are already in ruin, so the Doomers no longer need to get involved to make things worse. Right now, the Brotherhood is working on destabilizing the first-world countries so they can ruin them from the inside as well. That's Navuh's main strategy. They're using pedophile rings to gather blackmail material on influential people—politicians, business leaders, and anyone else with any power and influence."

Ell-rom's expression darkened. "How many of those perverted people are out there?"

"More than I ever imagined, and I'm mad at myself for thinking that it was a fringe problem or a conspiracy theory. The numbers are staggering. Hundreds of thousands of children are being exploited, and the Doomers are riding the worst of the wave. The more depraved the act, the more control they gain over these people. It's all part of Navuh's plan to destabilize societies from within and bring about the fall of humanity."

Ell-rom looked confused. "What you describe is horrible, but I don't understand how it can bring about the fall of civilization. My impression is that most people are decent."

Kian drew a deep breath. "Most people are indeed decent, but they are easy to manipulate, which is the gods' fault for designing them that way. The Brotherhood is using the blackmail material they collect to influence legislation, redirect resources, and corrupt institutions. The goal is to create chaos and decay in any way they can. More wars, more civil unrest, fewer children born, etc. A weakened humanity is easier to control, and that's what Navuh's goal has always been. To have every human on Earth enslaved to him and to worship him as a god."

Ell-rom frowned. "What can we do about this? How can we stop it?"

"Killing Navuh is the best option and will probably lead to the Brotherhood falling apart. His adopted sons would fight among themselves for power or split apart, with each taking a portion of the warriors and resources. They will still pose a threat, but divided, they will not be as strong, and we might be able to take them out one by one until they are down to small bands of bandits roaming the world."

"Then what's stopping you?" Ell-rom asked as Anandur drove into the keep's underground parking.

"We can't get to Navuh." Kian sighed. "We don't have enough warriors. We can't nuke the island either, because many of the people living there don't deserve to die, and I don't even want to think what it would do to the surrounding islands. The nukes of today are more precise than they were during WWII, so the fallout might be minimal, but still. Not something I'm comfortable with."

Ell-rom nodded. "I understand now. You are hoping that my talent can kill him from afar."

"It would solve my biggest problem." Kian let out a breath. "Two of my biggest problems. If you can kill from afar, you might be able to get rid of the Eternal King as well, and that would be fantastic not just for Earth but the entire galaxy."

Ell-rom snorted. "No pressure. No pressure at all."

16

MORELLE

Morelle was fascinated by the toy representation of Annani's living room that Allegra had created. She and Evie sat on a thick mat spread across the floor, oblivious to the adults around them.

Watching them play was heartwarming. The girls were so serious about the toy furniture and dolls, which Allegra was arranging to mimic the scene in the room she was in.

Morelle wondered which doll was supposed to represent whom.

None could match the regality Annani projected or Amanda's polished beauty, but she and Syssi were a little easier to portray using dolls that had been crafted by humans. It looked like so much fun that she was tempted to join the girls on the floor and play with their dolls, but it would be too embarrassing.

Perhaps some other time when she wasn't there to be tested.

It occurred to her that playtime could be even more fun for the girls with dolls that looked like the immortals, and perhaps Brandon could suggest it as a project to some of the creatives in the clan.

Was fashioning dolls a difficult thing to do?

Morelle had no idea. The more she learned, the greater her lack of knowledge seemed.

"I need to thank you," Syssi said, leaning over to kiss her cheek.

"For what?" Morelle turned to her, surprised by the sudden show of affection.

"For giving me and Amanda an excuse to take Fridays off work." Syssi's eyes sparkled with amusement. "We were already working half days on Fridays, but now that Amanda is obsessed with testing your abilities, she decided to change our schedule. We'll be working four days a week at the university, and Fridays will be dedicated to you."

"I'm honored," Morelle said. "And I would be delighted to spend more time with you and your girls." Her gaze drifted back to the children, noting how carefully they'd been positioned away from the fireplace.

The dangerous stone mantels had been replaced in every house that had children throughout the village, including Annani's, because she often entertained the little ones at her place.

"Come have tea," Annani called from the couch,

gesturing toward the elegant spread on the coffee table that her Odus had prepared. Delicate sandwiches were arranged on silver platters, their crusts perfectly trimmed, accompanied by an assortment of small cakes that looked almost too beautiful to eat.

As Morelle settled beside her sister, she marveled at how wonderfully different life in the village was from her life in the temple. There, her and Ell-rom's meals had been eaten quickly and in silence, mostly in the animal enclosure. The Kra-ell subsisted on blood, and no one in the temple complex needed food delivered to them other than the animals that were kept there as a convenient blood supply for the younger children and sometimes also for older ones when hunting was not possible for whatever reason. The Head Priestess had put Ell-rom and Morelle in charge of feeding the animals, so they could eat the fruits and berries that had been brought in as their feed. They often hid some of it under their robes to bring to their room, even though the priestess had forbidden it.

Here in Annani's village, eating was an occasion for gathering, for conversation, and for strengthening bonds.

"Are you nervous about today's testing?" Annani asked, pouring tea into fine china cups.

Morelle accepted her cup and inhaled the fragrant steam. "A little," she admitted. "Drawing on your power is intense." She glanced at her sister.

"I will need to be very careful not to draw too much."

"Do not fear, Morelle." Annani's voice was firm but gentle. "I have more than enough to spare, and we need to understand the limits of your ability."

"I know you can spare it, but what if I can't contain it? What if I channel too much and hurt people or myself?"

Amanda had designed a series of tests to measure her ability on different weights and distances—how heavy an object Morelle could move and how far she could move it while drawing on different power sources. The scientist in Amanda wanted precise measurements in controlled conditions, and they both wanted safety, but Morelle wanted it above all other considerations, while Amanda was willing to take more risks.

"Good point." Annani lifted one of the tiny sandwiches off the plate. "I am glad that you are not as impulsive as I am. That you are careful."

"I have to be," Morelle said. "Amanda calls Ellrom and me the Power Duo, but other than the danger of draining someone of their power or myself, I don't see how my ability could ever be useful. I can't bring down buildings or demolish bridges. I can only drain power from people I'm near, and I will never get close enough to the Eternal King to use it against him unless he comes to Earth, and I hope he never does."

The only reason her grandfather would do that was to find her and Ell-rom and kill them, but since he supposedly never soiled his own hands and preferred to send others to do it for him, the chances of him coming here in person were negligible.

Then again the Fates, or the Mother of All Life, had designed Ell-rom and her to have unique powers for a reason, so maybe that possibility wasn't as far-fetched as she thought.

Morelle set her teacup down and turned to Syssi. "I have a question. Would it be possible for you to have a vision about the Eternal King and whether he has any notion of ever visiting Earth?"

Syssi looked thoughtful, absently stirring her tea. "I could try." She looked up. "It's so strange that Earth is hidden from the seers on Anumati, but Anumati is not hidden from me."

"I wondered about that." Morelle leaned forward. "Why do you think that is?"

"It is the Fates' doing." Annani set her cup down. "The blocking seems to work only one way. Like a one-way mirror."

"Or a shield," Syssi said. "Perhaps Earth's magnetic field blocks it from seers on other planets, and Anumati doesn't have one."

Morelle reached for a sandwich, considering what Syssi and Annani had said. "I wonder how the gods discovered Earth if their seers couldn't see it. They came here for gold, but with how vast the galaxy is, I doubt they stumbled upon it by chance. Something must have indicated the presence of gold to them, but it wasn't their seers."

Annani turned to Amanda. "Is life possible on planets without a magnetic field?"

Amanda tapped a finger on her lower lip. "Earth's magnetic field protects us from charged solar particles and cosmic rays, but it's not essential to life. Come to think of it, the lack of such protection on Anumati might be the reason that the gods chose to live underground. On the other hand, the Kra-ell and all other life forms on Anumati seem to have no problem existing on the surface, so perhaps they have a natural immunity to radiation."

"It makes sense," Annani said. "What does not make sense is that the gods did not have natural protection against the radiation as well, which might indicate that they were not indigenous to Anumati. That is why they chose to live underground and why they needed gold to protect their aboveground vehicles and interstellar ships from radiation."

The only thing Morelle understood from her sister's speech was that the gods might not have been native to Anumati.

"The Kra-ell believe that they and the gods originated from the same people and that the gods accepted a bargain from the trickster that offered them knowledge about gene manipulation, while the Kra-ell refused it because they wanted to live authentically and naturally."

"Fascinating." Syssi reached for the teapot and refilled her cup. "The things you can stumble upon when you let your mind wander. Maybe the genetic manipulation cost them their natural protection from radiation."

Amanda shrugged. "Or maybe the Kra-ell myth is not true. I kind of like the hypothesis that the gods were not native to Anumati and came from somewhere else in the universe."

Syssi arched a brow. "Why?"

"I would like to believe that the entire universe is brimming with life."

"The Fates work in mysterious ways," Annani said. "Perhaps they had a hand in creating this protection, knowing that Earth would need to be a sanctuary someday."

Amanda glanced at the children playing on the floor before returning her gaze to her mother. "I bet there are many sanctuaries like Earth out there. Many places that the Eternal King can't see. I hope the rebels on Anumati know of them and can use them to hide."

Morelle liked the idea of Earth itself helping to protect them from harm, both natural and unnatural. It was shielding them from radiation and also from her evil grandfather. She thought about her power. Was her ability to draw energy from others and redirect it really so different from what Earth might be doing with its magnetic field, redirecting harmful radiation away from the planet's surface?

Maybe understanding how Earth protected itself might help her and Ell-rom understand their abilities better. Perhaps other paranormal talents as well.

No one had ever said anything to that effect, but as someone who knew next to nothing, she had the advantage of thinking freely without being burdened by accepted dogmas.

"I hope Ell-rom is okay," Annani said. "He is about to be tested as well, and I worry about what it might do to him."

Morelle nodded, her throat tightening. She'd wanted to go with Ell-rom to the keep, to support him as he tested his deadly power, but he'd refused her, and he'd refused Jasmine as well. "He's so gentle by nature," she said. "Even knowing these men deserve death for what they've done, it must be so hard for him."

"That gentleness is what makes him perfect for his talent," Annani said. "He will never abuse his power or take pleasure in dealing death. He will do what needs to be done, quickly and mercifully."

"Still..." Morelle glanced at the clock. Hours yet until dinner, when she'd see her brother and be able to gauge how he was handling this. "I worry about the toll it might take on his spirit."

"Kian is with him," Syssi said. "He might not seem like the nurturing type, and he's not, but he knows how to motivate people. He will give Ell-rom the strength he needs."

Annani nodded. "I agree with Syssi. Kian is not going to let this break Ell-rom."

Amanda put her teacup down. "Now that we've solved all the mysteries of the universe, it's time for testing. I set up the equipment outside." She looked at Syssi. "Are you going to stay here to watch the girls, or are we going to leave the Odus in charge?"

"I'll stay," Syssi said. "You don't really need me out there. Do you?"

Amanda leaned to kiss her cheek. "I always need you, but I can manage without you."

17

MAX

Max walked into Kian's old office in the keep, pulled out a chair, and sat down at the conference table. The room smelled faintly of furniture polish and coffee—Okidu's work. Kian's butler had arrived earlier to prepare the office, and he'd left the space spotless and well-stocked with refreshments.

When Onegus had explained to him why Kian was bringing Ell-rom to the dungeon, Max finally understood things that hadn't made sense to him before. First, he'd wondered why so many humans had been brought to the keep instead of being disposed of. It wasn't as if they could learn much from them. Then Onegus had instructed several Guardians to go over the human prisoners' recent memories and write down what they had seen.

The evidence was damning, the scope of their

crimes defying comprehension, and since it had been confirmed by several Guardians, it was indisputable. Now that Max knew what Ell-rom was about to do, it all made sense.

The prince was not a hardened warrior, and killing for sport was not something that was up his alley. He had an amazing ability to kill with a mere thought, but he needed to test it, and for that, he needed victims who deserved killing without a shadow of a doubt.

The talent was enviable and useful, and Max found it odd that it had been bestowed on someone as squeamish about killing as the prince. And yet, the Fates' guiding hand and the many blessings they had showered upon the clan over the past few years were hard to deny, so the prince might still have an important role to play in the grand tapestry of the clan's destiny.

The sound of four sets of footsteps in the corridor announced the arrival of Kian, Ell-rom, Anandur, and Brundar.

As Max rose to his feet to greet them, Kian entered with Ell-rom at his side and the brothers behind them.

"Good afternoon," Max said. "The coffee is freshly brewed, and Okidu left some refreshments."

"Maybe later." Kian turned to the prince. "This is Max, the other Guardian who's going to accompany you and Jasmine to her father's cabin tomorrow."

Max extended his hand. "It's my pleasure, Your Majesty."

The prince grimaced. "Please, call me Ell-rom." He shook Max's hand firmly.

"Very well. It's a pleasure to officially meet you, Ell-rom."

The prince's expression didn't change. He still looked like there was something sour in his mouth. Jasmine must have told her mate about her displeasure at meeting Max on the cruise, and he couldn't really blame her. His behavior had been inexcusable.

"I'll leave you two to get acquainted," Kian said. "I need to speak with Onegus." He gestured to Anandur and Brundar, who followed him out of the office.

Great. Now, he was stuck with the guy who could kill with a thought and who had no reason to be nice to him.

The silence that fell was deafening.

Ell-rom stood near the door, his discomfort evident in every line of his body, and Max had a feeling that it was not just about the prince's animosity toward him. The guy was about to do something that would have been difficult for most anyone, let alone a civilian who'd been raised to be a cleric.

"If you have any questions for me, now is probably a good time," Max offered, expecting questions about his history with Jasmine and preparing to apologize and explain.

"Tell me a little about yourself." The prince's request surprised him. "Who are you when you're not being a Guardian?"

Max blinked. "I..." He moved to the coffee service Okidu had left, more to give his hands something to do than from real thirst. "Would you like some coffee?"

"Yes, please."

As Max poured two cups, he gathered his thoughts. "Right now, I don't have much of a life outside the force, but it wasn't always like that. I've done a lot of things during my five hundred and twenty-three years of life, but my first job was on the force. I joined a little over five hundred years ago and served for seventy-two years before retiring."

Ell-rom accepted the coffee. "What did you do after you retired?"

Max smiled. "Believe it or not, I was a stage actor for a while. I even joined the opera, but I never got any leading roles, so I moved on."

"An actor and an opera singer?" Ell-rom's cool demeanor cracked slightly. "That's unexpected. It would seem that you have more in common with my Jasmine than either of you realize."

"I know. I heard her singing at the wedding and then at Rob's induction ceremony. She's amazing."

Ell-rom beamed with pride. "She's extraordinary." He took a sip from his coffee. "What did you do after you gave up on acting and singing?"

"I built homes. For most of my life, I was a stonemason." Max pulled out a chair for Ell-rom and one for himself. "There's something deeply satisfying about building things, creating something permanent and beautiful that brings utility and joy to others." He paused, cradling the paper cup between his palms. "Sometimes, I miss it. The simplicity, the camaraderie with other builders, the satisfaction of creating something that lasts. It's very different from what we do now."

"Rescuing trafficking victims?"

Max nodded. "That's more fulfilling in many ways, but it's very taxing mentally. The things we see, the evil we encounter—it rubs off on you after a while." He studied Ell-rom's face. "I've lived for a long time and seen a lot of crap. But it's all new to you. You are still soft."

Ell-rom seemed taken aback by Max's straight talk, probably not expecting a lowly Guardian to talk to him so plainly. "I guess I am. Were you ever soft? Or were you born tough?"

Max laughed. "We are all born soft, or at least most of us are. Time and experiences harden us, hone us. Warriors are like swords. They start soft and malleable, but with repeated strikes of the hammer, we become sharp and deadly."

Ell-rom nodded. "I like the analogy. I can think of a sword as something beautiful, not just as an instrument of death."

"I'm glad I could help." Max leaned back in the chair. "Those monsters deserve killing, Ell-rom. Don't feel sorry for them. Think of them as cancer cells and of yourself as the medication that eradicates them. If you leave them alone, they will kill the organism. You are necessary to saving it."

The prince smiled. "This one is not as good. Anyone can kill, which means that there is nothing special about my kind of medicine."

Max chuckled. "Regrettably, I don't have any smarter analogies. I wanted to impress you with how deep of a thinker I can be, but the truth is that I'm a simple guy."

"I doubt that's true." Ell-rom was quiet for a moment, staring into his coffee. "Why did you come back to the Guardian Force?" he asked finally. "Why return to this darkness?"

"Because I was needed and also because I had to get out of Scotland, and joining the force here seemed like a good idea."

"What happened in Scotland?" Ell-rom asked.

"I made a mistake. One that cost me a friendship." Max sighed, the old guilt rising. "I betrayed someone who was like a brother to me because of a woman. I wasn't young so I don't have the excuse of youth. But I was competitive, always had to win. I didn't realize—or maybe I didn't want to realize—that Din was in love with Fenella. I just saw it as a challenge."

"I assume you won?" Ell-rom's tone was neutral.

"I got the girl, lost my friend, and learned too late what really mattered." Max shook his head. "It happened fifty years ago, and Din still won't speak to me. Not that I blame him. Moving here was partly about escaping that constant reminder of my inexcusable mistake."

Ell-rom didn't look surprised by the revelation. "I was told that the woman looked a lot like Jasmine."

Max frowned. "Did Kian tell you about that?"

"Jasmine did. Amanda told her not to get upset over the way you reacted to her and explained why. Not that I accept it. I think it was immature of you, and given that you have lived centuries longer than I have and have vastly more life experience, you should know that."

Max met Ell-rom's gaze directly. "You are absolutely right. It was unfair and unprofessional of me. Jasmine didn't do anything to deserve the cold shoulder I gave her, and I should have apologized a long time ago."

"It's never too late, and you will discover that Jasmine does not hold grudges. She will forgive you easily." Ell-rom smiled. "I imagine carrying that guilt for fifty years is its own kind of punishment. You really should let it go. Your friend should have forgiven you a long time ago, and the fact that he didn't indicates that he might not have been as good of a friend as you thought he was."

"You know what? You are right." Max shook his head. "The training you got seems to have made you a good counselor. Have you thought about combining your occasional death-ray service with consulting? It could provide you with a professional balance."

Ell-rom gaped at him, looking unsure if Max had been serious or had meant it as a joke.

"I'm serious, Ell-rom. One does not preclude the other. We have only one counselor in the clan, and she is overworked because she takes care of the trafficking victims we rescue. Your services would be in high demand."

The prince shook his head. "I know so little of Earth's customs. How can I give advice to earthlings?"

"You just gave me excellent advice. You might want to take a couple of online classes first, or maybe more than that, but hey, you're immortal, so there is no rush."

"True." Ell-rom lifted the paper cup to his lips.

Max had hoped the prince would be cheered up by their talk, but he still seemed pained.

"These men chose their path," Max said. "They knew what they were doing was wrong. They knew that they were destroying these children, and they didn't care and did it anyway. By stopping them, you're saving countless others."

"I know." Ell-rom's voice was barely above a whisper. "It shouldn't be as hard as it is. I guess I need some of that hammering you mentioned before I turn into a sharp blade."

18

ELL-ROM

The conversation with Max had helped settle some of Ell-rom's nerves, but as Kian led him down the keep's corridors toward the cells, anxiety crept back in. His palms were sweating, and he felt nauseous.

"We'll start with something simple," Kian said, pulling out his phone and bringing up a photograph. "I want you to try directing your ability at this man."

Ell-rom stared at the image of an ordinary-looking middle-aged human. Nothing about him suggested the monster he apparently was. "I can't," he said. "Not without verifying his guilt myself."

Kian's expression hardened. "The test is to see if you can affect someone you've never met, using only an image. We need to know if your ability works at a distance." He paused, meeting Ell-rom's eyes. "The clan would never ask you to execute an innocent person. The Guardians have thoroughly verified his crimes. He's a monster."

The logic made sense, but something in Ell-rom still resisted. But hadn't he just been talking with Max about trust and necessary evils?

Taking a deep breath, he nodded. "I'll try."

He focused on the photograph, directing his death wish toward the man it depicted. Nothing felt different, though. There was no surge of power and no burning in the back of his eyes like when he'd killed that attacker in the alley. He knew even before Onegus's voice sounded in his earpieces that it hadn't worked.

"No effect," the chief said.

"Try again," Kian instructed. "This time, think about what he's done. The children he's hurt. The innocent lives he's ruined all for his sick pleasure."

Ell-rom closed his eyes, trying to summon righteous anger and channel it toward the photograph.

Still, he felt nothing.

"Nothing," Onegus confirmed.

Suddenly, fear gripped Ell-rom. "What if I accidentally killed someone else? Can we check the other prisoners?"

He hadn't felt anything, so probably nothing happened to anyone, but he couldn't be sure that the same reaction would take place each time he used his talent. He didn't remember feeling anything special when he'd killed that first guard, but then he still didn't remember anything from his life in the temple, only the bits and pieces he'd seen in his dreams and what Morelle had told him.

Luckily, she'd retained all of her memories.

"No one died," Onegus confirmed after a moment.

It was both a relief and a frustration. Why wasn't his ability working?

"Let's try something more direct," Kian said, leading him toward one of the heavy metal doors lining the corridor.

When the door opened, and Ell-rom got a look at the interior, it was nothing like he'd imagined. Instead of the dark, dank dungeon he'd expected, the cell was clean and modern, with cream-colored walls and new fixtures. The prisoner lay on a bed, lightly sedated and shackled.

"Tell us about the children you molested," Kian commanded, then turned to Ell-rom. "Look into his mind and see for yourself."

As the guy mumbled incoherent words, Ell-rom approached the bed hesitantly, looked down at the portly human, and reached out with his mind to access his memories.

The images that flooded his consciousness were worse than anything he could have imagined, and as bile rose in his throat, he yanked himself out of the monster's mind and struck with his death wish without giving it a second thought.

The man's eyes went blank, his body slack.

Dead.

Ell-rom felt no remorse, only a cold satisfaction that shocked him. Was this what Max had meant about becoming a blade?

"Damn it," Kian muttered. "I wanted you to try it from a distance first. Come on." He guided Ell-rom to another cell. "You need to control your temper."

Outside, Kian put his hand on Ell-rom's shoulder. "I'm sorry. I shouldn't have snapped at you. How are you feeling? Are you okay?"

"Yes. Surprisingly. I can kill monsters like him all day long and feel only satisfaction."

"Good." Kian clapped his shoulder. "Then let's continue, but this time, let's test the distance."

Ell-rom nodded. "I'll do my best to control the death ray."

The next prisoner looked equally ordinary and equally human. Regrettably, monsters didn't come with horns or with a tattoo on their forehead proclaiming them demon-spawned.

Ell-rom wouldn't have given the man a second glance on the street.

When Kian ordered the man to talk, Ell-rom hesitated before entering his mind, the horror of the previous one's memories still fresh in his mind. But he had to do this.

As he reached out again, accessing the human's memories, the flood of them hit him like a physical blow, and as the bile rose in his throat again and he yanked himself out of that cesspool, he couldn't hold it back this time.

Doubling over, he vomited onto the floor but managed to keep his death wish from striking.

"I'm so sorry," he gasped. "I'll clean that up." He wiped his mouth on his sleeve.

"Leave it," Kian said firmly. "The Guardians will handle it. You need some air." He steered Ell-rom toward the exit, his grip supportive but urgent.

As they waited for the elevator, Anandur walked over to a vending machine that was tucked into a corner and returned with a cold can.

"Drink this." He popped the lid. "It will help settle your stomach and wash away the bad taste."

"Thank you." Ell-rom gulped the sweet drink, the carbonation helping eliminate the acid taste in his mouth.

"You looked awesome when you killed that first bastard. Almost demonic. I never imagined that you could look so scary." He affected a shiver.

Kian shot the Guardian a warning glare, but Ell-rom shook his head. "It's alright. Jasmine told me how I looked when I killed that vagabond in the alley."

After they emerged from the keep's underground parking, Anandur drove Kian's vehicle aimlessly through the city streets, taking random turns while Ell-rom watched the normal world pass by outside and wondered who among the people shopping, walking dogs, living their lives, were evil like those in the keep's dungeons.

He had a feeling that he would never be able to look at humans again without thinking that some of them were monsters or all of them.

Gradually, though, his breathing steadied, and his heart rate normalized. The horrors he'd witnessed began to fade, though he knew he would never be rid of them no matter how long he lived.

After what felt like at least an hour, Kian shifted in his seat. "Try again," he said. "Think about the prisoner whose memories you saw. Think about justice and deliver it."

Ell-rom closed his eyes, picturing the man's face, remembering the atrocities he'd seen in his memories. This time, when he sent out his death wish, something felt different. A connection, almost like a thread stretching across the distance.

Kian pressed his earpiece. "Onegus?"

"Dead," came the reply. "Instantaneous."

Relief and something like pride crossed Kian's face. "Good. That will be all for today. I'm taking Ell-rom back to the village and we will continue testing on Monday." He turned to Ell-rom. "After you and Jasmine return from the cabin."

Ell-rom nodded, still processing what he had done.

His ability worked at a distance. He could deliver death from miles away. It should have terrified him, but instead, he felt a sense of peace.

He was delivering justice to those who had forfeited their right to life through their own evil actions.

"You did well," Kian said softly. "I know it wasn't easy."

"It was much easier than I thought it would be."

The city continued to drift past their windows. Somewhere out there, children were safer because two monsters would never hurt anyone again. It wasn't what he'd planned for his life to be about, but perhaps it was what he'd been created for all along.

Not a weapon of mass destruction but a precise instrument of justice. A blade, yes, but one that was wielded with purpose and control.

19

KYRA

Kyra sat at her desk and scanned the latest intelligence reports while trying to ignore the way Zara kept glancing at her when she thought Kyra wasn't looking. The whispers about her strange abilities had grown louder lately, especially after her performance during the last raid.

She shouldn't have been as obvious, but lives had been at stake, and that was more important than hiding her oddities.

"A few of the new guards at the compound aren't normal," Zara said. "I don't know how they do the things they do, but I must assume drugs. People can do extraordinary things when they are high."

"Like what?" Kyra asked.

"One of our watchers saw a guard lift a truck to get a bottle of coke that had rolled under it. He held it up with one hand and reached for the bottle with the other, and he didn't even seem to strain too hard to do that."

That would have been an impressive feat even for her, so she doubted that the report had been factual. "Maybe you should check the watcher for drugs. He must have been hallucinating."

Zara put her hands on her hips and struck a pose. "And what about the guard who jumped from the roof and kept running to catch a kid who'd been throwing rocks at their windows?"

Kyra's throat tightened. "What did he do to the kid?"

"Nearly tore off his ear and then kicked him so hard in the ass that he nearly shattered the boy's pelvis. Rashid took care of him."

"Good." Kyra rubbed a hand over her chin. "Maybe they are enhanced with steroids or something like that. The regime has been experimenting with drugs and conditioning for years."

She wasn't sure about what she'd just said, but someone had obviously done something to her to make her abnormal. Until now, though, Kyra hadn't encountered anyone else who could do the things she could.

"I don't know about that." Zara's dark eyes fixed on her. "You can do strange shit, and I know for a fact that you are not taking drugs."

The accusation hung in the air between them.

Kyra kept her face neutral, but her heart rate accelerated. "What are you suggesting?"

"Nothing." Zara looked away. "Maybe some people are just stronger and faster than others."

Soran entered the tent, breaking the tense moments and bringing with him the scent of wood smoke. "The weapons shipment to the post arrived last night," he said. "But that's not the interesting part. Those new guards unloaded three tons of cargo in under an hour. No machinery, just pure manpower."

"That's impossible," Kyra said, even though she could envision several people like her doing just that.

"Is it?" Rashid's voice came from the tent entrance. The healer stepped inside, his weathered face grave. "As impossible as wounds that vanish within hours? As impossible as surviving falls that should kill?"

Kyra's fingers brushed against her pendant, seeking comfort. "We need to focus on the intelligence. Given the elite guard, the prisoners that arrived last night must be important. What do our watchers inside the compound report?"

Soran gave her a look that spoke volumes, but she ignored it. Let them suspect what they would, but she wasn't going to admit anything.

He pulled out a chair and sat down. "They overheard the prisoners being questioned about resistance cells across the region and about safe houses we didn't even know existed. Someone is coordinating a massive intelligence operation."

"The new commander," Kyra said. "Everything has changed since he arrived. The guards are different, the security protocols are enhanced, and our people are getting caught at twice the normal rate." She studied the papers, trying to piece together the puzzle while ignoring the weight of their stares. "Show me the new patrol patterns."

Soran produced a map marked with red lines. "They've completely restructured their rotations. No blind spots, no gaps in coverage, and they are actually doing their jobs instead of playing cards and shooting the breeze like the old guards. Even the unenhanced ones are out of our league."

There was a note of desperation in his tone that she could understand but didn't accept. Every organization had weaknesses. It was just a matter of finding them.

Kyra stood, pacing the length of the tent. "Where there is a will, there is a way. We can't storm the place like we used to, but we can nip at their heels, so to speak, and find out what's so special about them."

Zara snorted. "Whatever they are taking, I want some of that."

Soran pinned Kyra with a hard stare. "If you know something about these enhanced soldiers, now would be a good time to spill it out."

Kyra turned to face them. "I've fought beside

you for fifteen years. I've bled for our cause. I've saved your lives more times than I can count. And you are questioning me?"

"We're grateful for your service," Rashid said. "But the knowledge you are keeping to yourself might be crucial to our success. Who are these soldiers? What are they capable of?"

Kyra let out a breath. "I don't know, and that's the truth." She braced her hands on the desk, studying the map to avoid their gazes. "I can no longer deny that I'm different, and in many ways I'm similar to those new special guards, but I don't know why or how it happened. I woke up in an asylum nearly twenty-five years ago with no memories, and abilities I couldn't explain. Those abilities allowed me to escape that hellhole and take other imprisoned women with me. They led me to the resistance. I don't even know my real last name or where I came from. The others called me Kyra, but even that might not be my real name. Now you know exactly what I know, and if you care for me and value my life, you won't tell anyone about what I just told you."

Each of the three punched a fist against their chest.

"Your secret is safe with us," Rashid said. "You are our secret weapon."

Zara nodded enthusiastically. "We couldn't have pulled off half the missions we have without you and your special abilities, but you are just one woman, and there are several enhanced soldiers in that compound. I say that we should move out of here before it's too late and establish a new base far away from here."

Kyra traced the patrol routes with her finger. "We can still do this. We just need to spend more time gathering intelligence."

"Are you going in yourself?" Rashid asked.

"I'm the only one who has a chance against them. I can switch places with one of the maids and spend some time mopping floors while observing and listening. No one ever pays attention to the cleaning staff."

They had two people working in the compounds—a kitchen assistant and a maid—who provided them with intel about the comings and goings in there, but neither had her superior hearing and eyesight. There was so much more she could learn than they could.

"What if you're caught?" Zara asked. "They might recognize you as one of them."

The question struck a chord of fear in Kyra but also intrigue. There had to be a connection between what happened to her in the asylum and these enhanced soldiers.

"Then I'll finally have some answers," she said, with more confidence than she felt.

As the meeting wound down, Soran lingered behind. "Can we talk?"

Kyra nodded even though she would have preferred not to have that talk with him.

He waited until they were alone. "You know I trust you with my life, right?"

"Of course. But?"

"But I'm worried. It can't be a coincidence that you have those special abilities and now these enhanced soldiers show up in our territory."

"You've known me for fifteen years. If they were looking for me, they would have found me a long time ago. It's a coincidence."

"I don't think so." He stepped closer. "We might not have been the only ones who noticed your abnormalities. Our enemies might have noticed them, too. That might be why they are here. They might have come for you specifically, Kyra, and it would be a great mistake for you to walk into the lions' den and give them what they came for."

Kyra sank into her chair, suddenly exhausted. "I don't think they are here because of me. I've been careful, and this place is in the middle of nowhere, which is why the regime chose it as an interrogation center. In either case, I have no choice. I have to find answers, and I'm the only one who can do that."

20

JASMINE

It was still dark outside when Jasmine and Ell-rom left Brandon's house. Settling into the SUV's back seat, she stifled a yawn and allowed her eyelids to succumb to gravity's pull. The familiar scent of leather seats and Ell-rom's cologne wrapped around her like a cozy blanket.

"Tired?" Ell-rom's voice was soft as she leaned against his arm.

"Mmm." She snuggled closer. "This is an ungodly hour to be awake."

Max slid in beside her, and she tensed momentarily, remembering his not-so-friendly attitude from before. He'd apologized to Ell-rom for how he'd treated her, but he hadn't apologized to her yet.

Besides, having any guy who wasn't her mate sit so close felt awkward, uncomfortable to the point that she felt her skin prickling. It reminded her of what Margo had said about fated mates. Once they were bonded, they couldn't feel attraction toward anyone else and were even repulsed by members of the opposite gender.

Evidently it was true because, under different circumstances, she would have found Max attractive. He smelled of soap, shampoo, and cologne, and his clothes had been freshly laundered. There was nothing about him that should have repulsed her.

"You can sleep on the plane," Anandur said as Brundar took the passenger seat. "It's a five-hour flight to New Jersey."

"I like flying," Jasmine said.

Generally, that was true, but today she was flying to meet her father and confront him about her mother's fate, and she was scared of what she was going to learn.

Beside her, Ell-rom shifted. "I've never experienced taking to the air before."

"Actually, you did." Jasmine lifted her head to look at him. "We didn't drive you here from Tibet. You flew."

"I was in stasis and unaware." His fingers drummed nervously on his thigh. "How safe is this mode of transportation?"

"Very safe." She covered his hand with hers, stilling the nervous movement. "Safer than riding in a car."

"Look on the bright side," Anandur called from

the front, waggling his eyebrows in the rearview mirror. "You'll get a chance to join the mile-high club. That should distract you from worrying about flying."

As Max snorted beside her, Jasmine felt her cheeks warm up.

Ell-rom's brow furrowed in confusion. "What kind of club is that?"

Anandur's grin widened. "It has to do with having first-class lie-flat seats with privacy partitions. You can do a lot of naughty things provided that your thralling and shrouding ability is any good and you can maintain it while doing other things. It requires skill."

As understanding dawned on Ell-rom's face and a deep blush spread across his cheeks, Jasmine couldn't help but find it adorable, especially given how uninhibited he usually was in private. But that was the thing—Ell-rom was a very private person, and doing what Anandur had suggested required a risqué character, which her prince lacked.

"I... that's..." he stammered, then gathered himself. "Even if I could thrall the other passengers, Max and Brundar's seats are right behind us."

"You might be able to thrall us," Max said. "You are half god after all."

Ell-rom shook his head. "I can't. I tried."

"No need," Brundar spoke up unexpectedly, but his usually stoic expression remained unchanged.

"I intend to put my earphones on and catch up on the latest movies."

Given the look Anandur cast his brother, he was just as surprised by his declaration as everyone else in the car.

Max's shoulders shook with laughter. "I intend to do the same with the earpieces that William designed. They filter all outside noise."

Jasmine felt a flutter of excitement in her stomach. Pressing closer to Ell-rom, she brushed her lips over his ear. "It could be fun," she whispered. "A little adventure."

"I don't think so," Ell-rom said with as much indignation as he could muster, given his slightly elongated fangs.

Max snickered on her other side. "A piece of advice, Prince. Never say no to your lady. Whatever she wants goes."

Anandur lifted his bushy red brows, looking at Max through the rearview mirror. "As the only unmated guy in this car, I don't think you are qualified to give advice, but I happen to agree."

When Ell-rom stiffened, and not in the way Jasmine would have liked, she patted his thigh. "We were just teasing, love. And anyway, we need to talk about strategy and how we are going to approach my father when we surprise him in the cabin. It's not like he's expecting us."

"Simple," Anandur said. "You got confused about the dates and brought your boyfriend and his two bodyguards to the cabin on the wrong weekend."

That was actually not a bad idea. Kian had explained that it would be best to get her father in a relaxed mood before asking him questions, so he wouldn't put up mental barriers. She even planned on purchasing a fine bottle of whiskey on the way to help things along.

"It would go well with my story of being a prince," Ell-rom said.

"You are a prince." She lifted her face and kissed the underside of his jaw. "Literally and figuratively."

The conversation lulled as they merged onto the highway, streetlights casting intermittent shadows through the windows. Jasmine let her eyes drift closed, idly playing with Ell-rom's fingers.

She thought back to the lullabies she'd listened to on YouTube last night, some in Farsi and some in Kurdish. She hadn't found the one her mother used to sing to her, but she was pretty sure that it sounded more Farsi than Kurdish.

The Farsi language lent itself to gentle, rounded vowels. It felt as if the words curled in on themselves, soothing her in a melodic arc even if she hadn't understood the lyrics. Kurdish had sharper consonants, a subtle friction hidden in the words, and it gave the melody a slight edge—less polished.

"First time flying and joining the mile-high club

on the same day," Anandur mused, looking at Ell-rom through the rearview mirror. "Lots of excitement."

"Please stop saying that," Ell-rom said, but there was no real heat in his voice. "Not happening."

"Just trying to help you focus on something other than flight anxiety."

"Yes, because what you suggest is so relaxing."

Jasmine chuckled. "I'll probably sleep through the entire flight. I want to arrive refreshed and alert. Wake me when we get to the airport." She settled more comfortably against Ell-rom's shoulder.

21

MAX

Max squinted at the partition between the first-class seats, fighting his curiosity even as he made his way toward the bathroom. One quick glance wouldn't hurt, would it? But when he peeked over, he found Jasmine sleeping peacefully while Ell-rom watched the same mindless action movie Max had abandoned.

Settling back in his seat, Max tried to focus on the film again. The special effects were impressive enough with buildings exploding in hyper-realistic detail and stunts that looked impossibly real, but the plot was laughably thin. Brandon had been right about the decline in quality. It felt like the studios were deliberately aiming for the lowest common denominator.

"They really think people are stupid," he muttered.

On the other side, Brundar grunted in what might have been agreement.

When they landed and picked up their rental car, the mood shifted, growing somber. Jasmine stared out the window, looking tense, and Ell-rom's hand hadn't left hers since they'd gotten in the car.

The silence was suffocating, and Max missed Anandur and his quirky, sometimes offensive humor, regretting that he had to stay behind. Now, he was stuck with Brundar, doing his usual impersonation of a statue in the seat beside him.

Max cast him a sidelong glance. "You have to admit that rides are more entertaining with your brother around."

Brundar's eyes flicked to him briefly before returning to his vigilant watch of the side mirror. The stoic Guardian's silence and impassive expression were dismissive.

Sighing, Max reached for the radio. A familiar melody filled the car, one of those classic songs that everyone seemed to know. Without thinking, he started singing along, falling easily into the rhythm.

Then Jasmine joined in, harmonizing perfectly. Their voices blended and soared, filling the car with a sound that made even Brundar's stern expression soften slightly.

When the song ended, Ell-rom applauded. "That was incredible!"

Another familiar tune started, and Max caught Jasmine's eye in the rearview mirror. She grinned, and they launched into it together. They were both trained singers, so harmonizing was as easy as breathing, and soon, the tension was gone from the car.

Max couldn't remember the last time he'd enjoyed singing with someone. For decades, he'd only been singing in the shower, and not very often at that.

Finally, a song neither of them knew the words to came on, breaking up their impromptu concert. The silence that followed felt different than before, warmer, more companionable.

Max took a deep breath. The moment felt right for the apology he still wasn't sure how to phrase. He hadn't been offensive to Jasmine on the cruise, he'd just projected animosity. How was he supposed to apologize for that?

"I owe you an explanation," he said, meeting Jasmine's eyes in the mirror. "I should have been much nicer to you on the cruise, and I want to assure you that the reason I was standoffish had nothing to do with you and everything to do with my own issues. You just look a lot like someone who caused me a lot of pain a long time ago, but mostly, you remind me of my own weakness and stupidity."

That hadn't come out right, but he didn't know how to say it better.

"I know the story," Jasmine said. "Or part of it anyway. Were you in love with her? The woman I remind you of?"

Max chuckled humorlessly. "Love would have at least partially justified my behavior, but I wasn't in love with Fenella. She was gorgeous and sexy as sin, and I just had to have her." He gripped the steering wheel tighter. "Din, my best friend, was taking things slow with her, but I thought that he was just being timid. I had no idea he was actually in love with her, and I thought nothing of seducing her. Looking back, I realize that she played us both, enjoying the power she had over the two of us. I tried to explain myself to Din and help him see that she hadn't felt anything for either of us, but he refused to listen."

"What happened to the girl?" Jasmine asked.

Max shrugged. "I don't know. She's probably a grandmother now, if she's still alive. I stayed away from her after I realized how hurt Din was, but I went to the pub she worked in a year or so later, and the barman told me that she went on a self-discovery backpacking trip to India. You are probably too young to know that, but it was a thing in the seventies."

Jasmine smiled apologetically. "You are right. I didn't know that it was such a popular destination for the hippie generation. So, what did you do? Just avoid brunettes ever since?"

"Gorgeous, curvy brunettes are my kryptonite,"

he admitted. "I learned I couldn't trust myself around them, so I kept my distance. It was easier than facing my own weakness."

"I see." Jasmine smiled at him through the rearview mirror. "I guess I should feel flattered by your animosity."

"There's something to that. If you were ugly, I wouldn't have tried so hard to avoid you."

She laughed. "So, it is my fault after all?"

He was making a mess of this apology thing. "I didn't mean it like that."

"I know," Jasmine said. "I'm just messing with you. Anyway, you've made up for it with that harmony of 'Sweet Dreams.' It was pretty amazing."

"It was," Max agreed. "You have serious pipes."

She waved a dismissive hand. "You've heard nothing yet. You should join me next time I perform in the village. Do you know 'The Phantom of the Opera'? I love that duet, and singing it with someone who can actually hit those notes would be a real treat."

Instead of answering, he started singing the part of the phantom.

For the next hour, they cycled through various musical theater numbers, their voices blending and separating in complex harmonies, and even Brundar seemed to enjoy the performance, his foot occasionally tapping to the rhythm.

It wasn't until they turned onto the gravel road

leading to the hunting cabin that reality intruded again. The music faded, replaced by the crunch of tires on loose stone and the weight of the revelations awaiting them inside.

22

JASMINE

Jasmine's good mood from the car ride faded as they approached the cabin.

It had felt good to clear the air between her and Max, but the truth was that singing with him had done a much better job at smoothing things out than his half-assed apology. He was a damn good singer, but he was bad with words.

Oh well, no one was perfect.

Except for her prince, who was everything she'd ever wanted in a mate and more, and knowing that her father would try to find fault in him put her in a combative mood before she even stepped foot in the cabin.

Ell-rom pulled out the teardrop translating device from his pocket and hung the string it was attached to around his neck. He was making good progress with his English studies, and he'd managed without the device on the flight, but he wasn't confident enough to face her father without it.

She should have thought to ask for translation earpieces for her father, but it was too late now. Besides, they were proprietary technology, and William might not have approved of letting her father use them.

"What is the name of the country I'm supposed to be the prince of?" Ell-rom asked, his fingers fidgeting with the device.

"It's a national secret," Max replied from beside them. "That way, you can avoid lying and messing things up because you have no clue what you're talking about."

"Got it." Ell-rom centered the device carefully on his chest.

Jasmine placed her hand on his arm, feeling the tension in his muscles. "My father is going to be unpleasant. Don't take it personally. That's how he is with everyone."

Except for the adopted sons that he adored. He was nicer to them than even to her stepmother. Maybe he was just a misogynist, and he only liked the company of men. That actually made sense since his favorite pastime activity was hunting with his buddies.

As they approached the front door, she was suddenly gripped by fear. Why hadn't her father come out to see who was driving up to his cabin?

There was nothing else around, so anyone arriving with a vehicle was coming to see him.

The sound of wheels on the gravel drive should have at least brought him to the window. What if something had happened to him? A stroke, a heart attack...

Despite their strained relationship, the thought of losing him sent panic through her chest. He was all the family she had left.

She rushed to the large plant pot by the door—empty as always except for some dirt—and tilted it slightly to retrieve the key hidden underneath. Her hands shook as she inserted it into the lock, but before she had a chance to turn it, the door swung open, and she found herself face to face with her father.

He wore a sleeveless shirt and sweatpants, his cheeks flushed in a way that suggested he'd been drinking. Relief flooded through her, quickly followed by tension.

"Jasmine? What are you doing here? I thought it was Ray." He frowned. "Didn't I tell you that I was using the cabin this week?" His tone carried the familiar note of disapproval.

She forced surprise into her voice. "It was this week? I thought it was the next one. Didn't you tell me that you were going the second week of the month?"

His lips twisted in that expression she knew all too well—the one that said she'd failed him yet again. "You've always had a knack for messing up dates and appointment times. You're such a scatterbrain. No wonder you couldn't apply yourself to anything other than acting."

As always, the words hit their mark. No matter how many times she told herself his opinion didn't matter and that her life choices had been the right ones for her, each criticism still cut deep.

Jasmine plastered on a smile. "Well, maybe it's a lucky coincidence. You get to meet my boyfriend." She turned to make the introductions. "Eli, this is my father, Boris. Dad, this is Eli." She gestured to Max and Brundar. "And these two gentlemen are Eli's bodyguards. Maximilian and Brundar."

Her father's eyes narrowed with suspicion. "Why do you need bodyguards?"

"Eli is a prince," she said, watching his reaction carefully. "And before you ask, I can't tell you of which country. He's traveling incognito."

"I thought he worked for that matchmaking company, Perfect Match." Her father's frown deepened, and she could see him searching for ways to find fault in her story.

Jasmine took a deep breath, lifting the paper bag she carried. "Let's go inside, and I'll explain. I brought a bottle of fine whiskey that I'm sure you'll enjoy."

The whiskey wasn't just a peace offering. It was part of her strategy. After a few drinks, her father was always more talkative and less guarded, and since he seemed to have already started on some, her job should be easier.

As they followed him inside, the familiar scent of the cabin sent a pang of nostalgia through her—wood smoke, old leather, and the lingering aroma of coffee. Nothing had changed since her childhood. The same worn furniture and the same faded photographs on the walls. She had a few fond memories of the place. Her father had had his better moments from time to time. When she was young, he still believed she would make something of herself. Make him proud.

"Still drinking Lagavulin?" she asked, pulling the bottle from the bag.

His eyes lit up at the sight of the expensive scotch. "I'm surprised you remember what I like."

Jasmine ignored the jab. "Should I get glasses?" she asked, already moving toward the kitchen cabinet where they'd always been kept.

"Yeah, sure." Her father sat down on his favorite leather chair and motioned for the men to sit down, pinning Ell-rom with a hard stare despite being slightly drunk. "So, Eli. Jasmine tells me that you are a big honcho in that matchmaking scheme. Is that true?"

"Partially," Ell-rom answered, or rather the teardrop did.

"What's that?" Her father pointed at the device.

"It's a translator," Ell-rom said. "I'm in the

process of learning English, but I'm not proficient enough to have a conversation."

"What language do you speak?" Her father was still eying the device suspiciously. "It sounds like that fake Klingon language from *Star Trek*."

Jasmine laughed, but it sounded false even to her own ears. "It does, right? That's what I told him."

She walked over with the glasses, and the familiar dance of pouring drinks, making small talk, and waiting for the right moment began. But underneath it all, her heart was racing with anticipation and fear. When it was done, she would either have answers about her mother's disappearance, or she would find out that her mother was truly gone and the woman in Syssi's visions had been someone else.

23

MAX

Max waited patiently as Jasmine and Ellrom engaged in small talk with Boris, using the opportunity to take light reconnaissance dips into the man's mind. The surface memories were mundane—fragments of television shows, an argument with his current wife about his increasing alcohol consumption, worries about a failing investment.

Beside him, Brundar maintained his characteristic silence, present but unobtrusive. They'd agreed to follow Syssi's intuition about Max taking point on the thralling, with Brundar as backup if needed.

As the whiskey level in the bottle dropped, Boris grew increasingly animated, his words beginning to slur. Max hoped that the man didn't have any hunting plans for the day. Mixing firearms with this much alcohol would be dangerous, and he was quite sure it was also illegal.

"You know, Dad." Jasmine's voice carried a forced casualness that made Max wince internally. She either wasn't that good of an actress, or her father was stressing her out. "Eli asked me about my mother, how she died, and where she was buried. I was so embarrassed because I couldn't tell him a single thing. Don't you think it's time you told me what really happened to her?"

"No." Boris's response was sharp, and he emptied his glass down his throat and reached for the bottle again.

The question should be enough to bring old memories to the surface where Max could take a peek at them. He seized the opportunity and delved deeper into the man's mind.

The first memory hit him like a physical blow—raw anguish and panic as a younger Boris frantically called the police about his missing wife, then the desperation in his voice when they told him he had to wait twenty-four hours to file a missing person's report. The image of him rushing out of the house with little Jasmine and driving around with her in the back seat, then running around with her hugged to his chest while showing Kyra's photo to anyone who might have seen her.

The memory of little Jasmine crying for her mother twisted something in Max's chest. Then came the scene of Boris clutching Kyra's photo at night and sobbing into his pillow.

"They took her!" The words echoed through the memory, repeated desperately. "She said that they would come for her. What am I going to do?"

"Max?" Jasmine's worried voice pulled him out of Boris's head. "What's going on?"

He met her concerned gaze, then looked at Boris with newfound compassion. "Someone took your mother. Who took her, Boris? Who took Kyra?"

"Her family." The words seemed to be torn from him. "She said that they would come looking for her and that if they found out that she had married a Christian, they would kill her."

"But they didn't," Jasmine protested. "She sent you signed divorce papers from Iran."

Lost in the haze of whiskey and old grief, Boris didn't notice his daughter's inexplicable knowledge of events he'd never shared with her.

"They must have forced her to do that and then killed her. She said they would." Tears tracked down his weathered face. "They killed my Kyra."

Max felt his own throat tighten as Jasmine moved to embrace her father. The man folded into her arms, decades of grief pouring out in harsh sobs.

The scene shifted something in Max.

He'd come prepared to find a difficult man, perhaps even a cruel one, based on how Jasmine had described him. Instead, he found someone broken by loss, someone whose harshness might have stemmed from the pain of unhealed wounds.

When Jasmine turned to Brundar, her own cheeks wet with tears, Max already knew what she would ask. "Can you make him forget?"

Brundar nodded, understanding what she was asking. Taking away those old memories of pain was impossible, but Brundar could erase the memory of this meeting and of Boris telling his daughter about her mother.

Max studied Boris's face, seeing now how the years of carrying this burden had carved deep lines around his mouth and eyes. The man had lost his wife and had probably lived in fear of her family coming after Jasmine. He had pushed his daughter away not only because she reminded him so much of Kyra but also because he was afraid that if she was taken from him, he would break apart and never come together again.

It was a cowardly notion, and Boris should have been stronger for the sake of his daughter. He should have showered her with love to compensate for the mother she'd lost. Instead, he had remarried and hoped his new wife would fill the void Kyra had left behind.

He could have done better, but he was just a flawed man, and Max still felt compassion for him.

The revelation that Kyra's family had taken her changed everything they'd thought they knew. If her relatives had initially taken her against her will, perhaps she had later chosen to stay with them to protect Boris and Jasmine.

As Brundar moved closer to Boris and started whispering soothing words that Max was surprised the Guardian was capable of, Jasmine walked over to her mate and sat down beside him.

When Ell-rom wrapped his arm around her, she turned her face into his chest and cried.

It seemed that Kyra's story was much more complex than they had expected. More pieces of the puzzle had been discovered today, but, regrettably, none that pointed toward where she could be found.

24

JASMINE

Jasmine wiped tears from her cheeks as the four of them walked from the rental car toward the restaurant. She probably had raccoon eyes from her running mascara. It was supposed to be waterproof, but tears were not made of just water. Emotional tears contained stress hormones and proteins in addition to water, and those could dissolve any kind of eyeliner or mascara.

"Are you okay?" Ell-rom asked.

She nodded. "My father's breakdown shattered the image I held of him through all these years. In a way, it's a relief to know that the cold, unemotional man who seemed to take pleasure in criticizing my every choice was a sham. But it's hard to see that the real man underneath is still grieving. Still bleeding."

Her father was drowning in grief and guilt. He'd lost the love of his life and couldn't bear to fully love the daughter who reminded him so much of her. Maybe his attempts to force her into a conventional career path hadn't been about control but about trying to protect her in the only way he knew how.

"He loved your mother very much," Max said softly as he held the restaurant door open. "He's still heartbroken over her loss so many years later."

"I know." Jasmine sniffled, following him inside.

When they were seated, she looked at Brundar. "I'm glad you made my father forget. How did you do that? Did you plant new memories in his head?"

She expected a nod or a shake of his head, but for a moment, Brundar didn't react, maintaining his usual silence. Just when she thought he wouldn't answer her at all, his pale blue eyes met hers. "I made him forget that you were there. That's why I took the empty whiskey bottle you brought for him. I didn't want to leave any trace of your visit." He paused. "I also planted a mental suggestion for him to accept that it wasn't his fault that Kyra had been taken, and that he couldn't have done anything to prevent it."

Jasmine frowned. "Does he blame himself for it?" Her chest tightened at the thought. "Why would he?"

"Your father believes he should have taken Kyra

more seriously when she warned him about her family. He thought that she was being melodramatic and that the worst-case scenario would be her family disowning her. They were affluent and influential, and he refused to believe that they would stoop to the barbaric custom of what is called honor killing in that region." Brundar paused, probably feeling out of sorts after having said so many consecutive words. "He blames himself for not taking her somewhere safer, like South America or some other place where information about people wasn't so easily obtained. He's carried that guilt ever since. I hope I eased his burden."

The Guardian fell silent.

"Poor man," Ell-rom said, squeezing her hand. "I understand why he would feel that way. If someone took you from me because I wasn't vigilant enough, I would blame myself as well."

Max was still staring at Brundar in amazement, no doubt surprised by the stone-faced Guardian's show of empathy. It seemed that like her father, Brundar was projecting a certain image to protect a softer inner self.

Had he also lost a loved one?

Empathy was often the product of suffering. There was a powerful connection between personal adversity and one's capacity to understand others. While people could develop it through observation, there was nothing like personal experience to gain visceral appreciation for the pain of others.

"Let's order." Max lifted the laminated menu. "I'm starving."

"We should call Kian," Ell-rom suggested. "Let him know what we discovered."

"It can wait." Max was still scanning the menu. "As emotionally earth-shattering as today was, we didn't learn anything that will help us find Jasmine's mother."

"I've always thought he resented her," Jasmine said quietly. "That he blamed her for leaving us. I even read about how people's grief often turned to resentment, blaming the deceased for not taking better care of themselves or for being careless. I thought that was how he was dealing with her death. Then, when I started to suspect that she was still alive, I thought he was angry because she'd left him."

Ell-rom wrapped his arm around her shoulders. "He did an excellent job of bottling up his feelings, and I'm sure he thought that he was protecting you by shielding you from his pain."

The same had occurred to her. "In his own misguided way, by pushing me toward a 'safe' career and being critical of my choices, he was trying to make sure I would be okay if something happened to him. The funny thing is that despite my questionable career choices, I took care of myself and never asked him for financial help or any other kind. I've been independent for years." She sighed. "I was also so angry about the way he judged me. It feels good to let go of this anger."

"Parents often express love in ways their children don't understand," Max said, leaning over the table so he was closer. "Immortal mothers, in particular, are very clingy. That was another reason for my move here. My mother stayed in Scotland."

Jasmine appreciated his attempt at humor, but all his comment had achieved was to make her miss her mother even more.

"You are lucky that you still have your mother and will have her forever. You should be thankful."

Ell-rom nodded in agreement. "My mother was distant and seemingly unfeeling, even more so than Jasmine's father, and I still miss her and wish she was alive."

Even Brundar seemed to agree.

"Is your mother still around?" Jasmine asked the Guardian.

"Thank the merciful Fates, she is. She attended my wedding and Anandur's."

Max put the menu down. "The thing about your father's memories that struck me most was how desperate he was to find her. He called hospitals and police stations within a hundred-mile radius of your house, and he drove around for days, showing her picture to people in supermarkets, clothing stores, beauty salons—everywhere she used to shop. He wasn't just going through the motions—he was frantic."

"I wish..." Jasmine stopped, collecting herself. "I wish I could tell him that she's alive. That she didn't die like he believes."

"We don't know that for certain," Max cautioned.

"But Syssi's visions say she is."

"They show someone who looks like you leading Kurdish rebels," Max said. "It's compelling evidence but not proof. You shouldn't raise his hopes only to have to shatter them later."

Her father was also married to another woman now, and bringing her mother back from the dead might not be the best idea for him.

Kyra might have remarried as well.

When the waitress appeared, Jasmine was grateful for the interruption.

"There's one thing that doesn't add up," Ell-rom said after the waitress left. "If her family took her to punish her for marrying outside their faith, why bother to send divorce papers? It was an act of kindness toward your father that must have come from her, which means that they didn't kill her. Maybe that was the price they demanded."

Max nodded. "That would explain a lot, including why she never contacted you even after getting free. Perhaps she was protecting you from her family."

Jasmine wondered at the twists of fate that had taken both of her parents away from her.

They each kept their distance to protect her. One physically and the other emotionally.

25

DROVA

Drova stared at the textbook in her lap, the small script blurring as her mind wandered back to the horrors she'd witnessed during the mission. The comfort of her bedroom, with its soft bedding and the ridiculously huge teddy bear that Phinas had gotten her, felt like she'd been transported to a different dimension after what she'd seen.

Becoming a Guardian had seemed like the perfect fit for her, and to be offered a spot in the training program at her young age was a great honor and a vote of confidence she didn't deserve after the stunt she'd pulled. She loved the uniform, the respect, the purpose, but most of all, she loved being close to Pavel and having him look on her as an equal and not the kid he humored because she was their leader's daughter.

Now, though, she wasn't sure it was where she

belonged, and that uncertainty felt like betraying everything she was supposed to be as a Kra-ell.

Her mother would be ashamed if she knew her daughter's thoughts. Jade was a true warrior, unflinching in the face of evil. And Pavel…oh, Mother of All Life, Pavel. He would be appalled.

He'd tried to comfort her after the mission, telling her she'd get used to seeing such things, but she didn't want to get used to seeing children suffer. She didn't want to become numb to it.

No one should.

Evil. It was pure evil, and it still clung to her as if she had somehow taken part in that, had a hand in it, when all she had done was save those kids.

That was the cost of doing the right thing, though.

Someone had to save them, and as a compeller, she had abilities that made her invaluable for the rescue operations. Her role in the last mission had been minimal, but there was so much more she could do.

She could make traffickers reveal their networks, force abusers to confess their crimes, and help traumatized victims feel safe enough to talk.

The sound of footsteps in the hallway pulled her from her thoughts. They didn't belong to her mother or to Phinas, and she was surprised when Parker appeared in her doorway, his lanky frame filling the space.

"Hey," he said. "Sorry to barge in on you, but Phinas told me to just go ahead." He gestured to the books scattered around her. "I came to collect those. I'm sure you cannot wait to get rid of them now that Kian has commuted your sentence."

Drova closed the book but didn't offer it to him. "I want to keep them." She gestured for him to sit on her bed, which was made with military precision like it always was. Her mother would be livid if she didn't make her bed first thing in the morning upon waking up. She also had to keep her room neat at all times.

Parker sat down, or rather plopped down in astonishment, with his eyebrows arched so high that they were almost touching his hairline. "You hate studying. That's why we chose it as your punishment for compelling us to do your bidding. Cheryl was sure you'd kiss me on both cheeks when I told you that I came to take them away. Lisa bet on one cheek, and I said you wouldn't kiss me at all." He grinned. "Winner gets cupcakes from the losers."

Drova smiled. "Are you so sure you'll win?"

Parker laughed. "If I hadn't told you about the bet, would you have kissed me?"

"No."

"Then I win."

When she didn't laugh, his smile faded, and he studied her face. "What's wrong? You look like you haven't slept for days. What happened?"

Her first instinct was to say that nothing was wrong or that she was tired after a week of training, which she was, but her fatigue wasn't physical.

Parker wasn't a warrior and had no plans to become one. He dreamt of becoming a great businessman like Kian, so he wouldn't judge her for having doubts, and she could confide in him.

"My first mission was much more difficult than I expected. It left a sour taste in my mouth that I can't seem to wash out."

"That bad, huh?"

She nodded, hugging the textbook to her chest. "My father was a cruel despot, but compared to what these monsters do to children, he was a saint." She shuddered. "Pavel says that I'll get used to it, but I don't want to. I don't want to become so hardened that seeing such things doesn't affect me anymore."

"Then don't," Parker said. "Being affected by cruelty doesn't make you weak. It makes you human."

"I'm not human," she reminded him. "I'm Kra-ell. Being a warrior is everything I am. If you haven't noticed, none of the purebloods have any desire for education. The closest to scholars we have are our priests, and except for the prince and princess who were acolytes but have no wish to guide us, we have none. My mother knows some of the Kra-ell history, and she teaches the kids what she knows, but that's about it. We have no scientists, no engineers, not even doctors or nurses. By the clan's standards, we are savages."

Parker remained quiet for a long time, probably because he knew she was right, and he couldn't argue the point with her.

"What about all those Kra-ell hybrids that Igor sent to study in universities?"

She smiled sadly. "You said it. He sent the hybrids who had so little Kra-ell blood in them that they looked fully human. The rest of us remained ignorant." She tapped the stack of books on her desk. "I'm probably the wrong person to start an educational revolution among my people, but it needs to be done. After all, wasn't the rebellion on Anumati all about giving the Kra-ell access to the same opportunities as the gods?"

Parker scratched his head. "I think it was also about giving the non-royals access to the elite universities that only the royals got to go to. I overheard my dad telling my mom about that."

"Whatever." She waved a dismissive hand. "It just reinforces how important education is. The problem is that I have a rare gift, and as a compeller, I can do a lot more good with that than as a scientist or a teacher. The other problem is that I really hate studying. I lose concentration, and I get bored and restless."

He let out a long breath. "I don't know what to tell you. You are right about your compulsion ability being an asset to the force. You will need to find someone else to lead the educational revolution."

She regarded him for a long moment. "So, you're saying that I just need to toughen up and keep going?"

"You're a compeller, and that's rare and valuable. But you also deserve to be happy. No one can decide for you. I can make one small suggestion, though."

She arched a brow. "Like what?"

"Keep the books and study as much as you can. That way, you are leaving yourself the option of doing something else. Give yourself more time, not to get numb to the horrors but to learn to focus on the positive side of rescuing these kids from hell. If after several more missions, you decide that this is not for you, you can ask Onegus to move you to the Saviors Division."

She snorted. "As if rescuing victims of trafficking is less traumatic."

"I think it is," Parker said. "But what do I know? You should talk to Peter. He's done both."

"Thanks," she said softly. "That was a lot of good advice."

Parker shrugged, but she could see he was pleased. "That's what friends are for, but you shouldn't look so surprised."

"Well, you're just fourteen, so it is surprising that you are so smart."

He dipped his head. "Thank you."

26

KIAN

Kian smiled at the sight of his daughter sprawled on the couch. She'd fallen asleep while watching her favorite show, at first just closing her eyes and letting her head loll sideways, then sliding all the way down and continuing to sleep.

"You should put her in bed," he told Syssi.

"She needs to get a bath first." Syssi leaned over and picked up Allegra's little hand and kissed the back of it. "Is it just me, or is she growing too fast?"

"She is definitely growing too fast." He wrapped his arm around Syssi's shoulder. "We need another baby. Should we visit Merlin and ask for another course of potions?"

Syssi looked surprised and delighted at the same time. "There is nothing I would love more than having another child, but I doubt Merlin's potions were the reason we got pregnant with Allegra. It was just a lucky coincidence."

"I say that if it worked once, it might work again. I'm willing to go through the ordeal of drinking the nasty stuff if you are."

"Of course, I am." She shifted onto his lap and wrapped her arms around his neck. "Do you want to start working on it right away?"

Kian felt his fangs start to elongate, along with another part of his anatomy. "I would be delighted, but didn't you just say that Allegra needs a bath?"

Syssi cast their daughter a loving look. "She can skip one night if it's for a good cause, but we need to put her in bed first."

He was about to move Syssi off his lap so he could take Allegra to bed when his phone buzzed in his pocket.

"People have the worst timing," he grumbled as he pulled it out. "It's Ell-rom."

Syssi tensed. "Maybe they have news about Kyra."

Nodding, he answered the call, and then both of them listened to Ell-rom's report about what Jasmine's father had revealed, and when he described how emotional Boris had gotten, Syssi wiped away tears.

"The poor man," she murmured. "It's hard to imagine that he's still grieving for Kyra even though he remarried."

Kian could understand that better than most. He no longer grieved for his first wife, but thinking about her always brought about a pang of sadness and regret.

When Ell-rom continued, saying that Boris blamed himself for not taking Kyra's warnings more seriously, Kian sympathized as well. There were enough what-ifs and should-haves in his life to fill several thick tomes.

"Thank you for letting us know," he told Ell-rom. "Have a safe flight back home, and we will talk tomorrow morning." He ended the call.

"I feel bad for Jasmine's father," Syssi said. "And for Jasmine. She must be so distraught after this visit."

"She's tough." Kian rubbed his wife's back. "She'll be back to her usual upbeat self by tomorrow morning."

Syssi nodded. "It's a gift to be able to do that. I find it much more difficult to change moods, especially after I learn something disturbing." She chuckled. "That's really not a good quality for a seer, but it is what it is, right?"

"The Fates are strange that way. Like them giving Ell-rom, one of the gentlest males I know, the ability to kill with a thought. He's better suited to be a priest."

"Wonder is another example," Syssi said. "She has the body and the strength of a warrior, but she can't tolerate violence."

"She chooses not to engage in it. Wonder is very capable of delivering it. She killed one of her attackers, and she handed Anandur and Brundar their asses."

Syssi chuckled. "I forgot about that. Anyway, I think I should summon a vision." She leaned away from him. "Would you mind if I do that while sitting in your lap?"

That was new. She'd never done that before, and usually, she didn't even want him in the same room.

"Is this a bribe so I won't object to you doing that?"

"Not at all." She shifted in his arms, settling into a more comfortable position. "I feel like experimenting. Now that you are not stressing me out with your antagonistic attitude toward my visions, I think that your presence might actually be beneficial to me attaining them. I draw strength from you."

"I was never antagonistic toward your visions. I just didn't like you summoning them because of how they drained you. I was afraid for you."

Her eyes softened. "I know, love." She cupped his cheek. "But that created negative energy that affected my ability. Now that you are more accepting, I can summon a vision right here in your arms."

"You also have Allegra here, and her presence enhances your results."

"True." She cast their daughter a fond look. "I'm going to have a good one."

As Syssi closed her eyes, Kian tried to remain quiet and to move as little as possible. He even tried to make his breathing nice and even.

It didn't take long for Syssi to go slack in his arms and for her breathing to slow down and deepen. To anyone else, she would have seemed asleep, but the rapid movement of her eyelids indicated that a lot was going on.

Long moments passed as Kian waited for his mate to wake up, and just as he was starting to get worried, she gasped and opened her eyes.

"What did you see?" he asked gently, trying to keep the urgency from his voice.

"Give me a moment to collect my thoughts." She reached for the forgotten cup of coffee on the table and took a sip. "How long was I out?"

"No more than five minutes."

"It seemed like much longer." She put the cup back on the coffee table. "I saw Kyra again." Syssi shifted in his arms so she could look at him. "At first, I thought that I was seeing the same vision again, but then I started noticing the differences. It was another dingy room with peeling paint on the walls and a small, barred window, but it wasn't the same room as before. Kyra was once again chained to the bed, but she wasn't drugged this time. She was bruised, her lip was swollen, and she had a black eye. The same man was there again, but this time he wore a uniform instead of a doctor's coat."

Kian tensed. "Was he beating her up?"

"Not while I was watching. He was just standing there and talking to her. He spoke in Farsi, and I could understand it this time." She rubbed her temples. "He said he was surprised to find her in Tahav, and he seemed very pleased with himself."

"Tahav? I wonder where it is." He lifted his phone off the table and typed in the inquiry. "It's a small town between Iranian Azerbaijan and the Kermanshah Province. It's in Kurdistan territory." He put the phone back down. "Did Kyra or the man look older in this vision?"

Syssi shook her head. "It was hard to tell with Kyra because of the bruising, but the man looked exactly the same as he did in the other vision." She frowned. "But maybe both visions are not from long ago like we thought. The television was playing in the background, and even though it was in Farsi, I recognized the speech the ayatollahs recently gave about Iran's nuclear capabilities. I saw it a day or two ago."

Kian sucked in a breath. "How is it possible? Your other visions of Kyra showed her among the rebels and in the previous one with the same guy when she was young. It doesn't make sense."

Syssi shrugged. "Maybe the man wasn't the same one, only looked like him. Maybe he's the son of the other one." She straightened in his arms. "But regardless of who he is, we know that the vision was current, and we have a location. Kyra is in Tahav."

"Daddy?" Allegra's small voice interrupted them. "My castle needs a princess."

She must have dreamt about building castles.

"It sure does, sweetheart. I'll get you a princess."

Allegra smiled, sighed, and went back to sleep.

Kian turned back to Syssi. "Did you see anything else?"

"The uniform he wore had an insignia. I don't know what it meant, but it looked like he was a high-ranking military, possibly Revolutionary Guard."

The implications were staggering. If the Revolutionary Guard was involved, getting Kyra out would be much more complicated than a simple rescue mission.

"We have to help her," Syssi said.

"I'm not sure that we should get involved. The Kurdish resistance Kyra's been working with might be already planning a rescue." Kian ran a hand through his hair. "I don't doubt your visions, but it is hard to know when they take place. Kyra might already be free."

Syssi shook her head. "I wouldn't be getting the same vision twice if there was no urgency and our help was not needed."

She was right, of course, and he was engaging

in wishful thinking instead of accepting what the vision was trying to tell them. If the man in the second vision was the same guy and not a younger relative who looked exactly like him, he was an immortal, and that meant that Doomers were part of the Revolutionary Guard.

27

ROB

Rob smoothed the crisp linen napkin in his lap for the tenth time as he and the others settled into a spacious booth in the upscale restaurant. Across from him, Margo displayed her usual casual confidence, with one hand resting on Negal's forearm and a smile on her face as she listened to Gertrude describe the chaos in the clinic when a bunch of Guardians returned from a mission in need of patching up.

Negal, who was wearing a suit with the ease of someone who had been wearing them for years, looked like a supermodel or an artificial intelligence creation—too handsome to be real and drawing the attention of people sitting at nearby tables.

For a guy who had spent most of his incredibly long life as a trooper in uniform, he certainly filled up that suit to perfection.

Their parents had already met Negal, but it would be the first time they met Gertrude, and Rob was nervous.

She looked beautiful, dressed in a simple yet elegant blue dress that complemented her dark hair and warm smile. She seemed determined to be a calming anchor for tonight, entertaining them with her stories of warriors who turned into petulant kids when they were patients. If only his mind could stop conjuring worst-case scenarios about his mother's reaction to his mate, he could actually start enjoying the evening.

Over the tinkling of piano keys in the background, Rob heard the clink of glassware as a waiter passed by, and his thoughts flickered to the last time he'd introduced a girlfriend to his parents. Lynda had charmed them almost instantly, but she was a con artist who had fooled everyone except for Margo.

His sister had been the only one who had seen through the act and saved him from making the worst mistake of his life.

The broken engagement and canceled wedding seemed like something that had happened a lifetime ago, but it had been only a little over a month, and his mother was worried that he'd fallen for Gertrude on the rebound.

"Relax," Gertrude murmured, sliding her hand over his, her touch sending warmth through him. "Everything will be okay. They'll love me."

She sounded so sure, but Rob knew better than to underestimate his mother's ability to find fault in all the wrong people. "I hope so." He forced a small smile.

His mother had been all for Lynda nearly until the end.

Across from him, Margo straightened, brushing a stray strand of hair behind her ear. "They're here," she announced, her eyes fixed on the doorway.

Rob turned to see his parents walking over. As usual, his father had that uncertain, slightly apologetic smile he always sported in new social situations, and the suit he'd chosen to wear hung loose on his thin frame.

Was he losing weight? Was he sick? Perhaps he should ask Bridget for a favor and have her examine his dad.

His mother looked as perfectly coifed as ever, with the same critical gleam in her eye. The contrast between them was as familiar as breathing, and Rob felt his stomach knot even further.

As always, she took in every detail at once, as if searching for imperfections.

"Mom, Dad," Rob said, rising from his seat with Gertrude following suit. "I want you to meet the love of my life, Gertrude."

His mother grimaced as if he had said something dirty, but she shook Gertrude's hand and murmured all the right things.

Gertrude inclined her head without a trace of nervousness in her expression, and Rob admired that—it took a special kind of calm to meet his mother's unwavering scrutiny.

His mother's gaze flicked over the other woman's dress, her hair, and then settled on her kind brown eyes, a tight smile stretching her lips. "Rob tells us you're a nurse?"

"Yes, I am," Gertrude said brightly. "I work in a private clinic that caters to a unique clientele."

The muscle in Rob's mother's jaw tightened almost imperceptibly. "You mean the Perfect Match secret compound employees?" she asked, lowering herself into the plush seat.

"Yes," Gertrude said cheerfully. "It's a large place."

"That no one's allowed to visit." His mother cast a reproachful glance at Margo. "I don't understand why they have such draconian rules. Your father and I would have gladly signed a nondisclosure agreement that covered all the bases. That's what most normal places do. What are they hiding in there?"

"A lot of proprietary tech," Rob said. "Many would love to steal it, and it is crucial to protect it at all costs. If the Chinese get their hands on the technology, they will build the same machines for one-tenth of the price and offer the service for a fraction of what Perfect Match is charging."

His mother tilted her head. "Would that be so bad? The consumers would love it."

"That's not how it works, dear," his father said. "Think of all the years and the enormous amounts of money that went into the development of this technology. The founders need to recoup their investment. That's what patent laws are about, but some foreign actors don't respect them."

Rob didn't like having to lie to his parents, but protecting the location of the village and the identity of its immortal population was nonnegotiable. At least the Perfect Match cover wasn't a complete fabrication. The technology existed; it belonged to the clan, and they were very secretive about it.

Margo cleared her throat. "I have a great idea for all of us to get closer. A spiritual retreat at Safe Haven, which is located on the beautiful Oregon Coast. Perfect Match sponsors it, and we can get free passes for all six of us."

Their father's eyebrows rose. "A spiritual retreat? We are not hippies, Margo." He chuckled. "Your grannie would have loved it, though, bless her soul. But we were born in a different generation."

"It's just a relaxing vacation," Margo said. "They have one-week programs and two-week programs. I can book us for the one week. Just walking on the beach there is a treat. Some yoga, some mindfulness, and gourmet meals prepared by a famous chef. We are going to have so much fun together."

"I don't think so," their mother said. "If you offered us a cruise, I would have considered that. But a spiritual retreat is really not my cup of tea."

Negal leaned forward and looked into their mother's eyes. "You are going to love every moment of it. You will find it transformative," he said in a tone that was as smooth as polished marble.

Was he thralling their parents?

As silence stretched over the table and both his parents stared into Negal's eyes, Rob exchanged glances with Margo and nodded.

They both watched as their mother's expression changed from doubtful to suddenly excited. "It sounds wonderful!" she declared, hands clasping in sudden enthusiasm. "When can we go?"

Rob exhaled, the tension in his shoulders lessening. Strictly speaking, the clan frowned on frivolous use of thralling—manipulating human emotions or decisions with supernatural influence—but given the circumstances, Negal had made a good call.

It was a good thing that the god didn't have to strictly abide by the clan's rules. He wasn't one of Annani's descendants, and although he was a guest in the village and his loyalty was expected, he was freer to do as he pleased than most of the other residents.

Margo clapped her hands. "As soon as I can get us in. The retreats always start on a Saturday, so I can probably reserve spots for next week. I don't think the place is as packed in the winter as it is during the summer months."

"Perfect," their mother said, a wide smile still plastered on her face. Her eager tone was a little unsettling. "Your father and I can't wait to spend a whole week with our children and their significant others."

Under the table, Gertrude gave Rob's hand a reassuring squeeze, and he shot her a relieved glance. Phase one of convincing their parents to come to Safe Haven was done. Now they just needed to find a way to break the news to his mother that she could become immortal and the method by which it could be done. That was the more difficult step, and he was happy to leave it all to Margo.

As the waiter approached with menus, his father cleared his throat. "So, Gertrude," he said, tugging at his tie. "Would you mind telling us more about your work? I'm curious how you ended up working for Perfect Match."

As Gertrude launched into a mostly fabricated story, and his mother continued to nod along with a serenity that was clearly thrall-induced, Margo and Negal shared an amused look.

It was a temporary fix, but it would keep dinner civil.

28

KYRA

The freezing early morning air prickled Kyra's skin as she approached the compound. Months ago, her team had planted a maid in there, and today, Kyra was going to take her place.

Parisa had Kyra's coloring and size, and in a society where women were second-class citizens at best, a maid with a mop in hand was invisible.

Kyra didn't move with her usual poise or her confident stride. Instead, she kept her head low, hunched her shoulders, and shuffled her feet. She also kept her expression timid even though only her eyes were visible above the scarf wrapped around the lower part of her face.

Her ID, a slim plastic card with a grainy photograph that could pass as her, sat tucked inside a small cloth pouch at her waist together with a few coins and a string of prayer beads—the tesbîh. She wasn't the praying type, but the beads would add to the submissive, pious image she was trying to portray.

A lone guard stood beneath the compound's archway, and as Kyra drew closer, he adjusted his stance, crossing his arms in a way designed to intimidate. The uniform he wore was crisp, not the sloppy type usually worn by the regular guards she was accustomed to seeing. It seemed that the new commander was keeping everyone on their toes.

"Papers," he demanded.

Kyra offered a timid nod, carefully avoiding direct eye contact. She drew out the ID card. With her general resemblance to Parisa and their similar build, it would be hard to tell that the ID was not hers even if he demanded that she remove her headscarf and show her face, but it was unlikely that he would do that unless he got suspicious.

The key was to project as much timidity as possible, which at the moment wasn't difficult because she was scared.

"Take your scarf off," he said, sending her heart rate into a gallop.

She widened her eyes, conveying her shock at the request.

"You heard me. The new commander is strict." He sounded almost apologetic.

Kyra nodded and, with shaking hands, removed the scarf from her face while looking down at the ground.

The guard took the card and held it up for a closer look. In the dim outer courtyard light, the photograph's details were murky at best, but he tilted the ID toward the sun. He leaned forward, tipping Kyra's chin upward with a rough, lingering touch that sent a hot wave of anger through her, along with a surge of panic.

"You look different from your picture," he said, his tone dripping with suspicion.

Kyra willed her body not to tense or recoil, even though part of her itched to twist his wrist until he screamed. "The picture is old," she murmured softly, lowering her gaze to the dusty ground. "I have given birth to two children since it was taken. That takes a toll on a woman."

His gaze flicked between her and the photograph, lingering on her face. After what seemed like an eternity, he dropped his hand with a grunt, probably finding her meek posture convincing.

"Arms out," he barked, stepping aside and motioning for a female to take over.

Kyra obeyed silently, extending her arms and bracing herself for the pat-down. The female was one she was familiar with, an old hag who liked to parrot the regime's vile propaganda and act as an enforcer of the modesty rules.

Luckily, the two of them had never been face to face, so the woman didn't know her. She should know Parisa, though.

Kyra remained silent and kept her eyes down as

the woman began patting down her shoulders and then moved down her sides. Her pouch was thoroughly inspected, and the woman nodded with approval when she saw the prayer beads.

Kyra had no weapons on her—no knives or guns, not even a sharpened hairpin. For this mission, her only defense was her own body and her training, her enhanced strength and reflexes that she hoped to conceal unless absolutely necessary.

She was here to learn and observe, not to stir things up.

The pat-down felt semi-thorough, as if the female was still sleepy and not in the mood to do her job. "She's clean," she said.

The male guard handed her ID back. "Go on," he ordered. "Report to Madame Afshar in the kitchen. She's short-staffed today."

Parisa was on the cleaning staff, which worked much better for what Kyra needed to do, but she wasn't going to argue. She'd start in the kitchen and slip out as soon as she could.

Ducking her head again in a show of thanks and obedience, she tucked the ID into her pouch and hurried through the tall, steel-reinforced gate.

Gravel crunched underfoot as she passed a series of parked military Jeeps. The building's high walls were topped by coils of razor wire, which had been added after her team's prisoner extraction.

An undercurrent of tension brushed against her heightened senses as she moved deeper inside the compound, and she tried to ignore the chill creeping along her spine. Somewhere in there, the new prisoners were being held. She could almost smell the faint metallic tang in the air—a smell that evoked memories of antiseptic hallways, metal restraints, and the glint of needles in the asylum, of which she only had vague memories.

Her pendant, hidden beneath layers of clothing, pulsed with a soft warmth. The subtle vibration seemed to resonate with her heartbeats, drawing her attention toward the eastern wing.

Before she followed that pull, though, she needed to report to the kitchen.

29

KYRA

The kitchen was chaotic, with staff in aprons and headscarves jostling around one another, shouting instructions and cursing in the early-morning rush. Steam hissed from large metal pots, and the scent of freshly baked bread permeated the air. Despite the frantic energy, the place was warm and inviting, and if Kyra hadn't been on a mission she might have enjoyed it.

Madame Afshar, the formidable head cook, was easy to spot. She had a presence that matched her stout figure, barking orders at an unfortunate young woman trying to scrub the counter with one hand while juggling a stack of baking trays with the other. When she spotted Kyra, she waved her over and pointed to a large tray loaded with breakfast items. "Take this to the officers' mess—third floor, West Wing. And hurry up about it!"

When the head cook added two steaming pots of tea, Kyra pretended to stagger under the weight, earning a smirk from the woman who had no doubt intended to test her.

Keeping her eyes downcast, Kyra murmured an apology.

"Just go!" Madame Afshar commanded, her voice echoing off the tiled walls. "Keep the officers' cups full and the mess clean. I don't want to hear any complaints about you."

Kyra bobbed her head in a silent "Yes, ma'am" and slipped away, carefully maneuvering around the other kitchen staff members who were moving between the boiling pots and hissing pans like an army of drunken flies.

No one gave her more than a cursory glance. Maids and kitchen workers came and went at all hours, and she was just one more in a never-ending stream of worker bees.

Clutching the tray, Kyra began the climb up several flights of concrete stairs to the West Wing's third floor. Even burdened as she was, her enhanced strength helped her navigate the steps quickly, and as she ascended, she caught snatches of conversation from behind closed doors—most of it meaningless chatter: complaints about duty rosters, arguments over petty grievances, and mostly gossip.

Then, a distinct male voice pierced the general noise. It was slightly accented as if Farsi wasn't his native tongue, although he spoke it flawlessly.

"Turmor is re-growing his toes," he said. "The idiot stepped on a mine. What did you expect to happen to him?"

Kyra felt her chest tighten. She moved more slowly, attempting to glean another snippet.

"…it takes time. It's not like a simple injury."

She wanted to linger, to press her ear to the door, but footsteps approached from the other direction, forcing her to keep moving.

The conversation proved that there were more people like her, people with advanced abilities that went beyond normal human limits, who could even regrow missing body parts. She hadn't known she could do that.

Finally, she reached the officers' mess—a large room lit by tall windows that overlooked the compound's central courtyard. There were three wooden tables, with at least half a dozen men in uniforms sitting and chatting.

Kyra lowered her head submissively and slipped in, serving coffee, tea, and bread to those seated at the tables. The hum of conversation buzzed around her, and she kept her ears attuned to pick up any mention of the new commander or the special prisoners.

A pair of soldiers near the window caught her attention. They were good-looking, tall, and imposing, but what made them stand out was the way they carried themselves, the way every move seemed too fluid, almost preternaturally smooth.

They were like her, enhanced.

These men had likely undergone the same procedures that had transformed her into the lethal weapon she was now, making them extremely dangerous.

"Where is the commander this morning?" asked a broad-shouldered officer, pausing mid-sip as Kyra refilled his cup.

"Attending a meeting," another replied. "He had his breakfast delivered to his office at dawn as usual."

Kyra worked her way around the room, offering tea and collecting empty plates. She kept the mask of a dutiful server, her shoulders slumped and her movements deliberately clumsier than usual.

The phrase "special division" flitted toward her from one of the conversations.

Did it mean people like her?

Her pendant radiated a low-grade warmth, an almost anxious pulse against her sternum as if urging her to remain on guard. She didn't need the reminder. Every nerve in her body was on edge.

When the breakfast service ended, a couple of the junior officers stayed behind, showing little interest in leaving. Kyra started to wipe down tables, feigning concentration on each crumb and drip of tea.

"Did you see what Sergeant Nazari did yesterday?" the shorter one asked in a hushed tone, believing only his friend could hear him. "He jumped down three stories and landed like a cat—walked away without so much as a limp!"

The other officer, a lean man with tense shoulders, shrugged. "If you know what's good for you, keep your nose out of their business and don't ask questions. Don't talk about the strange staff either." He leaned closer. "What if they are possessed?"

The other man laughed. "You and your stupid superstitions."

"They are not stupid. It is a known thing that the touch of a Jinn can give a man dark powers, and even more so to a woman."

"That I believe," the other one said and dropped his voice even lower. "I've heard rumors that the rebel women are Jinn touched. Some are even bulletproof."

As if reading her chaotic thoughts, her pendant warmed up. Were they talking about her?

Sensing that she'd lingered near them long enough, Kyra forced herself to keep moving, scrubbing away invisible spots. She needed more information, but she also needed to remain inconspicuous.

The conversation between the officers drifted onto other topics: the next supply shipment, the desertion of a soldier last week, speculation about how the commander managed to get so much funding from the government in Tehran.

It was all valuable information, but she still needed to get to the East Wing and find out who the new prisoners were.

Eventually the two stood and left, leaving half-eaten plates in their wake. Kyra placed the dishes onto the tray and returned it to the kitchen.

30

KYRA

In the supply room of the eastern building, Kyra loaded a cleaning trolley with brooms, rags, and disinfectants. The cramped space reeked of mold. It was no different than the countless other nooks and crannies she'd hidden in over the years on missions just like this one—blending into the walls under the cover of humility and listening for tidbits of information to piece together later.

Peeking out into the wide corridor, she verified that the coast was clear and pushed the cart out. Not that anyone would have raised a brow at a maid exiting a supply closet, but she didn't want to bump into anyone who might want to take a better look at her.

Act normal and keep your head down was a mantra that ran on repeat in her head.

A couple of ordinary guards came from around

the corner, the low timbre of their small talk unthreatening, and yet her heart pounded, and she gripped the handle of the trolley with a white-knuckled force.

Relax.

To them, she was nothing—just another woman in a shapeless garment pushing a squeaking cart with her eyes lowered in humble compliance.

Once the guards' voices faded, she took a deep breath and grimaced at the unpleasant scent. This building smelled even worse than the rest of the compound. Maybe it was an offensive mix of chemical disinfectants, the rot of neglect, or both. Or maybe she was registering the faint whiff of the human emotions permeating this space.

Fear, pain, despair, and their counterparts—hatred, greed, and cruelty.

The worst part was that the smell was familiar, and it evoked a surge of panic that Kyra couldn't afford to let distract her. She needed details about the prisoners behind the steel doors and perhaps some clues about what had been done to her.

Shuffling down the winding corridors, she encountered the same neglect she had seen in the other building. Nothing special had been done to fix the place ahead of the new commander's arrival. The paint on the walls was peeling away in scabs of green and yellow, revealing the dull cement underneath, and the floors, worn by decades of heavy boot traffic, bore scuff marks that no amount of scrubbing could fully erase. Many of the overhead fluorescent lights either didn't function or flickered as if they were in their last death throes, casting some areas in brightness and others in shadowy gloom. The effect was disorienting—like her disjointed memories—a few patches of clarity surrounded by stretches of dark unknown.

Two guards stood at the bottom of the concrete stairwell that led to the eastern wing's upper floors.

Kyra kept her gaze on her cart, and the guards barely glanced at her. She passed them without incident and climbed up, carrying her cart up the stairs and pretending it was a considerable effort.

On the third floor, a hush blanketed the corridor. Metal doors punctuated the walls, each with a small barred window near the top.

She turned a corner and nearly collided with a man whose uniform bore a colonel's insignia.

"Watch where you're going," he snapped, stepping aside.

What was that smell?

The colonel reeked of something that triggered a visceral fear and brought about an involuntary tremor, evoking memories she assumed were from her days in the asylum. Her memories of the place were murky, and she didn't remember how she'd gotten there or what had been done to her, or even how long she'd been imprisoned in the vile place. She barely remembered the route she'd taken in the final chaos when she'd freed the other captives and fled into the night or how she'd ended up with the Kurdish rebels. And yet, she remembered that smell.

Quickly lowering her eyes, she murmured an apology.

After a charged beat, he moved on, with an aide hurrying after him.

"Regarding the prisoner in cell twelve, sir, should we increase the dosage?"

"Not yet. The doctor wouldn't want her brain fried. We need to await his commands."

As the colonel and his assistant disappeared behind the corner, Kyra remained frozen momentarily.

Cell number twelve.

She had to see for herself who was held there. Gripping her cart, she wheeled it to the next corridor. When she was sure no one was watching, she parked it by a supply closet and continued walking.

Each door in this section also had a small, barred glass pane. She scanned the numbers by the frames: fifteen…fourteen…thirteen… twelve.

Standing on tiptoes, Kyra peered through the window, and her breath caught.

A woman lay shackled to a narrow cot, wrists and ankles held by thick restraints. Her dark hair clung to a pillow soaked with sweat, and tears and bruises marred her face.

Kyra had seen this kind of damage before—a mixture of chemical sedation and physical abuse she couldn't comprehend the purpose of, other than satisfying the sick pleasure of a sadist.

For a moment, Kyra's vision blurred. Emotions churned. Why did this stranger's face spark such a visceral reaction?

A swirl of memories battered at her mind: the asylum corridor, the doctor's eyes gleaming, her own screams sounding only inside her head.

Her chest tightened. What had they done to her and why?

As footsteps echoed in the stairwell, Kyra quickly stepped away from the window. With a shaky breath, she slinked back to her cart and pressed forward down the corridor, posture stooped and feet shuffling.

The guards tromped by moments later, paying her no mind. Only once they were gone did she allow the tremor in her hands to surface. Leaning momentarily against the trolley, she took a shallow, calming breath.

31

KYRA

Kyra ducked into an empty utility closet, shutting the door behind her. The air was stale, and the single bulb overhead cast a sickly yellow light. Still, it felt like an oasis of safety after what she'd encountered in the corridor, and she needed a moment to collect her thoughts.

Who was that woman in cell twelve? And why did she look so much like her? Was it her mind playing tricks on her?

She was well aware of her mind not being a hundred percent sound, probably the result of what had been done to her in the asylum, and seeing the bruised woman could have triggered memories of her own ordeal.

What if it wasn't her imagination, though? What if she was a sister or a cousin?

Did she even have relatives? And if she had, were any of them enhanced like she was?

What if she'd been born like that and didn't remember it?

They could have caught her and put her in that asylum to experiment on her to find out what made her different, and after she'd escaped, they searched for her relatives.

A shiver ran through Kyra, and she pressed a palm to her chest, feeling the comforting warmth of the amber pendant beneath her clothes. The stone pulsed faintly, but it had no answers for her.

On second thought, the theory that she'd been born that way didn't make sense. She'd been as helpless as the woman in cell number twelve before an unprecedented surge of strength allowed her to break free. She hadn't possessed it going into the asylum, or she would have been able to snap those chains before the surge.

She'd been so drugged that she could barely remember what she'd done, but she was pretty sure she'd snapped the necks of several guards. She'd been shot at, and she might have even been hit, but she didn't remember that or even how she'd ended up in the rebel camp.

Well, she knew how. Several of the women she'd liberated were rebels, and they had taken her with them. That was what they had told her once the drugs had left her system and she could think coherently again.

Her life before the asylum was like a black hole of nothingness.

It was as if she'd been born fully grown in that dingy room with a barred window. Naturally, that wasn't true, and the dreams she occasionally had of a girl with eyes just like hers were a hint of her past. Maybe the girl was a sister or a cousin. Maybe that sister or cousin had a daughter who looked just like her, and she was now imprisoned by the same monsters that had abducted her.

She had to take another peek at the woman to see if she really bore such a striking resemblance to her or if it had been a product of her imagination.

Kyra exhaled, leaning against the closet's grimy wall. She had to do something. If the colonel was throwing around words like tests and dosage, it indicated that he, or rather the one he called Doctor, might be doing the same thing to this woman that had been done to Kyra.

The question was the timing.

Had the woman already transformed? If so, she could be a great asset to the resistance. If not, extracting her while she was in the middle of her transformation might be risky. There could be dangers in halting the process midway.

On the other hand, could she leave the woman in the clutches of the sadist who was either beating her up himself or having someone else do that for no other reason than to satisfy his twisted desires?

Surely, the abuse had nothing to do with developing super abilities, and there were much easier methods to extract information from a captive.

Kyra cracked the door and peered out. Voices echoed faintly from the far end of the corridor. The colonel was somewhere downstairs, but guards came and went, and cameras loomed overhead, so rescuing the prisoner on the spot would be impossible. Kyra's best bet was to watch for an opportunity during medication rounds, but even that was reckless, given the enhanced guards on the premises.

Then there was the way her mind was misfiring, and she wasn't sure she could trust her own judgment right then. The place brought forgotten memories to the surface in confusing fragments.

A prick of a needle.

A cruel smile on the face of someone wearing a doctor's coat.

The change might have made her body nearly invincible, but it had messed with her head. To this day, she had memory issues, and not just from before the asylum or during her time there. That was why she made notes for herself that she regularly checked.

Steeling herself, Kyra eased into the hallway, pushing her cart once more. If she looked busy and preoccupied, no one would question her presence. She mopped the floors, wiped door handles, and shined the number plaques above the windows, giving herself an excuse to peek into the other cells, some of which were empty and some of which housed male prisoners who were not chained to their beds.

Half an hour passed with excruciating slowness. At last, a man carrying a tray of syringes and tiny cups of pills arrived, accompanied by two guards. She followed them with her mop, pretending to clean the new footprints they were making on the damp floor.

The colonel's earlier comment about drugging the woman replayed in her mind. Was the guy with the tray going to enter cell twelve even though the commander had told his assistant that the woman should not be drugged any further until the doctor said to do so?

Maybe the guy with the tray was the doctor.

Whenever the group entered a cell, Kyra paused to scrub or wipe a surface. When a door opened, a guard stepped in first to secure the occupant, followed by the guy with the tray, and then the door closed with the three inside.

They seemed to be taking forever, and in the meantime, Kyra's mind raced with the possibilities. The occupant of cell twelve might be a connection to her past, making this much more than an intelligence-gathering mission.

This had just become personal.

32

KYRA

It took the man with the tray forever to get to cell number twelve, and the more time passed, the more dangerous it was getting for Kyra. Someone would notice that she hadn't cleaned anywhere else and was taking too long in this corridor, and when they questioned her, they would discover she wasn't who she claimed to be.

She was so close, though, and her need to take another look at that woman was overwhelming.

Naturally, she'd cataloged each of the other prisoners, memorizing their faces and every bit of information she'd managed to overhear, thanks to her exceptional hearing. She hadn't dared to bring a notebook with her, which would have been helpful given the state of her memory, so instead, she kept repeating the descriptions and the information in her mind and making a story out of them.

She had learned this memorization trick from a television show she had seen a while ago. Making the information a movie in her head was immensely helpful in accurately recalling the details later.

The man with the tray and the two guards were taking far too long in cell number ten, though, and she was running out of patience. Maybe she should rush over to the door of cell twelve and peek through the small window again.

She could pretend to clean that door once more. It would be foolish, and she should wait until the three men were inside so she could spend more time at the window and listen to what they were saying, but she was impatient.

Pausing at the corner near cell eight, Kyra propped the mop handle against the wall as though she were taking a small rest. The corridor was deserted except for the occasional clink of metal, the hiss of old vents, and the muffled sounds of voices coming out of cell number ten.

After a moment's listening, she gathered her nerve and eased forward with a bottle of cleaning solution in one hand and a rag in the other. She stopped by cell eleven and quickly cleaned the door before rushing to her destination.

Rising to her tiptoes, she reached for the plaque above the window with her rag and peered inside.

Her breath caught.

The bruises were gone, which was impossible.

It hadn't been more than an hour, maybe even less, since she'd first seen the woman's face, and there was no way she could have healed so quickly. She still looked pale and gaunt, and she was asleep. Had she imagined the swelling of her cheek? The dark mottling? No sign of either remained.

The woman lay on her back, her head turned slightly to one side. Her face was unblemished, as though she'd never taken a blow. Now that it was clear, the resemblance seemed less uncanny.

They had the same dark hair, slender nose, and similarly shaped chins, but their similarities ended there. The woman's face was narrower, her lips were thinner, and she was more delicately built.

The sound of footsteps made Kyra stiffen.

She ducked aside, her heart hammering, and started rubbing her cleaning rag over a stain on the wall next to the door.

The guard passed her without a second glance, and as his steps receded, she chanced another look inside. The woman's eyes were open now, pale brown and glazed, gazing blankly at the ceiling.

She was still very much under the influence of drugs, and Kyra hoped they wouldn't give her any more or they might kill her.

Had the bruises never been there, and had Kyra projected her own experience on the woman because of their similar looks?

Or did the woman heal as fast as she did?

But if she had been changed in the same way

Kyra had, she should also have enhanced strength and been able to break free of the chains.

Maybe she didn't know how?

A swirl of half-buried memories tugged at Kyra—banging the cuff against the wall until the lock broke, her wrists that had been scarred raw, the blood flowing in rivulets down her hands. But then the healing had happened so fast that she'd thought she was hallucinating.

The prisoner blinked, tilting her head as if hearing something or sensing a presence. Kyra ducked to avoid direct eye contact, but curiosity won out, and she rose again, searching the woman's face for new clues.

The woman looked confused, her gaze flickering toward the door without focusing on it.

It was the effect of the drugs she'd been given.

When more footsteps echoed, this time from the stairwell, Kyra uttered a silent curse. Her time was up, and she needed to get out of there.

Leaping for her cleaning cart, she clutched the handle and then forced her racing heart to slow down and her feet to assume the shuffle she'd affected before. Once she reached the storage room again, she got inside and leaned against the door to take her first deep breath since she'd left its relative safety earlier.

A faint pang of remembered pain ran through her lower back where she'd once been struck by a bullet, yet within minutes, her body had expelled it, and her flesh had knit back together.

If the woman had healed just as quickly, she would have been another product of the same program that had changed Kyra from a regular human to something more.

What was she supposed to do, though?

Rescuing the woman was impossible, with the compound being guarded by elite forces who seemed to have undergone the same type of transformation. For all of Kyra's strength, she wasn't a match for an entire unit of enhanced soldiers.

A confrontation would be suicide.

She closed her eyes, mind sifting through potential strategies.

They couldn't keep the woman imprisoned here forever. This wasn't an asylum, and prisoners came and went. Perhaps her team could snatch the woman when she was being transported to another facility.

It would be much less risky than attempting to storm this place.

If the woman was a fellow rebel, she could join Kyra's team, and with her enhanced abilities, she could become an invaluable member. Hopefully, she could also fill in some of the missing pieces of Kyra's shattered past.

33

KIAN

Okidu knocked on Kian's office door before pushing it slightly open. "Mistress Syssi requested I inform you of the guests' arrival."

Kian had heard the doorbell, so sending Okidu hadn't been necessary. He just needed to finish reviewing the counteroffer Shai emailed him Friday night.

"I will be right there," he told his butler.

"Of course, master." Okidu probably bowed, but since the door was only opened a crack, Kian couldn't see him. "I shall inform Mistress Syssi."

The counteroffer was for a prime piece of land that could be developed into a gated community the size of a small town, and Kian was considering the option of building a new place for his people. There was really no need for a new location, and the village was big enough for their needs. Still, most of his business decisions were based on gut feelings rather than logic, and even though the price was more than what made sense to spend on an undeveloped parcel of that size, the location was perfect for the clan's needs, and his gut told him to go for it. Perhaps he would just sit on it and let it appreciate. He could always decide later what he wanted to do with it.

Reluctantly, he closed his desktop computer, rose to his feet, and headed for the living room. He would take another look at it later.

As he stepped into the family room, the first thing that struck him was the easy camaraderie between Jasmine and Max. It seemed that they had ironed out whatever animosity had lingered between them, and they now looked as if they were the best of friends.

"Good morning," he said as he sat on one of the armchairs. "How was your flight back?"

"Great," Jasmine said. "Thank you for the first-class tickets. I slept for four hours straight, which is all I need now. Being immortal rocks."

She seemed upbeat, considering the emotional visit to her father's cabin. Then again, Jasmine was an actress, and putting on a face was as easy for her as breathing.

"I'm sure everyone wants coffee." Syssi walked in with a carafe in hand.

"Please," Max said. "I didn't sleep during the flight, and I need it."

Kian was surprised that Syssi had opted for a simple drip instead of showing off her cappuccino-making skills, but he didn't mind the drip. It seemed appropriate for the occasion.

"Okidu is warming up croissants," she said as she poured coffee for their guests first and then for Kian and herself.

He took the cup, impatient to be done with the small talk and the pleasantries so they could be done with the report, and he could go back to go over the counteroffer and decide whether the land was worth the money.

Oh, hell. Who was he kidding? He'd already made up his mind about buying it. The only question was whether he would sit on it, build a new place for his clan, or develop it for sale.

He cleared his throat, drawing their attention. "I appreciate you all coming here this morning. I want to get a handle on things as soon as possible and decide on a course of action."

Jasmine set her coffee down, folding her hands in her lap. "My father believes that my mother's family came for her. He said she'd warned him that they might do something drastic if they discovered she'd married a Christian, but he admitted that he never took her seriously. He's been drowning in guilt ever since she was taken, and he believes that they killed her. I wanted to tell him that they hadn't and that she was still alive, but I didn't want to get his hopes up."

Max leaned forward, clasping his hands between his knees. "Boris was beyond distressed—there's a lot of pain bottled up inside him. He ranted about how she'd left him vulnerable, how he'd spent months searching. Ultimately, he believed her family forced her to sign divorce papers before killing her, but that makes little sense to me. If her family were so horrible that they were willing to kill her for marrying someone they disapproved of, they wouldn't have bothered to get her a lawyer and have her divorce him. My bet was that they wanted her to marry someone else, someone of their choosing, and that they needed the divorce to make it possible. They probably also threatened her with harming her daughter if she ever gave Boris or Jasmine a sign that she was alive."

"That's the most logical explanation," Kian agreed. "But given Syssi's visions, that's not how the story went."

Syssi nodded. "My latest vision showed that Kyra was held as a prisoner in Iran. At first, I assumed it was another vision showing the past, but a recent news broadcast was playing in the background, so I realized that it couldn't have been more than a few days old."

Jasmine tensed. "What did the vision show you about my mother?"

Syssi winced. "She was once again chained to the bed, but she wasn't drugged this time. She was bruised, though, and the same man from the other vision was there again, but this time, he wore a uniform instead of a doctor's coat. He said that he was surprised to find her in Tahav and seemed very pleased with himself. Kian searched for the name, and it's a small town in the north of Iran, somewhere between Iranian Azerbaijan and the Kermanshah Province."

"And?" Jasmine tapped her foot on the area rug. "I can sense that there is a big reveal coming up."

Syssi nodded. "The man didn't look a day older than in the previous vision. It was a little harder to tell what age your mother was, given the bruising on her face, so she could have been much older. But since I think the fake doctor was a Doomer, it's not a stretch to assume that he induced her transition when he forced himself on her. Your mother might be an immortal already."

Jasmine gasped, her hand flying to her chest.

"How could they have known about Kyra?" Ellrom asked.

"It might have been a fluke," Kian said. "She was probably put in an asylum to be brainwashed to forget her husband and child, and someone working there might have been a Doomer. He would have had no idea that she was a Dormant or that she transitioned to immortality later, or he wouldn't have let her go. He would have taken her to the Doomers' island to become a breeder for Navuh's mercenary army."

Syssi shivered. "Maybe that's where she is?"

Kian leaned over and patted her hand. "You heard him say he was surprised to find her in Tahav. It's not a name you've heard before, so you couldn't have just superimposed it on the vision."

"Right." Syssi rubbed her temples between her thumb and forefinger. "But now that he knows she's immortal, that's exactly what he will do. We might already be too late."

Jasmine's jaw tightened. "Maybe she had a rough transition that caused her memory loss? Or maybe that is what all the drugs they pumped into her were for. They wanted her to forget about her family so she would be more agreeable to the arranged marriage, but then she transitioned and escaped. The bastard found her somehow, and now she is at that accursed island, and there is no way for us to get her out of there."

Kian regarded Jasmine's stricken expression and wished he could give her a glimmer of hope. "Kyra might still be in Tahav, Jasmine. Otherwise, the Fates wouldn't have given Syssi so many visions about her. They were trying to convey a sense of urgency, and we should send a team to that place as soon as possible."

Jasmine's eyes brightened. "You are right. The Fates need us to find my mother so she can help us find Khiann. It's all connected."

"We have to operate under the assumption that her captors are well-funded and well-connected,"

Max said. "A mission inside Iran is tricky; if the Brotherhood is involved, that's even trickier."

Kian let out a breath. "Her family might have connections to the Brotherhood, and they might have used its help to smuggle her out of the country. We have our resources that we can mobilize."

Turner knew people, and Kian was confident that the guy would find a way to smuggle a team into Iran. The question was how quickly those resources could be mobilized.

Getting people and equipment into Iran shouldn't be more complicated than operating inside Russia, and they had sent two chartered planes full of Guardians and military equipment to Saint Petersburg.

Kian ran a hand over the back of his neck. "We need to assemble a team as soon as possible, which is a problem because I don't know if Onegus can spare anyone."

Max lifted his hand. "I would like to go, provided that Onegus can release me from my post at the keep."

Kian nodded. "You're in. I'll talk with Onegus. We need more people, though."

"I'm going," Jasmine declared. "And don't even try to dissuade me. I'm great with disguises, and I can act my way through anything. I can color my hair, wear local clothing, keep my face covered—whatever it takes."

Ell-rom gave her a supportive squeeze of the

shoulder. "I'm coming with you, and that's not negotiable either."

Kian's gut clenched. His mother wouldn't like her brother going on a dangerous mission even though he was probably the most lethal weapon in their arsenal.

He rose from his armchair. "I need to plan this with Onegus and Turner, and time is of the essence. I'll let you know when we are moving out, but be ready to go on a moment's notice."

Max rose to his feet. "I would like to join the meeting if you don't mind."

Kian was about to say that it wasn't necessary, but after a pointed look from Syssi, he nodded. "Right now, I'm just going to call them and schedule a time. Go home and freshen up. I'll let you know when and where the meeting will take place."

Thankfully, neither Jasmine nor Ell-rom demanded to be present as well.

34

MAX

When Max followed Kian into Onegus's office, Turner was already there. They were fortunate that it was a Sunday and the strategist was home. Otherwise, they would have been forced to wait for him to return to the village from his downtown office or meet him there.

Noting how the chief's usually pristine desk was covered in mission reports and personnel files, it was clear to Max that Onegus was also working overtime instead of resting on the weekend, probably because of all the extra work he had with establishing the new division.

The guy needed an assistant, and the clan needed more Guardians, but there were no more to be had. There wouldn't be any in the foreseeable future, unless they revived the Doomers they had placed in stasis and compelled them to join the clan in the fight to improve humanity, instead of their original programming that called for enslaving it.

In fact, that wasn't such a bad idea. Toven might not agree to lead a mercenary army with his compulsion power, but now they had Drova on the force, and Igor's daughter might not be as squeamish about who she led. On the other hand, she wasn't all that trustworthy either, so possibly that wasn't such a great idea.

"Kian, Max," Onegus said, rising to greet them. "Please sit down." He gestured to the vacant chairs across from his desk, the third occupied by Turner. "So let me get this straight." He cast a tired look at Kian. "You want to assemble a rescue team to get Jasmine's mother out of an Iranian prison?"

Kian nodded and looked at Turner. "In my opinion, it will be easier to infiltrate them and do whatever we want there than it was to run the rescue operation in the heart of Russia. They are poorly organized, and the people are very responsive to bribes. The problem is that we don't have time to prepare. We must assemble a team before Kyra is taken to the Doomers' island. Once she's there, getting her out will be nearly impossible."

Onegus arched a brow. "The Doomers' island?"

"Yeah." Kian leaned his elbow on his knee and his chin on his fist and relayed the main points of the conversation they'd had earlier and the conclusions they'd arrived at. While Onegus was listening with an unreadable expression, Turner was taking notes.

When he was done, Onegus sighed. "I understand the urgency, but I can't spare any Guardians right now. With the force split into two teams and some guarding the prisoners in the keep," he glanced at Max, "I just don't have enough fighters. This mission will need more than two or three Guardians. You need a large team to storm a compound that might have several Doomers operating within its walls. It's also not a quick operation that can be done in a day. Taking flight times into account, we are talking three days at the minimum, probably four. I would have to cancel a lot of missions to give you what you need."

Turner shifted in his chair. "What about the Kra-ell? I mean the ones who are not yet serving on the force."

Onegus turned to look at him. "They have no training."

"Actually, they do," Turner said. "Just not Guardian training. They trained in Igor's compound, and they're natural warriors, stronger and faster than immortals, and they're also resistant to thralling and compulsion. There is no one better to fight Doomers."

Onegus shook his head. "They trained with swords, staffs, and hunting rifles in Igor's compound, and they obeyed his commands because he was a compeller and gave them no choice. They are undisciplined, and we can't provide them with even rudimentary weapons training."

Kian waved a dismissive hand. "They are natural soldiers, and if I get Jade or Kagra to come along, they will keep them in line. The problem is their appearance. They're too distinctively alien—too tall and too thin. Their enormous black eyes can be hidden with big sunglasses, and we can put them in baggy clothes, but that's a good disguise for one person. A group of extremely tall and thin people all wearing sunglasses would look suspicious, and since we are sending them to Iran, it's not like we can put them in team uniforms and present them as a Chinese basketball team."

"You can put them in Revolutionary Guard uniforms," Turner said. "Even if they look suspicious, no one will dare to ask them anything."

"That's an option." Onegus leaned back. "I can also spare Yamanu, and he can shroud everyone. I only use him occasionally when massive thralling and shrouding are necessary, and I don't have anything of that size planned for next week."

Having Yamanu on the team was a game changer, and Max was glad the head Guardian was available. The downside was that Yamanu would get to lead the team, and Max had hoped to do that.

"There's another advantage to using Kra-ell

warriors," Kian said. "Their presence doesn't trigger a warning response in other immortal males."

"That's a good point." Onegus turned his screen to show them a roster of available Kra-ell. "Would you consider taking some of the females?"

Kian usually didn't like sending females on missions that involved Doomers. Still, given that Kra-ell pureblooded females could handle themselves against the most vicious of Navuh's males, he might be okay with that.

The boss winced but then let out a breath and nodded. "I need to get over my instinctive resistance to including females in combat missions, and the best way to do that is by reminding myself that Jade saved me from Igor. I've never seen anyone move like that. The Doomers wouldn't know what hit them. But that will be up to Jade, of course."

"Right," Onegus agreed, then a grin spread over his face. "Can we equip the Kra-ell females with personal cameras and record the Doomers' reactions?"

Kian snorted. "I like the way you think, chief."

"There's one more thing to consider," Turner said, his expression serious. "If we're right about Doomers being involved, this could be bigger than a simple rescue mission. It could be a good opportunity to gather intelligence about their regional operations. So, if at all possible, we may want to consider grabbing at least one of them, preferably the leader, and bringing him back to the keep for interrogation."

Kian nodded. "An excellent suggestion, Turner."

It was, but putting a Doomer in stasis in the middle of a battle would be tricky. Perhaps they should bring tranquilizing darts with them. The other problem would be making the Kra-ell use them. Those people were vicious predators, and once they smelled blood, they wouldn't stop to consider who they were going to kill and who they were going to capture.

Except for Jade, perhaps. She was a professional.

Turner considered his notes while everyone waited for him to continue. "We will need to get the team as close to the compound as possible for the extraction. That means a transport chopper or two, depending on the team size and how many additional passengers we'll pick up. I can probably arrange for a couple of Russian-made transport choppers commonly used by the Iranians and have them painted to look like Revolutionary Guard equipment. We will also need authentic-looking uniforms to complete the illusion. This will give our team an edge as they approach the enemy."

Turner consulted a map of the region on his laptop. "If we can have the choppers wait for us near the Turkish border, the flight path is well within the equipment's range."

Onegus nodded. "Good plan."

Turner continued without responding to the praise. "We need to fly the team to Turkey on a private flight. With Yamanu on board, they won't need documentation, but just in case, we should provide them with fake Iranian identification."

Max quickly counted in his head as Turner flipped to a new page on his yellow pad. "The clan's jet should suffice," he said.

Onegus shook his head. "We need the eighteen-seater to accommodate the team and several guests. I hope Kalugal doesn't have plans to fly anywhere next week. We need his jet."

"What size team are we planning?" Kian asked.

"A small squad of Kra-ell should suffice," Turner replied. "Five to six warriors plus Jade or Kagra. This is a surgical grab-and-go operation, so a large force would be a hindrance."

"Plus Yamanu, Ell-rom, Jasmine, and me," Max added.

Onegus's eyebrows rose. "You're taking Jasmine? Is that wise?"

"Kyra is her mother and besides the fact that she insisted, she may be needed to assist with Kyra," Kian said with a grimace. "And where Jasmine goes, Ell-rom follows."

"At least he's not helpless," Max muttered. "That special ability of his could come in handy."

By now, many of the Guardians knew about the prince's deadly ability, but it was still being kept a secret from the rest of the clan. To Turner's credit, his face remained impassive apart from a raised eyebrow. But Max did not doubt that he would query Kian for the details in private later.

"We haven't fully tested the range limits of Ell-rom's talent yet," Kian said. "That's why I was keeping it under wraps. And we don't know whether it would work on immortals, but he's half Kra-ell, so his strength alone should be enough."

It was easy to forget that Ell-rom had Kra-ell blood that made him stronger and faster than the average immortal or even a god. He was so well-mannered and mellow.

"You should also have a compeller with you," Turner said. "We don't know how many Doomers are there, and Yamanu can't hide the team from them or thrall them."

Kian winced. "I can't ask Toven or Kalugal to go to Iran to rescue one woman who might not even be there."

Remembering his earlier thoughts, Max smiled. "What about Drova? She singlehandedly took care of the Doomers in the last operation, and she performed well under pressure."

Kian shook his head. "She's too young to join a mission like this."

"That is something for Jade to consider and decide," Turner said. "In the Kra-ell culture, Drova is considered ready for battle."

"Are you going to speak with Jade, or should I?"

Onegus asked Kian as if it had already been decided that Drova would join their team.

Kian looked resigned. "I see that I'm overruled. I will call Jade and Yamanu. I want you to concentrate on the logistics and getting the team out as soon as possible."

35

KYRA

Kyra woke well before dawn, the chill biting through the thin canvas walls of her tent, and as she rose from her cot, the low-pitched whistle of the wind teased the edges of her hearing. She pressed a hand to the pendant resting against her sternum, feeling the gentle thrum of warmth that never entirely left her and taking solace in its presence.

It was early even for her, but she needed the head start.

Mornings were the best time to slip into the compound with the rest of the staff without drawing attention. Early mornings were also the best time to check on the prisoner in cell twelve.

After pulling on the shapeless black dress and headscarf that was part of her disguise, she headed out.

Despite the cold, the air was crisp and fresh,

and she let herself enjoy it for a moment before rushing to the communal bathroom. Her reflection in the dingy mirror over the sink startled her, not because of the disguise she wore but because of the haunted look in her eyes.

It was difficult to witness the extent of the cruelty inflicted on that still unnamed prisoner and then breathe a sigh of relief after the near-miraculous healing. The woman's torment would be repeated tomorrow, and the next day, her sadistic abuser relishing in her ability to erase the physical signs of his abuses so he could do it all over again.

There were other missions. Other prisoners. Twelve wasn't the only woman in there, and she wasn't the only one getting beaten, but she was getting the brunt of the sadistic efforts, and Kyra was drawn to her as though by a magnetic pull.

Twelve reminded her so strongly of herself that she felt compelled to look out for her even if there wasn't much she could do until the woman was moved to another facility.

Her people wanted to know why she would risk her life to do no more than watch the woman suffer abuse from afar. They wanted to know why she insisted the fate of a single prisoner mattered more than the broader war they were fighting.

How could she explain that she was selfishly trying to save herself?

How could anyone truly grasp the all-consuming need that drove her toward that cell?

She would do it again today, trek on foot into the low valley housing the compound and spend her shift, or rather Parisa's, with her head bowed, arms loaded with cleaning supplies, careful to avoid direct eye contact.

The risk was immense, and the frustration of doing nothing to rescue the woman was driving her half mad, but she didn't want to risk anyone else, and it was crucial to find out the exact time they would move the woman so her people could ambush the transport and rescue Twelve.

In the meantime, she was gleaning more intelligence about the schedules, the watch rotations, and the purpose of the enhanced soldiers. It seemed like a waste to station them in this area. The Kurdish rebellion had been going on forever, and she found it hard to believe that the regime planned a severe crackdown on them and had brought these enhanced humans for that purpose. As superior as they were to normal people, there weren't enough of them to make much of a difference.

She met Soran at the edge of the camp, as he had requested. He was leaning against a battered truck, arms folded over his chest, expression somewhere between anger and resignation.

"Why are you going in again?" he asked,

dispensing with any preamble. "You realize that we need to plan the next supply run?"

Kyra nodded. "You can be in charge of that, with Hamid and Zara doing the actual runs."

Soran's mouth tightened. "Zara is mad that you're neglecting your job. She says that you are losing your mind." He let out a heavy breath. "I'm not trying to undermine you or question your judgment. But you're risking yourself needlessly. Parisa can do what you're doing in there, watching and listening and gathering information, but no one can take your place here."

She shoved her hands into the folds of her dress, resisting the urge to argue. "Everyone is replaceable, Soran, and you are a very capable man. It's time that you took command."

He narrowed his eyes at her. "Why? Are you planning to leave us?"

"Of course not, but contrary to what you and the others think, I'm not indestructible, and one day, I might encounter a bullet I can't dodge. I want to have the peace of mind of knowing that this place will not fall apart and that you can continue our work. You need to start taking on more responsibilities."

"What if I fall too?"

She put her hand on his shoulder. "When I fall, you should start training your replacement. That's how it works, and that's what good leaders do. We plan ahead."

He shook his head. "Why now, though? The same was true yesterday, and the week before, yet you didn't insist then on leaving me in charge. So don't tell me stories, Kyra. For some reason, you are obsessed with that new prisoner. I need to know why."

"She's like me," Kyra finally admitted in a hushed voice. "She heals faster than normal. I've seen her bruises vanish. They are doing to her what they did to me, and as horrible as it is, we need her. Imagine having two of me. The things we would be able to do. That's why I must find out exactly when she gets moved, and I don't trust anyone else to do that." She adjusted the headscarf. "I also need to find out what they did to me, and that place has the answers."

Soran pushed off from the side of the truck. "Then we should storm that place and take her now."

"We can't." Kyra shook her head. "I can't fight all those enhanced soldiers alone, and the rest of you will have your hands full with the regular guards. We need to be patient and wait until they transport her out. That's our only chance, and I won't blow it by going in too soon."

He looked like he wanted to rail at her but settled for a reluctant nod. "Fine. I guess I need to thank you for the promotion."

Kyra smiled. "No need to thank me. You've earned it, and you're ready."

36

KYRA

Kyra arrived at the compound's perimeter under the gauzy light of dawn, slipping into her daily routine and ensuring the guards became accustomed to her presence. Her ID had only needed to pass muster the first time. Despite the new commander and his team of well-trained soldiers, the place was still poorly administered and prone to staff turnover. No one paid too much attention to paperwork when they got to know the people.

She just had to avoid the commander.

The pat-down for weapons from the female staff member at the gate was perfunctory. The woman just patted her shoulders and sides once and waved her through. She had her own problems—lack of pay, fear for her children, the rising cost of essential goods.

The truth was that very few people were

zealous about their politics or even their religion, and most were preoccupied with daily survival. The problem was the leaders and what mayhem they wanted to stir up in their never-ending pursuit of greed and power.

Once inside, Kyra gripped the handle of the broom trolley that had now become a better friend to her than her favorite dagger, which she'd left under her mattress at the camp.

The familiar whoosh of overhead fans, the metallic clang of spoons on breakfast trays, the hiss and pop of old equipment—it was all so normal and routine that it was hard to believe the evil that lived in the East Wing.

The corridor where the special prisoners were kept smelled of mold and fear no matter how much cleaning solution she used to scrub the floor and the peeling walls.

Along the way, she gathered tidbits of intelligence from open doors and overheard conversations, which were of little interest to her. Pushing her cart along the third floor, she passed cell after cell until she reached the one marked with the number twelve. She listened for footsteps to ensure no one was nearby and stopped under the pretense of cleaning a scuff mark on the floor near the door. When everything remained quiet, Kyra rose on her toes and peered through the small glass window.

The woman was awake, lying on her side this

time with just one wrist and one ankle shackled to the frame. She was stripped down to a thin shift, and a new bruise was splashed across her left cheek. The prisoner's eyes seemed to stare at nothing, but a flicker in them suggested she wasn't as broken as she looked. There was defiance there, a tiny ember she still clung to.

Kyra silently prayed that it wouldn't be extinguished before she was saved.

I'm here. I see you, she wanted to tell her. *You're not alone. Hold on a little longer. Help is coming.*

But there was no speaking to the woman through the thick door without alerting everyone else, so Kyra had no way to communicate that salvation was near. *Not soon enough.* So, she merely observed, sending positive energy to her sister-in-pain and hoping she felt it somehow and it helped her endure.

As footsteps echoed off the walls, Kyra quickly returned her attention to the scuff mark, scrubbing vigorously, and when the footsteps passed without halting, she risked another glance in the window.

The woman shifted her gaze as if she sensed someone was watching her, and a small smile curved her lips. Perhaps it was only wishful thinking, but Kyra's heart leaped at the thought the woman felt her gaze and knew that she had a friend on the other side.

Reluctantly, she forced her eyes away.

Too long at the door would raise suspicion.

Guiding her trolley, she headed down the corridor and around the corner. She wanted to smash that door open, throw the woman over her shoulder, and sprint out of the compound, but she wasn't suicidal.

During the midday break, Kyra collected her lunch from the kitchen and found an out-of-the-way corner in the utility room to rest. She had to maintain the charade that she was a lowly maid who needed a few minutes to catch her breath and liked to eat in solitude.

Most of the others gathered in the kitchen to eat and gossip, but she couldn't mingle with the people who knew Parisa and might realize she wasn't her despite the similar build and face covering.

She wondered how Soran was managing without her. Was Zara giving him a hard time for not talking sense into her?

Probably.

The entire region was on high alert, resources were scarce, and there were bigger fish to fry. They were counting on her for the more significant objectives, and she was letting them down.

Kyra pressed a hand to her pendant and murmured a small prayer for the safety of her people and success in rescuing the woman and the other prisoners as soon as they were moved out of this place.

Her moment of peace was shattered by a bark of laughter in the corridor that she recognized by now. With her heart kicking into overdrive, she edged closer to the door.

"Yes, sir," a man said, voice dripping with a subservient mixture of fear and awe. "I'll ensure that your instructions are followed to the letter." The footsteps receded, and the conversation was lost in the shuffle of other voices echoing in the hallway.

What instructions?

Were they going to do something to the woman in twelve?

There was no way Kyra could return to that corridor without arousing suspicion. She had to move to the West Wing and mop the floors there. Could she pretend to have forgotten some cleaning implement or solution on the third floor in the East Wing?

Her gut knotting with worry, Kyra made her way to the western building and started her methodical progression on the floors.

The officer in charge of staff stopped by her when she was on her knees, scrubbing a stubborn stain on the first floor.

"Make sure to do a thorough job today. We need the facility spotless by the end of this week. Gleaming everything, am I clear?"

"Yes, sir," she murmured meekly, nodding but not raising her head.

A few minutes later, as a group of guards passed by her, she heard them talking about the commander preparing the facility for higher-ups' visit. This could mean one of two things: The higher-ups were arriving because of the prisoners currently held in the facility, or they were bringing a fresh crop of detainees with them.

The commander might want to remove the current prisoners before the visit and ship them out, as the day of their transport was approaching.

The problem was that they might get rid of the prisoners by killing them instead of shipping them out. She prayed they would keep the woman alive for the same reason they'd once kept Kyra: to harness her potential and use her however they wanted.

The drugs, the beatings, and the violations were meant to break Twelve's spirit so she would obey them, but it seemed like she was holding on. The question was how long they would keep trying before deciding she would never break and then disposing of her.

37

KYRA

When the guards' shift change approached the outer gates, it was time for Kyra to leave. She silently pulled off her apron and folded it neatly, placing it in the supply closet for tomorrow's use. Then, head bowed, she slipped out into the open air. The sky burned gold as the sun prepared to set, and dust swirled around her boots, the same dust she'd spent all day wiping from the compound's floors.

She kept her shoulders hunched as she approached the perimeter checkpoint, offering a small nod to the guard who waved her through. It was much easier to get out than it was to get in, and for a moment, she entertained the idea of smuggling Twelve out of there by trading places with her. If she did that near the end of her shift, no one would notice until the next day when the sadist came to take his twisted pleasure from the woman again and realized it wasn't the same one.

To anyone else, they would look similar enough to avoid notice.

Getting into the cell shouldn't be too tricky, and sabotaging the surveillance cameras was as easy as disrupting the compound's internet connection. Their system was simple, the kind anyone could buy in a store or order online. The more she thought about it, the more sense it made to her, except for the detail of her taking Twelve's place. Her people would never agree, and she couldn't pull this off alone.

Someone had to disable the internet just long enough for the switch, and someone also needed to meet Twelve outside the gate and lead her to the camp.

She could lie to them and omit the part about taking Twelve's place, but after working with these people for so long, Kyra wouldn't betray their trust.

Was there another way to do it?

The guard recognized her because she wore the same clothes each time she passed through his checkpoint, walked with the same shuffle, and gave him the same timid hand wave. That was why he'd let her through without verifying her identity. Another guard would not do that.

Still, Twelve looked a lot like her, so even if he

asked to see her ID, he would probably not notice the difference. Then again, if the same guard was manning the checkpoint, he would notice Twelve's shorter stature and her different posture and gait.

When Kyra arrived back at camp, she found Zara, Rashid, and Soran waiting in her tent. Zara looked exasperated, standing with her arms crossed over her chest, while Soran wore his usual slightly worried expression, and Rashid was frowning.

"What's going on?" She removed her headscarf and tossed it on her cot.

"We have intelligence from Erbiz," Zara said.

"And?" Kyra pulled out a chair and sat down. "What's the intel?"

"The Revolutionary Guard Corps is building an encampment on the hills south of there."

"I'm surprised that they didn't just evacuate the people of Erbiz from their homes and take over. That's what they usually do."

"What are we going to do about it?" Soran asked.

"What do you think we should do?"

"Question the workers they hired or send one of ours undercover," he answered without pause, as if he expected her to ask him exactly that.

"There you go." Kyra waved a hand. "You know what to do and can handle it without me."

"That's not the point." Zara's voice trembled

with barely suppressed anger. "We need you. You're our leader."

Kyra closed her eyes, struggling to maintain calm. "We are all in this together, and no one appointed me as your leader. I just took control when Dosdan was killed. Any one of you could have done that." She turned to Soran. "I was thrown headfirst into the water without knowing how to swim, but you have the benefit of stepping up with me still around to guide you."

"Why are you talking like that?" Zara squeaked. "Are you dying or something?"

"Not as far as I know." Kyra pulled the pendant from inside her blouse where it had been warming her skin. "I'm guided by intuition as much as strategic thinking, and both agree with my decision to accelerate Soran's training as my replacement. We are not the military and don't follow strict protocol, but I don't appreciate you three questioning my decisions."

Soran raked a hand through his hair. "People look up to you."

"They also look up to you." She cast the three a hard look. "Unless you have anything of substance to report, this meeting is over."

Rashid winced. "We can't afford to lose you."

None of the three moved an inch.

"You are leaving us in the dark," Zara said. "You are not telling us your plans, and that's not okay. As you said, we are in this together."

They were more right than they were aware of, but after their combined attack, she wasn't going to tell them about her latest plan. Besides, she was still working on it.

Kyra fought to keep her expression schooled. "You know my plans. When they move the prisoners, we attack the transport. In the meantime, I'm collecting information about the methods they used to turn that woman into someone like me."

Letting out a breath, Rashid plopped down on a stool. "And how's that going? Did you steal any of the drugs they are using on her or are you about to?"

She shook her head. "Two guards always accompany the guy who administers the shots."

"So, how are you going to find out?"

He was right, of course. Even if she managed to snag a sample of the drugs they used, she had no access to a laboratory that could analyze it and tell her what was inside. And even if she did, she would fear sending it to them and pointing a big arrow at herself.

"I might overhear something. People like to talk, and the cleaning staff is practically invisible. No one pays me any mind. They treat me the same as they treat a broom."

Soran exhaled in frustration. "So you will continue like this until they transport her out?"

Kyra pulled her fingers through her hair, combing it to give herself a moment to collect her thoughts. "That's the only viable strategy, and I don't think it will be much longer now. They're preparing the place for someone's important visit, and I'm betting they will move the prisoners out before that."

"Okay." Soran sat on one of the folding chairs. "Let's plan for next week." He cast her an accusing glance. "With you just as an observer. But if you catch me messing up too often, it will prove you are needed."

"She's always needed," Zara grumbled as she sat down.

Kyra gave her an appreciative smile before shifting her gaze to Soran. "If you mess up on purpose, I'll know. So don't try it."

"I won't."

Hours later, the meeting wound down, and a hush settled over the tent as Zara gathered her notes.

Soran rolled his shoulders, stiff from sitting for too long on the uncomfortable folding chairs. "So, how did I do?"

"As well as I expected you to do. You are ready to take over."

He didn't look happy with her answer. "At least we have a plan for the next few days. Zara will lead the supply run south, and Hamid will gather intel on the new squads." He looked at her for a long moment. "We're all invested in you, Kyra, and if you think this woman is crucial to our cause, we'll follow your lead. We don't want to lose you. Don't let your guilt from the past drive you to do something reckless."

It took her a second to speak. "I'm not feeling guilty, Soran. I'm haunted. That's different." She rose to her feet. "I'll see all of you tomorrow."

38

KIAN

Kian leaned back in his chair, exhaling slowly as his gaze swept over the group assembled before him. The floor-to-ceiling windows let in the late-afternoon light, but it would get dark soon, and the forecast promised rain. He hoped he would be done with the meeting before that and not get soaked on his way home.

"What's the weather like out there?" Yamanu asked.

Onegus pushed a folder toward him. "Cold at night and warm during the days. It's an inland area, so it doesn't get the tempering influence of a large body of water. It's all in the file."

Yamanu grimaced. "Mey ordered snow clothing for me online and paid for expedited delivery. Oh well, I guess I can use it on our next ski vacation."

Onegus frowned. "I didn't know you were planning a skiing vacation."

Yamanu flashed him a smile. "I didn't know either."

Kian cleared his throat. "Let's go over the plan from the top."

He glanced at Onegus, who set down his notepad. The chief rubbed a hand over his square jaw and nodded. "We gathered intel on the town of Tahav, located in northwestern Iran. It's a small town of about twelve thousand people, with a nearby military hub of the Revolutionary Guard. It's not a big place, but the intel suggests that they use it to interrogate political prisoners, those who oppose the regime, though it's not a permanent holding facility. We assume that's where Kyra is, but since we are going solely based on Syssi's vision, that might be completely off." He cast an apologetic look at Kian. "I'm not doubting her vision, but it could have been about something that happened in the past or has not happened yet."

Kian nodded. "I'm well aware of that, but given the intensity and the number of times Syssi has had visions about Kyra, I believe that they were meant to impart a sense of urgency and to guide us to her."

Onegus tapped the folder in front of him. "I agree, but I just thought it was important for everyone present to know this might end up in nothing."

"I'll take Syssi's visions to the bank," Yamanu said. "It's like having a window into the future."

Onegus continued his briefing. "We will fly you on Kalugal's jet to eastern Turkey, to an airport near the Iranian border. Turner has arranged for two transport helicopters to take you from there straight to Tahav. They will come equipped with Revolutionary Guard uniforms to change into."

Max leaned forward, resting his elbows on the table. "Are they the stealth type?" he asked. "I mean the choppers."

Onegus shook his head. "They are old model transport birds, the kind the Revolutionary Guard would have used to transport troops in the area. This should help with the element of surprise. They will be painted to look like the Guards' machines, so there's that."

Turner seemed to have contacts worldwide, which didn't surprise Kian. As a Special Ops guy who'd served for two decades, he'd gotten to work with all types of international players. Kian was always amazed anew by what Turner could arrange on short notice. The guy was invaluable, and yet again, Kian silently thanked the Fates for bringing him to the clan.

"They'll be noisy fuckers." Max cast Jade and Drova an apologetic glance. "Pardon my French." He turned to Yamanu. "Can you shroud these large choppers?"

Yamanu pursed his lips. "I can cover them visually. I'll project an illusion that melds with the sky, so from the ground, anyone watching will see empty space. But I can't cover the engine noise. If I attempt that, I'll have to split my energy in multiple ways, and that would weaken the overall effect."

Kian frowned at that small snag. "So, we can't do anything about the sound?"

Yamanu leaned back in his chair. "Sorry, boss. I can reduce the visible signature, but acoustic illusions are a separate form of mental manipulation, and doing both simultaneously at that scale would push it even for me. I can try partial muffling, but I'd rather not. If the illusions flicker in and out, we'll be spotted. I prefer to maintain focus on the visuals."

As Onegus continued, Kian observed the team. Jade looked as formidable as ever, and she would be an asset to the team. Drova was a surprising bonus. When Max had proposed using her on this mission, Kian didn't expect Jade to agree, but to everyone's surprise, she was on board with the idea as soon as he suggested it. He hadn't had to do any convincing. The rest of the Kra-ell seemed serious and eager, and Kian knew all too well how lethal they could all be. Ell-rom was gentle and lacked combat training, but his unique killing-with-a-thought ability could prove an essential element in their arsenal and might decide the battle. Jasmine was the only weak point, but she had to be there.

Onegus tapped a pen on his notepad. "The

Iranian air-defense network in that region is demolished or severely undermined. Some say it was an internal sabotage, others say it was a foreign strike, but either way, it makes infiltration by air possible in a way it wasn't a short time ago." He smiled at Kian. "The Fates indeed work in mysterious ways."

Kian chuckled. "Talk about massive prep work. All this just so we can rescue Kyra, but then a lot is at stake. If she is the key to finding my mother's one true love, no amount of effort to get her out of there should be spared."

Murmurs of agreement sounded around the table, surprisingly from the Kra-ell group as well.

Everyone was rooting for his mother to get her love back.

"The team will approach low and fast at dusk," Onegus said. "Yamanu will cover the helicopters from eyes on the ground, and the birds will be well away by the time anyone wonders where that noise is coming from. The choppers will drop you off over the ridge, a couple of clicks away and downwind. Chances are that little, if any, noise will make it to the compound." Onegus paused to sip some water.

"The pilots will wait for your return to the landing site and, if needed, will take off and land at the alternative pickup zone." Onegus pointed to a spot marked on the plan he was holding up for all to see. "While Yamanu will maintain full shrouding, the Kra-ell team led by Jade will take down all the active eyes, both on the ground and in the watchtowers."

The Kra-ell warriors sat up a little straighter when mentioned, and Drova looked excited but scared.

Looking directly at the young compeller, Onegus's tone became a little softer as he addressed the teenager. "You have proven yourself well in your last mission, but I don't want you engaging the enemy. You will stay by Jade's side at all times, and you will carry a miniature megaphone with you. From now until you land at the destination, you will practice key command words in Farsi so that you know all of them by heart and can pronounce them with the correct accent to ensure none is misunderstood. You will issue compulsion commands only if and when Jade, Yamanu, or Max instruct you to do so. Are we clear?"

To her credit, Drova didn't wilt under the chief's attention, and nodded.

Onegus raised his eyes and focused on the entire group. "Apart from that, this is a standard infiltration mission. You grab and you go."

Max let out a wry chuckle. "There is nothing standard about infiltrating a Revolutionary Guard stronghold halfway around the world. No big deal, though. Maybe next time we can pick an easy job, like eliminating the regime's nuclear power."

It was obvious that Max was trying to lighten the mood, but Kian didn't find the suggestion funny. Perhaps the clan should do something about those madmen creating nuclear bombs to eradicate all the infidels. They wouldn't even care if those bombs killed half their population, along with all the nonbelievers that they hated so rabidly.

Right now, though, he needed to focus on saving Kyra, not the entire world.

Kian managed a small smile in return. "They won't expect an elite commando-type raid. They are used to dealing with the Kurdish resistance forces, which are amateur soldiers. Brave and committed, no doubt, but amateur nonetheless." He turned to Jade. "Are your people okay with a helicopter flight?"

The Kra-ell had a problem with deep water, and they hated sea voyages. There were no reports of them having difficulty during the flights that had brought them to Southern California, but a helicopter wasn't a charter jetliner.

Jade leaned forward, her long raven ponytail sliding over one shoulder. "My warriors and I are more than ready. I took several simulator classes on flying a chopper, and I enjoyed it very much. I don't foresee my people having a problem with charging ahead as soon as the helicopters touch the ground." She smiled at him, full of fangs. "We will be thrilled to leap out even before touchdown, and if the choppers bring us next to the compound walls, we will take the enemy by surprise. The Doomers won't anticipate our presence or our strength."

Her team of two hybrid males and four full-blooded females all flashed their fangs in agreement.

"We can handle an entire squadron of Doomers if it comes to that," Jade said.

The female was Kra-ell to the bone—direct, fierce, and unafraid of armed conflict. Hell, she was eager for it.

"The base will probably not have a whole squadron of Doomers," Kian said. "We suspect some, but it will mostly contain well-trained human troops."

Jade nodded. "My people will gladly tear Doomers and human soldiers to pieces. We just need to know who not to hurt by mistake."

There was one problem with her boasting, and Kian needed to point it out. "How many of your people can handle a gun?"

"Aside from me?"

He nodded.

"All can shoot, but only Anton, Dima, and I have experience with automatic weapons. We are all lethal with throwing knives, though, long knives, hand-to-hand, and our fangs and claws." She assumed a vicious smile. "And we are fast. The Doomers won't see us coming."

Max let out a low whistle. "I almost feel sorry for the poor bastards. Almost."

A hint of humor flickered in Jade's dark eyes. "They have no idea." Then her expression sobered. "We need to know who not to kill. How do we tell friend from foe?"

"It's simple," Max said. "Everyone in uniform is an enemy, and also anyone shooting at us."

"One more point I should make clear," Kian said. "It is crucial that the Doomers don't find out about the Kra-ell. Anton and Dima can pass for humans, but the rest of you need to wear dark glasses. The tactical vests should conceal your thinness, and if you tuck your hair under your helmets, you will look like young male soldiers."

Jade leaned back. "That's all fine, but what about our fangs? We can't hide who we are."

"All who see you fight must die. The disguise is only meant to hide what you are from those you decide to leave alive. That means immediately confirming each kill, especially the Doomers, because they can regenerate from most injuries, and then doing so again before clearing the compound. Is that clear?"

Kian paused and took the time to look at each of the assembled company, securing a nod before continuing. "And one more thing. Before you leave, find out where the security footage of the facility is stored and make sure to destroy it in a manner that will make files and image retrieval impossible. We leave no evidence behind."

"How about we just burn the place down?" Max asked. "That will be faster and more effective."

"Not a bad idea," Onegus said. "That would eliminate the bodies of dead Doomers and save you the trouble of torching each one individually. Just make sure that no innocents are hiding inside before you do that." He turned to Yamanu. "Will you have enough juice to hide the explosions?"

"Sure thing, boss."

39

MAX

Jade appeared to be super excited about finally seeing some action. It sucked being a warrior and not getting to fight. She could join the Guardian force and accompany them on missions, but there wasn't much bloodshed during those, so it wasn't what she was thirsty for.

Max stifled a chuckle. Thirst took on a whole new meaning in reference to the Kra-ell. During the clan's liberation of Igor's compound, Jade had drained Igor's second-in-command by drinking his blood. She hadn't killed him, though. He'd convinced everyone that he was a good guy who'd been a helpless pawn and was now working as a gardener, doing community service in the village.

The liberation had been such a glorious operation, and Max would have loved to do the same for the entire oppressed population of the region they were about to infiltrate, and restore freedom, democracy, and fundamental human rights, but they had neither the manpower nor the strategy to attempt a revolution.

"So, to summarize," Jade said. "We secure Kyra, aim to capture the leader of the Doomers at the compound, leave no one alive that saw us in action, destroy all recorded evidence of the mission, and withdraw immediately."

Max snorted. "Are you sure we can't take down the ayatollahs while we are at it? If we are already there, why not free the oppressed Iranian population and the Kurds? You know, tick off a few items on the to-do list. Maybe rescue a city or two while there as well." He was only half joking.

How hard could it be to remove a few rotten old men?

Onegus cracked a smile. "As much as we would like to, we can't solve all the world's problems, Max. It's not as simple as picking off the top leaders." He sat forward, resting his forearms on the table. "You kill one tyrant or a dozen, and others step in to fill the void. The root of the evil isn't just a single personality. It's a system and culture of corruption, fear, and brutality. Changing that requires more than a band of immortals playing vigilante."

"So true and so frustrating," Kian said. "We have the power to do many things, but the deeper we wade into Earth's geopolitical messes, the more convinced I become that lasting change requires more than brute force or a single decapitating strike. Look at Navuh. We want him gone, but killing him doesn't guarantee the Brotherhood's fall, even if we could get to him. One of his adopted sons might step up, or an ambitious commander. With enough charisma, it's possible to lead the Brotherhood without the benefit of compulsion. As impossible as it might seem, the next leader might be worse than Navuh."

Onegus regarded Kian with a contemplative look on his face. "Navuh is at the root of some of the most sophisticated child-trafficking rings and destabilizing operations that stem from them. If we take him out, we will hamper a huge chunk of the organized network and the Doomers who run those abominations."

Kian waved a dismissive hand. "Those will continue without Navuh. But that's a conversation for another day. Right now, we are here to talk about extracting Kyra."

Onegus nodded. "Let's return to the infiltration details. The plan is to fly from our airfield to the airport in eastern Turkey. The local contact arranges for us to be picked up and flown to Tahav." He turned to Yamanu. "Once the choppers are in the air, you start the illusions. It's a long flight, so preserve your energy."

Yamanu nodded. "I will need to shroud the choppers both ways and also cover the operation.

This is going to stretch my ability." He turned to Max. "Can you shroud?"

Max winced. "Only myself and perhaps one other person."

"You're no help." Yamanu looked at Jade. "You?"

She shook her head. "We have our version of shrouding and thralling, but it doesn't work like yours. It's not going to help you."

Onegus waited to see if Yamanu wanted to add anything else, but when he shrugged, indicating that he was done, the chief continued, "If the intelligence we have is correct, the compound is not heavily guarded—some soldiers, but not a full complement. They might call for reinforcements, though, which is why speed is essential." He looked at Max. "Get into as many heads as you can until you find one that can tell you where Kyra is. That's much faster than using brute force to get people to talk."

Max nodded. "I know. Yamanu will be busy, Ell-rom and Jasmine can't thrall, and Jade's people can't either."

"I can compel, and of course, so can Drova," Jade said. "My ability is weak, but hers is formidable. Drova can compel answers from the humans and the Doomers." That was a relief. Max wasn't a strong thraller and didn't want to be solely responsible for extracting the information.

"It is not how I saw Drova's role, but that is a great idea that may save us precious time," Onegus said. "Max and the both of you go to work on finding Kyra right away while the rest of the team fights the guards. You will split into two squads. One will protect Yamanu so he can keep his shroud up, and the other Ell-rom and Jasmine, as neither has combat training."

Jade inclined her head.

Max wondered if Ell-rom needed protection. They still didn't know if the guy could kill more than one person with a thought because there had been no time to continue his testing. Perhaps this mission would provide the perfect opportunity to do just that.

If Ell-rom could take out an entire squadron of soldiers with just a thought, the Kra-ell would have little left to do.

They would be so disappointed that Max almost hoped Ell-rom's ability wasn't that good.

Almost.

Perhaps after the mission was done, he would show Ell-rom pictures of the ayatollahs and tell him how many people they'd killed and maimed, hanging human rights activists in barbaric public spectacles. It might be enough to activate his death ray.

40

KIAN

"The choppers will land about two miles from the southwestern corner of the base. There is a hill there that will provide cover." Onegus flicked on the screen behind Kian and pointed at a grainy picture of the compound. "This looks like an adequate flat area. It's expansive enough for both choppers to safely land and take off simultaneously, even with the expected winds. We don't anticipate any challenges at the landing zone, but if you have to hold off an attempt to take down the choppers, plan B is to fly to the compound, drop off the team, and continue here." He motioned to a spot that was a few miles away. "The extraction window is tight. You'll have about an hour before reinforcements can arrive from the nearest outpost. Possibly less if the Iranian chain of command is functioning."

"Understood," Jade said. "Do we cut their electricity? Destroy their communication ability?"

Onegus shook his head. "We don't have info on the layout, and you'll have no time to deal with that. It's a shock and awe type of operation."

Yamanu and Max nodded.

Onegus tapped the map. "After you find Kyra, immediately button up the scene and retreat to the choppers. If, for some reason, you can't make it back to the helicopters, commandeer whatever vehicles you can and head out into the mountains toward the alternate pickup zone. And if that is not feasible, find a spot you can defend." He pointed at several possible locations. "We will extract you from here, but let's hope that's not going to happen."

Max let out a short laugh. "The moment they see Jade's warriors bounding around with their fangs exposed, they will run for the hills, but you can't allow anyone who saw you in action to escape, and once you are done, you need to destroy all evidence of your attack."

Kian raised his finger to focus everyone's attention on him. "I want to remind everyone that if the opportunity presents itself to grab a Doomer for later interrogation, try to get a senior one. The foot soldiers are rarely well informed."

"Let's talk timeline," Onegus said. "Departure is five o'clock tomorrow morning. Okidu will take you to the airstrip. Flight time is about eighteen hours, including a refueling stop."

Jade pursed her lips. "It gives me a little more time to train my people so they can at least identify safety switches, reload mags in a pinch, and fire short bursts."

"Do I get to carry a gun?" Jasmine asked.

The chief arched a brow. "Do you know how to use one?"

She shook her head. "I do, but only a handgun. My father took me to this hunting cabin when I was little, but he didn't let me touch his rifle. Also, I don't know if I will be any good under fire. Shooting at a range is very different than actually aiming at people."

Onegus glanced at Ell-rom. "Max and your mate will protect you."

Ell-rom winced. "Supposedly, I know how to use a sword and a dagger, but since I don't remember that, I'm not going to risk it, and I certainly don't know what to do with a gun."

Kian cast him an amused smile. "I suggest that you get a crash course and Jasmine a refresher. You have a few hours, and it's not as difficult as it sounds. But if you prefer not to carry, you don't have to. You are a weapon yourself."

Ell-rom nodded. "I keep forgetting that."

The poor guy wanted nothing more than to forget what he could do, but his ability might be needed to protect the lives of his team members.

"Let's continue," Onegus said.

As they ran through the final details, an uneasy sense of finality settled over Kian, and he laid his hand flat on the table, glancing around at his people. "This mission is personal. Syssi's visions have pointed us toward Kyra, and we hope to find her in that compound. Let's offer a prayer to the Fates and the Mother of All Life for a successful retrieval of Jasmine's mother and everyone returning unharmed."

After a short moment of silence, Onegus rose to his feet. "I think we've covered everything. Let's head out."

After everyone left, Kian turned to look outside, but night had fallen and the automatic shutters had come down, so he didn't know whether it was raining.

He walked over to his desk, pulled out the bottle of whiskey in the bottom drawer, and poured himself a shot.

His mother had set a broad mission for her children to advance humanity and protect it from the twisted manipulations of Navuh and the other followers of Mortdh, but they were nowhere near achieving their goals. Perhaps rescuing Kyra would have ripple effects that none of them could imagine that would somehow bring the clan closer to eradicating evil from the world.

It was an absurd thought that one woman could be the key to salvation, but with so many of

Syssi's visions centering on this one person, that person had to be of vital importance.

But how?

Maybe Kyra would help them find Khiann, and he was the key to eradicating evil?

From his mother's stories, he seemed like a good guy, but he hadn't been a formidable god like Ahn or a genius like Ekin, so that wasn't likely.

It was still up to Kian and his clan to eradicate evil, and it felt like a Sisyphean effort.

All the lives the clan had saved from trafficking networks and twisted Doomer-run operations were small victories that chipped away at evil. But each time they cut off one head of the Hydra, another slithered forward.

Toven's words drifted into his head. *We need to cut off the entire serpent, not just a piece.*

But how to do that? Navuh's structure of darkness was anchored in centuries of cunning, infiltration, and cruelty, and every time Kian thought their archenemy was defeated or even just slowed down, he discovered that Navuh had managed to outsmart him once more.

Evil thrived in too many corners of the world, and the clan stepping in to rescue one woman was a drop in the ocean.

Yet that one life might matter immeasurably.

41

KYRA

As the rustle of her tent flap pulled Kyra out of her shallow sleep, she bolted up in bed with the dagger she always kept under her pillow.

"Don't kill me!" Zara threw her hands up in the air.

"Zara? What's going on?"

"Sorry about giving you a scare." The woman crouched beside her cot. "The supply run was successful. No ambush. But we've heard through the grapevine that new prisoners are about to be delivered to the compound. I thought you would want to know right away."

Kyra was immediately wide awake. She'd been expecting the current prisoners to be shipped out but not new ones to be delivered, not before the higher-ups' visit that had the entire staff in a flurry of cleaning activity.

Unless the higher-ups were arriving with the new prisoners, then it would all make sense.

Most of the cells were occupied, though, so if they were bringing in new people, they had no choice but to take the old ones out, and hopefully not with a shot to the head, but to transfer them somewhere else. The cells in the compound were meant for interrogation and not for long-term incarceration.

"When?" Kyra asked.

"Tomorrow. That's why I'm here instead of hitting the shower. They will most likely arrive in the evening because that's how long the drive from Abjid takes. We didn't get any information about who the prisoners were or who was bringing them in, but there is only one road they can take through the mountains, and we can stage an ambush there."

The question was whether to ambush the convoy on the way to the compound or on the way out, and Kyra preferred the second option. It might have been unfair, and the new prisoners might have been more important than the ones currently being held, but Kyra needed to save Twelve.

"Thank you." She got out of bed. "I'm betting they will have to empty the current holding cells to make room so that the same transport will be heading back with them, probably the following day. We will hit them on their way back. I am just hoping that Twelve will be among them."

It was a gamble, but it was also all she had.

"Wake up the others and tell them to come to my tent. We need to plan the ambush."

A mocking smile lifted Zara's lips. "Aren't you going to leave it up to Soran? I thought you wanted him to take the lead."

"I do, but this is still over his head." Kyra was already pulling on a pair of loose fatigues. "Tell the others to be here and then go to sleep."

"I want to be here." Zara crossed her arms over her chest.

Kyra arched a brow. "You can't keep going after a night mission. You'll have to sit this one out."

Zara shook her head. "I'm so pumped with adrenaline that there is no way I will be able to sleep. This is the biggest mission since we freed the other prisoners."

Kyra winced. "I'm surprised they didn't pursue us after that rescue and are still bringing people here. It almost feels like a trap."

Zara shrugged. "Those people weren't all that important, and we shipped them out the same day. Your decision to make our base here, right under their noses, was brilliant. All they can see are a bunch of refugees living in tents and half-ruined houses."

All their vehicles looked beaten up and old, with dents everywhere and missing glass in the windows. When used during the day, they rattled and groaned as if their engines were about to die. It was all for show, and once the noise makers were removed, they moved like the well-maintained machines they were.

"So, can I join?" Zara asked again.

"Fine." Kyra waved her off. "Go, now. I need to get ready. Oh, and tell Parisa to come here and get her things. I'm not going in her place today."

The woman was enjoying collecting pay for work she didn't do, so she wouldn't be too happy about returning to mopping floors.

A grin spread over Zara's face. "Hallelujah. Finally, this is over."

"Let's hope so." Kyra pushed her feet into her boots and collected her toiletries.

She hoped that this would be the end of her compound infiltration duties, and after this mission they would probably need to move their base somewhere else.

But it was worth it to free not just Twelve but also the other prisoners who'd suffered their share of incarceration in that vile interrogation center.

Regrettably, they couldn't save the incoming prisoners as well.

42

KYRA

The plan was straightforward. Hamid's group would block the narrow pass from above, forcing the convoy to slow or reroute, and then Kyra's team would strike from behind the ridge line. Ideally, they would isolate the prisoners' truck, free them, and vanish before the enemy knew what hit them.

Even if they called for reinforcements, none would arrive in time.

The rebels and the freed prisoners would be long gone.

Although communication with the scouts watching the compound was minimal and coded, the watchers still managed to relay pertinent information to the ambush team. The new prisoners had been unloaded from the van and brought into the compound, and those vacating the premises had been herded out. The watchers hadn't reported how many had been loaded into the vans, though, or whether any of them were females.

Kyra closed her hand over her pendant, which remained suspiciously cool against her skin. This was a good sign because heat often served as a warning, but it could also indicate a failed mission.

She was all too aware that the enhanced soldiers might be accompanying the convoy, but it didn't matter. She was going to face them, and she was going to achieve her objective despite them because she had no other choice.

Crouching behind a rocky outcrop, Kyra watched the pass below while dust clouds billowed from a winding road as the convoy approached. Beside her, Soran scanned the vehicles through a pair of binoculars.

She didn't need them to see the convoy clearly.

"It's them," he said. "I can see the van where they most likely keep the prisoners. There are bars on the windows."

Kyra's chest tightened. "Wait for Zara's signal." The plan was for Zara's group to spring the trap at the narrowest point of the pass, where the road was flanked by sheer rock walls, making it impossible for the convoy to outrun them. Then Kyra's group would swoop in from behind the ridge.

She glanced back at her fighters. Some of them

she'd recruited years ago; others were new, and this was their first dangerous mission. But everyone had to start somewhere, and there was no time for coddling.

The crackle of gunfire that echoed through the pass signaled that Zara's group had begun the ambush, peppering the lead jeep with bullets and forcing it to skid sideways. Meanwhile, Hamid's decoy team fired from the south, drawing away half the guards' attention.

This was Kyra's cue.

She sprang up from cover, leading her fighters down the slope at an angle so they'd be behind the second truck. The dryness in her throat vanished, and she entered the zone of intense focus. Gunfire rang out in staccato bursts, the sound reverberating off the stone. Fighters on both sides shouted, and muzzles flashed from the van's escort.

A bullet zipped past her ear, stirring dust, and she dropped into a crouch behind a boulder to return fire. Roshrud crouched on her right, steadying his aim.

The soldiers were quick to react, and she wondered how many of them were enhanced. Then she glimpsed one bounding from the lead jeep, moving with speed and agility that betrayed his identity.

Could a bullet kill them? Would it even slow them down?

She'd been shot in the past, and it had hurt, but it hadn't kept her down. Then again, nothing vital had been hit. If she aimed at the heart, perhaps it would be fatal or at least slow him.

Soran's voice barked out orders from behind a battered outcrop: "Kyra, push left! They're focusing on the decoy. We can get to the van now!"

She half-ran, half-crawled across the uneven ground, bullets ricocheting off the rocks. The enhanced soldier met her halfway, but instead of shooting her, he swung a baton at her head.

What the hell?

Did he want to capture her alive? Was that his plan?

Instinct guiding her, she ducked and spun instead of firing at him, blocking a blow that would have shattered the bones of an ordinary woman. A bullet wouldn't have slowed him down unless it was between the eyes, and her aim wasn't that good while fighting. The impact jarred her from shoulder to elbow, but she gritted her teeth, ignoring the pain. Catching him by surprise, she swiped his legs, twisting with more force than he'd expected from a woman. He went down but scrambled up terrifyingly quickly.

They exchanged rapid strikes.

His baton whistled past her skull, and she dodged and hammered a fist into his ribs, ignoring the logic that told her punching an enhanced soldier might not slow him down, but she still couldn't shoot him while fighting him hand to hand.

Kyra felt a satisfying crack of bone under her knuckles.

He grunted and staggered.

With him momentarily stunned, he provided her with the perfect target for a killing shot. She pulled out her gun and shot him point blank between the eyes.

No one should be able to survive that, not even an enhanced soldier, and for a moment, she felt a pang of sorrow for ending the life of someone like her, but then she reminded herself that he was nothing like her. He was a monster working for monsters who maimed and killed without remorse.

She whirled toward the van, scanning for danger, but her people had already taken care of the regular soldiers who had guarded its flank.

She sprinted, weaving between large rock fragments, until she reached the van's rear door. Bars covered the frosted window, and she glimpsed shapes inside, but there was no way for her to know whether there were more guards with rifles waiting for her inside.

Soran appeared at her shoulder and pressed a heavy wrench into her hand. "Padlock," he shouted over the din. "Do it. I'll cover you."

Kyra jammed the wrench against the lock,

using her supernatural strength to snap it. She heard metal groan and give, and the door swung open.

The interior was dim, but no one was shooting at her, which meant no guards were inside.

She scanned the detainees, looking for Twelve, but none of the faces matched the one she desperately needed to see. Some were lying on the van's floor, though, so maybe Twelve was among them. A slumped figure near the front of the truck had a sack over the head, and hope surged in Kyra's chest. She leaped into the van and yanked the sack off, but it was a man underneath, with bruises along his jaw and a livid gash across his temple.

Frantic, she forced herself to slow down and scrutinize each face. She'd seen these people through the windows of their cells. She recognized them.

They were all there except for Twelve.

Kyra felt faint.

She'd failed.

But this was not the time to fall apart. These people still needed her, and the young woman from room eight was cowering in the back like she was expecting another blow.

"Don't be afraid," Kyra said. "I'm here to free you. No one is going to harm you."

Her expression must have reinforced her words because the young woman, a girl really, let out a ragged sigh.

Behind Kyra, Soran covered the van's entrance with his rifle, scanning. "We have to hurry. The fighting is still intense."

"We need to carry some of them out. They are not in any shape to climb."

Nodding, Soran hoisted the older man, who could barely walk. Another rebel came to help and grabbed another prisoner. Kyra reached for the battered girl, cutting her bonds with a swift slash of her knife. The woman collapsed into her arms, letting out a sharp cry of pain.

"I'm sorry. You need to hold on for just a little longer."

The girl's lips parted, but no words emerged. A tear slipped down her bruised cheek.

"Come on!" Soran grunted. "Let's move."

Kyra hefted the girl, amazed by how light she felt. She let out a strangled whimper as some wound on her ribs jarred, but she clung to Kyra's shoulders.

With the others covering them, they leaped from the van and ducked behind an overturned crate. Gunfire erupted anew, possibly from the front position. A bullet ricocheted off the crate's side. Kyra shielded the girl with her own body. "Don't worry. I won't let them capture you."

Zara's voice crackled through the shortwave, "Retreat to the ridge behind the big boulder at coordinate three. Go now."

Soran fired a few covering shots while Kyra

carried the wounded woman across the rocky ground in a half crouch, with the two other rebels carrying wounded prisoners behind her, along with those who were able to walk on their own.

With each step, the girl's breath rasped, and Kyra glimpsed the tortured lines of her face. She was more badly hurt than Kyra had assumed. The daily torment must have accumulated. Scalding rage soared in her chest.

Somehow, they made it to Hamid, who offered them cover. Their people poured in one by one, slipping into camouflaged vehicles and lurching away from the intensifying firefight. The soldiers followed, but the rebels had planted explosives along the way.

Cars roared to life and sped off in zigzagging directions, kicking up dust. The entire scene was a storm of chaos—smoke drifting from a flaming jeep, the wails of wounded men echoing.

Inside the pickup, Kyra cradled the girl in her lap.

Despite the crushing disappointment over failing to save Twelve, she felt a wave of triumph.

The truck jolted over a rocky outcropping. Soran, from the passenger seat, glanced over his shoulder. "We need to get to the fallback position. The rest of them are scattering. Let's pray we're not followed."

Kyra exhaled and looked down at the unconscious woman, noticing how her clenched hands relaxed in slumber.

She could only imagine how much tighter the security in the compound would be after this operation. Her only option seemed to be to once again don the maid's outfit and somehow manage to trade places with Twelve.

43

MAX

Max sank into the plush leather seat and gazed around the cabin of Kalugal's jet.

Had the guy redecorated the interior?

He'd flown on this jet before but didn't remember it being so lavish—soft, cream-colored carpeting, overhead lighting, and polished walnut accents that gleamed under the ambient glow. The seats were arranged in pairs, each capable of reclining flat to allow for proper sleep, and Max was willing to bet that the overhead compartments contained down-filled pillows and blankets.

Kalugal wasn't the kind of guy who skimped on anything. Not bad for a former Doomer. Never mind that he'd made his money off the stock market using information he'd thralled from people's heads. There were worse ways to earn a living, and Kalugal's illegal activity was not such a big deal.

Hell, if the members of Congress used insider information to make shitloads of money on the stock market without consequence, then in his book, a three-quarter god with a bunch of rescued former warriors to feed was allowed to do so too.

Some seats faced each other across small tables with built-in screens, while others stood apart for those who preferred privacy.

Stretching out his legs, Max closed his eyes. They were heading to Turkey first, then on to their destination—an enemy compound in Iran where they planned a swift extraction of a prisoner, possibly of several, not to mention a Doomer or two. Except for the location, nothing about this mission seemed overly complicated, especially since they had assets like Yamanu and Drova with them. Between the shrouder and the compeller, what could go wrong?

He then remembered Ell-rom's unique talent. That weapon took their team's lethality to a whole new level.

Catching a murmur of conversation from the back, where Jade's team was sitting, he turned to look at them and was tickled by how excited they all seemed. Usually, the Kra-ell liked to project a stern or stoic front, but they weren't even trying to hide their awe. None of them had ever been on such a luxurious plane.

Jade stood in the center aisle, leaning over Drova and pointing out something on the touchscreen panel. The girl made a slight exclamation of wonder as she pressed the screen, and her seat started to recline. Jade flashed her a rare grin, then resumed her usual impassive expression.

Across the aisle, Ell-rom leaned over to talk to Jasmine. The two of them appeared calm, and Jasmine smiled at Ell-rom's comment, but Max didn't miss how Ell-rom's foot kept tapping the carpet in a restless pattern.

Everyone was keyed up.

Max rose and made his way down the aisle toward Jade. She wore a short bomber jacket that barely concealed her holster, and he was willing to bet she had several daggers strapped to her body. Her loose cargo pants could hide a whole arsenal of weapons, as did his.

Normally, passing through airport security with that arsenal would have been a problem, but Turner's guy had told them he would take care of everything and not to worry about the weapons.

Turner trusted the guy, and that was good enough for Max.

"Hey." He tapped Jade's shoulder.

She turned around. "What can I do for you, Max?"

"Mind if I ask how many of your team are packing firearms and how many are going old-school?" He jerked his chin toward the huddle of Kra-ell in the back.

Jade's eyes flicked toward her warriors, who had gone silent at Max's approach. "Anton and Dima are trained well enough to handle short-range rifles, but I made sure that the others refreshed their knowledge and know how to handle an assault rifle. Aim is a different issue, but I'm confident they won't shoot themselves in the foot. We prefer blades and have throwing knives strapped to our bodies where we can easily access them."

"Good." Max nodded. "I'd hate to rely on them for covering fire, only to find they can't shoot straight."

"They know their strengths," Jade said. "We'll rely mostly on speed and stealth. The rest is your job." She turned to her daughter. "And yours."

Drova had headphones on and was watching a movie, but she smiled and nodded, indicating she'd heard Jade.

Max wasn't comfortable with so much riding on the teenage compeller with a sketchy past, but he couldn't deny that she was indispensable.

"Compared to Drova, my job is simple. Catch the first human guard I encounter, who we haven't killed yet, and thrall him to see where the prisoners are kept. We need to get inside fast."

Jade's lips tightened over her elongating fangs. "My fighters have a taste for action, but I've told them we don't have time to play with our prey. They need to be quick and efficient."

Max glanced at the row of seats behind Jade, where the two Kra-ell hybrids were testing the seat recline buttons. Their eyes lit up in fascination, and their lips curled in goofy smiles as the seats glided back and forth. One of them noticed Max's gaze and immediately retracted the seat, looking embarrassed.

Dima and Anton, Max believed, were their names. He'd tried to memorize all the Kra-ell names, but he had a harder time remembering the females' names, or rather which name belonged to whom. Asuka, Rutza, Rishba, and Mehira, he believed, but had no idea who was who.

"They're excited, like kids with a new toy," Jade said. "But they are still lethal."

"I have no doubt." Max patted her arm, which earned him a raised brow. "Sorry. Old habit."

"Don't do that again."

"Yes, ma'am."

As she turned back to her team, Max continued toward Yamanu, leaning against the seat's headrest across the aisle from him.

"What's up, Max?" Yamanu asked without opening his eyes.

"I'm not used to this level of luxury. Did Kalugal have the interior redone?"

Yamanu shrugged. "Apparently, but I did not get the memo either."

"I sometimes forget how rich the guy is," Max said, then sighed. "I've made some questionable investments lately and lost a bunch of money."

"That's regrettable." Yamanu opened his eyes. "What did you invest in?"

"Stocks."

"You should follow Kian's recommendations. Shai posts them on the clan's bulletin board every weekend."

"I didn't know that." Max felt dumb. "I'll look into it."

"The plan seems easy enough," Yamanu said. "But I keep thinking about worst-case scenarios, like a squadron of Doomers. How many immortals can Drova compel at once?"

"We don't know," Max said. "But we are not relying just on her. We have Jade's squad, and we have Ell-rom."

Yamanu snorted. "We don't know the full scope of his talent yet or if he can function under fire."

Max glanced a couple of rows up. Jasmine and Ell-rom sat side by side, their heads close together, conversing quietly.

"I guess we are going to find out." Max pushed off the headrest and headed back to his seat.

After take-off, he adjusted the recline so he wasn't fully upright, but he wasn't ready to fall asleep yet.

Ell-rom seemed to have the same problem because he got up and walked over, resting a hand on the plush seat across from Max. "Do you mind if I sit with you? Jasmine fell asleep."

"Not at all." Max gestured to the seat next to him.

"It feels like the calm before the storm."

The man had zero combat experience and was obviously nervous, possibly because he was worried about Jasmine's safety.

"It's all going to be okay. We have it covered. It's a grab-and-go. We thrall or neutralize the guards. Drova compels any immortals we encounter, find Kyra, and get her out. We will vanish long before reinforcements arrive."

Ell-rom gave a slow exhale. "I know. Now I need to believe it."

"We've got a long flight ahead, Ell-rom. Try to get some rest."

44

KYRA

Kyra paused at the edge of the camp and adjusted her headscarf. Tents' canvases rustled behind her as Soran and Zara caught up, probably planning another attempt to dissuade her from going.

"This is insane, Kyra," Soran said, his voice low enough that no one else might overhear. "Wait a week until the dust settles. In the meantime, Parisa will collect intel for us like she has done for months."

Zara caught her elbow. "They'll be checking everyone now. They will order you to take your face covering off and realize that you are not Parisa. You'll get caught, and they will put you in a cell and abuse you the same way they are doing to that woman you are so obsessed with. And who is going to help her then?"

Kyra pulled her elbow out of Zara's grip. "They had me remove the face covering the first day I went, but the guard didn't notice anything. I'll be fine."

Her grip tightened on the small cloth bag at her hip. Inside it, she'd stashed Parisa's doctored ID, which had served her well until now and hopefully would serve her again.

She was tempting fate, but the pull inside her was too strong to ignore. She couldn't leave behind the woman in cell number twelve.

"Please," Zara pleaded. "Don't go."

They'd argued for hours the previous evening, but in the end, no one could sway her. No one else understood how crucial it was for her to check that Twelve was still there and see if there was a chance to free her.

"I have to do this. We need information, and Parisa is not good enough to collect it. Not the kind of information I need. You have your assignments. Go."

Soran shook his head but exhaled in resignation. "Just...be careful. At the first sign of trouble—"

"I know." She forced a tight smile. "I'll get what we need and slip out."

"Good luck," Zara murmured. Then she stepped aside, arms folded, a scowl etched on her face. "Come back safe, or I swear, I'll come after you and drag you out of that place myself."

"Don't you dare." She patted Zara's shoulder, turned, and walked briskly away.

It was still freezing this early in the morning, and Kyra nearly jogged to keep warm. Each step carried her farther from the half-ruined buildings of their makeshift camp into the rolling terrain that hid the road to the compound. She pulled her black scarf tighter around her face to shield it from the biting cold.

Every nerve in her body prickled with warning as she neared the compound, but that was nothing new. No matter how many times she'd done it before and the confidence she fronted for her people, everything inside her rebelled against walking into the facility and the ugliness it concealed.

Her senses were on high alert—ears straining for the hum of guard vehicles, eyes flicking to the horizon for any sign of unusual patrols. But it was quiet this early.

Perhaps too quiet.

By the time she arrived at the side gate, Kyra was already breathing shallowly, not from physical exertion but from the tension coiled in her gut. The guard on duty—a lanky, half-asleep soldier with a stained uniform—barely gave her a once-over. She dipped her head, offering the practiced meek nod that was part of her disguise. He waved her through with a bored grunt, and she exhaled in relief.

The cantankerous female tasked with patting down women staff for weapons did a more thorough job, but since Kyra had nothing on her, she passed the inspection without incident.

Inside, the atmosphere was different than usual. An undercurrent of agitation was palpable across the courtyard. People moved faster, hushed voices broke out near the main entrance, and she spotted a few uniformed guards hauling in supplies from the corner of her eye.

Kyra trudged across the cracked concrete yard with her head low and eyes downcast. The building's doors stood open, and she slipped inside, inhaling the familiar cooking smells from the kitchen.

Such homey smells in such a terrible place.

But then it wasn't terrible for everyone in here, just for the prisoners getting beaten and drugged on the third floor of the East Wing.

She made her way to the maintenance closet on the first floor to fetch a mop and a bucket. A small cluster of maids hovered by the sink, gossiping. They didn't seem more subdued than usual, yet their laughter was a little quieter, less boisterous.

Hopefully, no one would address her thinking she was Parisa. She would have to feign a cold and speak with a rasp so they wouldn't notice the different voice.

Filling the bucket, she never once lifted her gaze. If anyone recognized her as Parisa, they gave no indication. She got one annoyed glance for hogging the spigot, but that was it.

After cleaning the first and second floors and forcing herself not to rush through them, she finally ascended the stairwell leading to the East Wing's third floor, clutching the mop's wooden handle in her left hand, the bucket in the other, and several rags stashed in the belt tied around her waist.

At the landing, she paused, heart thudding for no apparent reason. The pendant felt warm against her skin, but no more or less than usual.

Kyra took a steadying breath and pressed forward.

The third-floor corridor seemed busy. Near the end, guards were posted, rifles slung across their chests, right next to the cell she needed to check on.

Damn.

Starting on the floor near the staircase, she listened to them talking, but except for a few Farsi and Kurdish words she recognized, the rest was unintelligible.

What language was that?

It was rough and clipped, but it didn't sound like Arabic or any of the region's other languages. Her memory itched at that odd accent, which was unpleasant and jarring, but she couldn't place it.

Thankfully, the guards moved to a different

spot, paying her little attention except for a curt bark to watch her step as she passed them. She didn't need to pretend when she flinched, but the servile nod took some effort.

She carefully guided her bucket and mop into the corridor section containing the row of cells she was interested in.

She hadn't gone more than a few paces when distant clanking and subdued shouts drifted in from a side corridor. The volume of the voices rose, and Kyra froze in place, sensing movement behind the thick walls.

Curving her shoulders in, she resumed a slow push forward while flicking her gaze toward the intersection ahead. That was when she saw them. Four young women with nothing but towels wrapped around their bodies walking in a tight group flanked by uniformed guards.

They must have been coming back from the showers.

They all looked terrified; one girl had fresh bruises on her forearm.

So, these were the new prisoners that had been brought in yesterday. They were too young and scared to be activists or rebels. They were probably brought here as playthings for the guards or as subjects for the same experiments she'd undergone.

Kyra swallowed hard.

One of the overhead fluorescent lights flickered again, momentarily casting a strobe-like effect on the scene. As the women were herded around the corner, she heard a cell door open, then another.

Kyra clenched her jaw.

She had to find out how they intended to use these new prisoners. Her heart was pounding so loud that she was afraid the guards would hear it, and if they were enhanced like her, they might.

She felt guilty for not doing something for the young women, but there was nothing she could do. She needed to be patient, gather every piece of information, and devise a sensible plan.

After what seemed like the longest time, the coast was finally clear, and she rushed to the door of cell number twelve with dread curling in the back of her throat. Was the woman still inside?

Kyra inched closer, the squeak of the mop head on the worn linoleum covering the slight noise of her footsteps. Then, another cluster of voices echoed nearby, words in Farsi, Kurdish, and that third, more guttural tongue mingling.

The hair on her arms stood on end. What if those were the ominous higher-ups?

Kyra swallowed, the sense of foreboding clenching her gut tighter. She had to see if Twelve remained locked in that cell or if they'd moved her somewhere else or gotten rid of her altogether.

Fear propelled her onward even though every muscle screamed for her to run the other way. She paused one last time, hugging the mop handle, and then pressed forward toward cell number twelve, but something stopped her from peeking in. A sense of foreboding and a slight warming of her pendant preceded the sounds of more footsteps approaching.

45

KYRA

Kyra kept mopping, moving away from cell number twelve, her knuckles white from gripping the handle. The wooden pole would snap from the pressure if she weren't careful.

She forced her fingers to loosen.

Someone important had just arrived. Even the demeanor of the guards shifted. Backs snapped straighter, hands quit fidgeting. All around, tension crackled through the air.

She focused on the soapy puddle by her feet, working the mop back and forth with feigned diligence and feebleness. Through the corner of her eye, she caught glimpses of a small entourage moving along the corridor.

One was the commander, but his stance was deferential in a way Kyra hadn't seen from him before.

A second figure stood out immediately. He wasn't dressed in standard fatigues like everyone else. Instead, he wore some kind of tailored dark coat, its collar high and stiff, with small silver pins glinting along one lapel. Two guards flanked him, each armed and wearing similarly dark attire without insignias. That alone was strange, but it wasn't what made Kyra's breath grow ragged with alarm. It was the man himself. Something about him made her skin prickle, and it wasn't his good looks or air of authority.

The commander sidled up to him and all but bowed his head. "*Amadan farman, aghayeh doktor,*" he said in a rushed tone. Kyra only caught fragments of what he said next, and she didn't fully understand what he was saying, but the context told her the commander was paying deep respect to the man he called Doctor.

The other responded in the same language she'd heard the guards speak before. He used several Farsi words that she could identify, like prisoners and schedule, but most of it was said in that unfamiliar dialect. It was harsher and guttural in places, pulling at the corners of her memory and stirring a sense of dread that made her palms sweat.

She hunched her shoulders, staying crouched over her mop. Her headscarf concealed her face, but they would see the fear in her eyes if they looked at her.

Just keep scrubbing. Don't look up. Don't twitch.

Still, curiosity warred with caution. Glancing up for a split second, she took in the doctor's face in profile. Sharp cheekbones, a slightly hooked nose, and lips curved in what appeared to be a permanent sneer.

He shifted a fraction, and she caught his eyes, dark-colored and intense. Something about those eyes lit a flare of recognition deep in her mind, but it balked at the memory as though a locked door slammed shut whenever she tried to glimpse behind it.

The commander answered with careful enunciation as if searching for the right words. "Yes… injections… tomorrow's procedure…" were a few terms Kyra recognized in Farsi. Then he slipped back into the other dialect, his tone hushed, as if fearful someone might overhear.

The man in the dark coat—the commander dressed as Doctor—clasped his hands behind his back as he surveyed the corridor. His gaze flicked from door to door, from guard to guard, as though assessing a laboratory setup. Kyra's lungs constricted at the clinical detachment that radiated from him.

She must have seen faces like his in the asylum, looming over her while she lay strapped to a bed like Twelve.

Kyra forced the thought away before it could paralyze her with fear.

She kept mopping, but she did it as unobtrusively as possible, making as little noise as possible. Yet despite her efforts, each pass of the wet rag squeaked across the floor. She willed her breath to steady and made her posture even more subservient.

"No mistakes this time," the doctor said in accented Farsi, and then lapsed into that unknown language again, issuing short commands that the commander responded to with hasty nods.

Stealing another sideways glance, she noticed that the doctor's entourage carried small black cases that could hold syringes, vials, or any number of instruments.

Her stomach lurched at the sight. He must be planning to begin his twisted transformation or experimentation on the new female prisoners that had arrived yesterday.

Why females, though?

If they wanted to create super soldiers, wouldn't it have been better to experiment on men?

Maybe it didn't work on males. Or perhaps they wanted women to use as spies. She knew better than most that women made better undercover operatives than men.

Kyra kept her gaze down, but her ears strained to pick up more words. The conversation drifted in and out, but she managed to glean that they wanted to watch the new arrivals for something, and then he said something followed by twelve.

A wave of nausea washed over her as old ghosts clamored in her mind. Had this so-called doctor been the one who had transformed her into what she'd become?

Suddenly, the corridor felt too narrow. The air too thick. She didn't dare stop mopping for fear of freezing in place, so she forced her arms to move—scrubbing, pushing, scrubbing, pushing—while her mind screamed for her to run.

As a guard stepped forward, delivering something to the commander, Kyra seized the chance to shuffle a few steps back, letting him pass between her and the doctor's group. She positioned herself near a wall, lowered her head, and continued her charade of cleaning the baseboards. If she could only stay out of their direct sight until they finished and moved on.

Moved on to what, though? Tormenting Twelve?

This doctor was conducting the same twisted experiment that had turned her into a near-immortal creature with preternatural strength and reflexes, healing far faster than any normal human.

Was he looking to refine the methods? Improve the results?

The entourage pivoted, preparing to continue down the corridor. The commander bent respectfully, gesturing for the doctor to go ahead. The man stepped forward, flanked by two guards, each with a firearm holstered at their hip.

A wave of relief touched Kyra—maybe he'd pass right by without noticing her.

But then the doctor paused, looking like a predator who had just sniffed prey, and his gaze swept over the hallway. Kyra bent over, wringing out the rag into the bucket of dirty mop water, trying to reinforce the perception of a lowly maid just doing her job.

She could practically feel his eyes skim over her, and her heart pounded so loudly she feared it would betray her.

He said something in that guttural dialect, an almost whispered question. The commander muttered a dismissive response in Farsi—perhaps clarifying that she was a nobody.

There was silence, a long pause. Kyra held her breath, every nerve lit, terrified that if he looked closer, if he saw her eyes, he'd recognize her.

After all, her eyes were very distinctive. Not many had gold flakes swirling around their irises.

She heard a faint snort, perhaps the doctor's reaction, before he resumed walking. The click of his polished shoes on the floor sent an ominous echo. The entourage continued forward, and the commander murmured quick apologies, promising everything would be ready. Kyra almost let herself breathe again.

Almost.

Then, the doctor stopped once more. She sensed the shift in the air as he turned back, looking over his shoulder. The need to look up and meet his eyes was overpowering, but she resisted, keeping her head down and scrubbing.

She felt his stare and could imagine his lips pressed together in a line of suspicion, his brow furrowed. Her pulse hammered so hard that her vision blurred at the edges.

Time felt suspended.

A second stretched into five, then ten. The hush in the corridor was deafening. She refused to look up, focusing on the swirl of dirty water around the rag she was dipping in the bucket. She concentrated on the beads of sweat forming along her temple, the dryness in her throat, and anything except meeting that gaze.

And then, mercifully, a single step sounded, followed by others, and they were walking away, their footsteps growing fainter as they headed around the corner.

Only when Kyra was sure they were gone did she slowly exhale.

She flexed her fingers, which had been clenched around the rag. She had to keep up the façade a little longer until the corridor was fully clear. Then she'd slip into the nearest supply closet and stay there until the monster left.

46

KYRA

Kyra steadied her breath as she ducked behind the narrow supply closet door, trying to gather the nerve to check on Twelve one more time. The corridor outside was mostly quiet now, with only the distant murmur of voices from somewhere near the stairwell. She suspected the so-called doctor and his entourage had moved on to check on the new girls.

This might be her only chance.

She emerged with her mop and bucket and headed toward cell number twelve. Her worst fear was that the woman was no longer there, and the prospect of finding the cell empty twisted Kyra's stomach.

Pressing the mop handle firmly, she shuffled quickly down the corridor. The one benefit of the doctor's visit was that he and his entourage had left many new footprints on the floor she'd previously brought to a shine, giving her a perfect excuse to clean it once more.

Two guards stood further up, engaged in a bored conversation. She kept her head down, eyes on the milky water sloshing in the bucket, and shoulders slumped.

A malfunctioning fluorescent light flickered for a second, like it was warning her, but she ignored it and parked her bucket by the skirting board. Running the mop across a patch of scuffed floor, she slowly slid toward the metal door and its small, barred window. She raised the mop handle, using its length to mask her sideways glance, and peered through the window.

The cell was dim, but enough overhead light revealed the same young woman lying on the bed. She wasn't chained and showed no fresh bruises, at least none that Kyra could see from this angle, but her expression was slack, and her eyes were unfocused.

She looked heavily drugged.

Her arms lay limply at her sides, suggesting that if she was free of restraints, she couldn't fight or try to break free in her current state.

Not that she could break the chains or that door down. Kyra doubted she herself had enough strength to do that.

It was a relief that the woman hadn't been

battered, but her drugged state was no less worrisome. What did they intend to do with her?

It was probably a matter of convenience. A compliant subject was easier to handle.

The sound of footsteps echoing behind her got Kyra to quickly move away from the door to concentrate on scrubbing the new footprints left on the floor she'd already cleaned.

The footsteps drew nearer, accompanied by a low hum of that unfamiliar language, and a chill slithered through her.

He was back.

She had hoped the doctor was busy elsewhere and that she could slip away right after confirming Twelve was still inside, but luck wasn't with her today.

She glanced out of the corner of her eye, only to see the dark-coated man getting closer. The commander and the rest of the entourage were with him, probably done inspecting the new prisoners and returning to examine Twelve.

Every nerve in Kyra's body screamed for her to run, but she would never outrun the enhanced soldiers or their bullets. If only one of her abilities was turning invisible, she would have vanished, but all she could do was keep up the ruse and remain crouched with the rag clutched in her hand.

"Let's see our favorite subject." The doctor

shifted from that foreign language to accented Farsi.

"Of course, doctor," the commander replied hastily.

Kyra's gut clenched at the thought of what was about to be done to Twelve, but there was nothing she could do to help her.

With any luck, they'd move on, and she could slip back into her hiding place in the supply closet.

But no one moved, and no one said a word either.

"You." A single word that cut through the corridor like a blade.

Her heart stuttered. She prayed he was addressing someone else—maybe the commander—but she felt a change in the air, as though his attention had landed on her like a hand tightening around her neck.

"I'm talking to you, woman. Look at me."

She was the only woman in that corridor. "Are you addressing me?" she asked in a trembling voice.

"Yes, you. What's your name?"

"Parisa, sir."

"Get up and face me, Parisa."

Kyra couldn't move. She couldn't breathe. She was paralyzed with fear.

"Now, woman!"

Closing her eyes, she rose to her feet and faced

him, keeping her shoulders hunched and her eyes downcast.

"Look at me!" The command snapped through the air like a whip.

She was going to die, and there was nothing she could do about that.

Lifting her head slowly, she opened her eyes and looked into his unsettling features, which were too handsome for someone as cruel as that.

He frowned. "Remove your scarf."

Kyra stiffened. She kept her voice low, attempting a timid accent. "I'm sorry, sir. I'm not allowed to show my face."

His stare darkened. "I said, remove it."

In a last-ditch effort, she pivoted abruptly, taking her mop handle with her. "Excuse me," she murmured, trying to edge past them as though she had urgent errands. "I must—"

Faster than she could blink, he blocked her path, stepping close enough that she caught the faintest hint of the soap he'd used. His hand shot out, seizing a fold of her scarf, and with one swift motion, he yanked it free.

The thin fabric scraped across her cheek, revealing her face.

A flicker of recognition sparked in the doctor's eyes, followed by a slow, almost pleased smile. "Well, this is unexpected," he said. "What a wonderful surprise to find you in Tahav, Kyra."

His lips curved further, and then his fist connected with her face.

The blow snapped her head sideways, white-hot agony exploding in her cheekbone. Stars burst in her vision, she tasted blood, and then her knees buckled and she stumbled, the pain dragging her down.

Kyra dropped to the floor; darkness swallowed her, and there was oblivion.

47

MAX

Max braced against the vibration rattling through his seat and tried to ignore the constant roar of the helicopter's engines. The earpieces he wore filtered out enough of the clamor to keep him from going temporarily deaf, but the low-frequency thudding of the rotor still vibrated in his ribs. He adjusted the collar of the olive-green uniform he'd put on less than an hour ago—a counterfeit Revolutionary Guard ensemble. It felt all kinds of wrong to wear it, almost like donning a Nazi uniform, but stealth and safety trumped all other considerations.

Across from him, Jade and Drova sat side by side. Their body language was more like two hardened warriors heading into a daunting trial rather than a mother and her young and inexperienced daughter.

They were both combat-hungry Kra-ell,

although Drova seemed a little nervous despite her fierce expression. He saw how her fingers clutched the harness as if it were a lifeline.

He stifled a chuckle. If the girl hadn't revealed her incredible compulsion ability by pulling stupid pranks, she wouldn't be riding a helicopter into enemy territory on a dangerous mission. She was only seventeen and should be focusing on getting her high school equivalency instead of going on missions.

He was grateful she was there, but he also felt a little guilty on behalf of the clan for dragging her into something she wasn't ready for.

Jade put a comforting hand on her daughter's thigh, a rare gesture. Drova's eyes widened, and she turned to look at her mother. Jade nodded and smiled, conveying her encouragement without saying a word.

They were all wearing earpieces with the channels open, so whatever she said to the girl would have been heard by everyone else. She chose to convey her encouragement through nonverbal facial expressions.

Drova released a breath and gave her mother a small smile in return. When she glanced at him, he smiled too, thumped his chest, and extended his fist to her in a gesture that was meant to say, I got you.

Drova returned the gesture and then turned to look out the window.

It was dark outside, a black void not even broken by the glimmer of stars because of the clouds.

Yamanu had cloaked them with his shroud, making them practically invisible to human eyes. However, they would still show up on radar. If they did, the pilots had a script they could recite about this being a secret diplomatic mission of whichever Iranian minister they were told to mention. A second helicopter trailed behind and below, also covered by Yamanu's shroud.

The mental strain emanating from their shrouder was almost palpable, but there was nothing any of them could do to help. The best thing was not to disturb him.

On the bench behind Jade and Drova, two Kra-ell fighters were checking their weapons and exchanging hand signs that Max didn't recognize. Probably some stealth Kra-ell warrior language.

Asuka laid several gleaming knives across her lap, even as the helicopter bounced and shook, and started sharpening one. The thing probably didn't need it, but it was probably her form of meditation before the battle.

Max regretted not having a sharpening stone so he could do the same.

Ell-rom and Jasmine sat close together. Their faces were mere inches apart, so they could converse without the benefit of the common earpieces' feed. Ell-rom's expression flickered between worry and resolve, as though he couldn't decide whether his presence on this mission was beneficial or detrimental.

"Everything okay?" Max said into the comm, turning his head so they would know he was addressing them.

Ell-rom lifted his eyes. "I don't know," he admitted. "A part of me is afraid that I might freeze when the time comes."

"You won't." Max tried to keep his tone reassuring even though he shared Ell-rom's concern. "We're going to thrall and compel whoever we can, subdue who we must, and get out. If all goes according to plan, you should have no cause to reach for your talent."

If Max could trust Ell-rom's ability, knowing he was their fallback would have been comforting. If they found themselves cornered by a squad of Doomers, Ell-rom could be the difference between victory and defeat.

Hopefully, his special talent wouldn't be needed, and if it were, he wouldn't hesitate to use it.

Jasmine placed a hand on Ell-rom's knee. "I'm just worried about whether Kyra is even there. For all we know, she was there sometime in the past or not yet. Syssi's visions don't come with a time stamp."

Max met her gaze. "The last one did. The television was playing in the background, and current events were being shown. That was not accidental. The Fates wanted her to know that Kyra needed help now."

"But what if she was there recently but has been moved?" Jasmine voiced the same concern all of them shared.

He shrugged. "Worst-case scenario, we confirm that she's not there, get intel from the guards about where she was moved to, and go look for her." He placed a hand over his chest. "I have a feeling that she is there, though. She is waiting for us even though she doesn't know we are coming."

He'd fallen asleep on the plane and dreamt about Kyra, a woman who looked a lot like Jasmine, with the same golden eyes and dark, rich hair but with a harder, fiercer expression. She stood on top of a hill, just like in Syssi's first vision of her, but her face wasn't covered, and she was looking straight at him. She didn't say a word, but the way she regarded him said that she counted on him to come for her.

He didn't put much stock in the dream. It was just a manifestation of the thoughts that had been occupying his mind for the past forty-eight hours or so.

But what if it wasn't?

It didn't matter. He was coming whether Kyra was waiting for him or not.

Jasmine nodded. "I hope you're right, because we can't fail. This is not just about finding my mother. It's about finding Khiann. That's why the Fates showed Syssi where to find my mother when she asked them about Annani's beloved."

The helicopter rattled as they hit a pocket of turbulence, and Max grabbed hold of the seat's edge to steady himself. He glanced forward to where the pilot sat behind the cockpit console, wearing a full Revolutionary Guard uniform like the rest of them. Turner's contact had arranged for these pilots—men who didn't ask too many questions as long as the pay was good and who weren't fond of the regime these uniforms represented. Next to him Yamanu, dressed similarly, kept his eyes closed, lips slightly parted in concentration.

The pilot's voice came through. "We're about ten minutes from our final approach. The other chopper is holding formation. You should get ready."

Jade turned to her Kra-ell team. "Dima, Anton, you go first. Secure the perimeter. Asuka and Mehira, back them up." Her gaze flicked to Drova. "Stay with me until we're certain there are no immediate threats, then do your job. Everyone, keep your comm channel open at all times."

Drova nodded so vigorously her helmet strap slipped across her cheek. Jade squeezed her shoulder and motioned for her to put her sunglasses on while pulling her own out of her pocket.

Ell-rom pressed the earpiece deeper into his

ear as if trying to block out the rotor noise that still slipped past the filters.

Jade nodded. "Don't stray from the plan. We secure the landing site, and as soon as everyone is on the ground, we double-time it to the compound. When there, they won't realize we're not who we appear to be until we're already inside. Drova's compulsion will take care of humans and Doomers alike, as long as they are in hearing range."

Drova pulled out a mouthpiece that was only slightly larger than a whistle but was a powerful voice amplifier. It was another technical gizmo from the prolific lab William was running.

Jade clapped her on her back. "I'm glued to you, Drova."

When the girl glared at her, Jade lifted a finger to shush her. "Not because you are my daughter but because you're our number one asset, and I need to protect you."

The helicopter veered left, a tilt that forced everyone to brace. Max felt rather than heard the engine shift as the helicopter began its descent. As if on cue, he felt an adrenaline surge, prepping his body to erupt into motion.

He forced his breathing to slow. This was nothing new. He'd been on many missions before, albeit in different places. But every mission was unique. You never knew when the unexpected would claw its way out of the shadows and tear the plan to shreds.

"Ninety seconds to the landing zone," the pilot announced. "Wind's picking up, but nothing we can't handle."

Jade shifted, glancing once more around the cramped interior. "Last reminder that if we get separated and things go badly, the fallback is the southwestern ridge."

Outside, the rotor wash churned dust and scattered pebbles in swirling gusts. The whine of the engines built to a higher pitch as the pilot slowed them, preparing to touch down. Max clenched his jaw, adrenaline lacing his veins.

"Approaching landing zone in ten... nine..." the pilot counted down.

Max's grip tightened around his weapon.

"Three... two... one..."

The helicopter touched the ground with a jarring thud, rotors still spinning overhead. Max could barely make out the silhouette of the ascending hill through the open door, but faint illumination from behind its ridge was a clear indication that they were in the right place. The compound lay beyond.

This was it.

"Go," Jade commanded, her voice sharp through the earpiece.

48

KYRA

Kyra's eyes fluttered open to hazy, overlapping shapes in a room she didn't initially recognize. Pain pulsed at the back of her skull, each beat intensifying until her vision blurred with it. She tried to breathe slowly, but the air felt stale in her nose, tainted with something metallic she knew all too well. Blood. Or maybe rust. She couldn't tell which was stronger.

Her mouth was so dry it felt glued shut. She swallowed once, failing to summon enough saliva to soothe her throat. Everything was dim, like a nightmare half-lurking in the corners of her consciousness. Her arms wouldn't move like she wanted. She tugged, too sharply, and a jolt of dull agony lanced her shoulder.

A surge of panic hit.

Chains. A rasping clank told her what she had already sensed. They were heavier than she remembered. The cold metal bit into her wrists, pinning her arms to the bed frame with no slack to spare. Her legs were similarly bound, ankles strapped in place. With every attempt to shift, the cuffs pressed into her skin.

She blinked, letting her eyes adjust to the gloom. The overhead bulb cast a sickly yellow light over peeling walls. A tiny portal near the ceiling was barred. Fresh iron, by the look of it, the metal glinting in the faint light.

The doctor.

That single word cut through the fog in her head like a blade. He had found her. Recognized her in the hallway, ripping away her scarf and calling her by name. She remembered the look of triumph on his face, then the sudden flash of pain.

After that, nothing.

A memory—or maybe a hallucination—flickered at the edges of her mind. Glimpses of a white coat from her nightmares, a smirking mouth, the prick of a needle sliding into her vein. She wasn't sure if it happened a minute ago or twenty years prior. Her thoughts felt scrambled, spinning just out of reach whenever she tried to pin them down.

A wave of nausea rolled through her gut.

She forced herself to breathe.

Focus.

She needed clarity, but the sedation that weighed on her was heavier than any chains. It clung to her limbs, pulling them into the thin mattress. She tried bending her elbows and testing the cuffs for a weak link, but the metal was thick and unyielding. This time, they'd accounted for someone with her strength. Not that she felt strong at the moment.

The drugs had siphoned out all her strength.

"Damn it," she croaked, voice barely above a whisper. The dryness in her throat made the words come out cracked and small. Another wave of panic washed over her. She forced a deep inhale, willing calm into her pounding heart. Panicking would do nothing but tighten the chains holding her.

From somewhere beyond the thick walls, a scream sliced the silence. It was distinctly female, echoing down a hall or maybe from a room next door. She froze, listening. She wasn't the only one trapped in this place. Something wretched tightened behind her sternum. She recalled the new girls the doctor had just brought in. What were they doing to them?

She tugged again, though she knew it was pointless. It was instinctive. She was like a trapped animal that would claw its way to freedom, even if it meant dying in the process.

A flash of memory returned. The door to her cell was identical to the one in the asylum, with its small barred window. Her arms were strapped to a gurney, a needle pricked her skin. The sensations merged with the present until she couldn't separate them. She had escaped that nightmare once, unleashing a strength she hadn't known she possessed—ripping away the restraints, snapping the lock. But it wouldn't happen this time. She could feel the difference. These cuffs were thicker, the frame reinforced, and the sedation coursing through her veins had robbed her muscles of their superhuman strength.

This time, though, someone knew where she was. Maybe her people would come to free her once they realized she'd been captured.

They would know as soon as night fell and she didn't return.

Her eyelids fluttered shut, dizzy with the swirl of drug-induced confusion. She wanted to believe a rescue was possible, but the two brain cells still functioning in her head knew the cruel truth. She might remain locked in this cell for weeks until her people staged an operation to free her.

She didn't deserve the sacrifice, the many who would fall.

They'd tried to warn her, and she'd refused to listen. It wasn't their fault that she was here, chained to a bed and drugged.

Another scream raked her nerves. She squeezed her eyes tight, wishing she could cover her ears. The chains clanked again as she shifted, painfully aware that her ankles and wrists were spread in a degrading, vulnerable position.

That was how they'd kept her before, wasn't it? In that asylum.

A memory surfaced of the doctor removing her clothes, half-lost in the haze. He'd pressed down on her stomach, sneering. He hadn't done it to examine her. Had he laughed? Maybe. She couldn't quite remember. But she felt the humiliation all the same. The memory burned, spurring her to twist again in the present, rattling the new restraints.

"*Khorafeh*," she mumbled under her breath—nonsense. Her mind spun in circles, mixing Kurdish, Farsi, and English in one swirl. If only she could stand or even sit up. But all she managed was shifting her hips a few inches. The bed frame creaked ominously. Every movement stole energy she didn't have, and the sedation made her arms feel like lead.

Cold sweat trickled down her temple.

She braced herself for the door to slam open, for footsteps to echo on the linoleum. She expected the doctor to stride in at any moment, or the commander, or one of those enhanced guards.

Kyra didn't want to think of the horrors awaiting her. The horrors she'd seen them inflict on Twelve.

A tear slid down her cheeks.

They were both doomed. No one was coming to save them.

A clatter outside the door jolted her, sending

her heart racing. She strained to listen, but it was only the echo of distant metal clunks. There was no sign of footsteps entering her cell. She should be thankful.

She turned her head, the slight movement draining her fragile reserves of strength. Her pulse throbbed painfully in her temple. The sedation pressed down on her, heavy and unrelenting, dragging her into a thick haze of half-sleep. She blinked, fighting it, but it was a losing battle.

Her mind drifted, images swirling. Distant in her memory, a small child's face—brown eyes with flakes of gold like hers, hair streaked with chestnut. In the vision or rather hallucination, she cradled the girl, singing her a lullaby. Or maybe that was a dream, too. Her reality was this vile nightmare with real chains and real pain.

She'd never felt so powerless.

"Help..." The word was a whisper, strangled and trembling. She wasn't even sure she wanted to be heard. Because who would hear her anyway? The only ears that might listen belonged to the bastards running this place.

Kyra sank into the darkness, a spark of defiance flaring in her chest even as her consciousness ebbed, and she was lost in that half-world between waking and oblivion.

She would endure just like she had before.

Clutching that final thought, she let the blackness swallow her once again.

49

MAX

Max crouched behind a low concrete barrier, his nostrils itching from the sharp tang of gunpowder thick in the air. Over the din of gunfire, the acrid smell of smoke, and the shouts echoing through the compound's courtyard, he could barely hear his own voice.

Their carefully crafted plan had fallen apart into chaos moments into its execution.

The trek from the landing site to the compound had been swift and uneventful. The Kra-ell warriors had scaled the watchtowers in seconds and taken out the guards manning them with no one any the wiser. Even Max, who had been listening for sounds of scuffles taking place, had heard nothing.

With Yamanu's shroud, the guards at the gate

had been dispatched with the same lethal speed. Things had been going to plan—until they hadn't.

When their team entered the courtyard, two Doomers spotted them and opened fire before his team realized they were dealing with Doomers, who weren't affected by Yamanu's shroud.

Yamanu had been hit in the neck, and his shroud had fallen apart. The Doomers' shots and shouts had alerted the rest of the force, and within seconds, a full-blown gunfight erupted.

The Kra-ell team had pounced without hesitation.

Dima and Anton had launched themselves among the soldiers, moving so fast their figures seemed to blur. Asuka and Mehira followed suit, their eyes gleaming with bloodlust as they bounded toward the Doomers. Max caught a glimpse of Jade's slender silhouette darting into the fray, a short blade in hand and a savage grin full of fangs curling her lips. The Kra-ell's demonic appearance was an unexpected advantage as soldiers screamed and ran in fear.

Max rushed to Yamanu's side.

"I'm okay," the guy assured him. "The wound is already healing. Give me a moment, and I'll continue the shroud."

"Don't. At this point, they know we are here. I'd rather you join the fray when you're ready."

"I will." Yamanu held a hand over the wound,

which seemed more serious than the guy was willing to admit.

Max helped Yamanu behind the concrete barrier. "Can you cover me?"

The guy was able to sit upright and hold his weapons steady by this point. "I will. Go."

Max turned to look for Drova.

They needed her to compel the Doomers, but so far, they had only encountered those first two who had been dealt with. He was sure there were more, though, and the human soldiers were a menace as well.

One command from Drova and this battle would be over.

He found her crawling on the ground.

"Drova!" her mother shouted into the comm. "Are you hurt?"

"No. I lost my loudspeaker." The girl sounded frantic. "I can't find it."

Could things get any worse?

A hail of bullets whizzed above Max's head, biting into the thick concrete he'd ducked behind and spraying a volley of rocks over his head and shoulders. Gritting his teeth, Max waited for the lull between bursts. "Use your voice without it!"

But Drova's panicked voice came over the line, "No one will hear me!"

As if to confirm her assessment, her words were drowned by the rifle racket.

From the edge of his vision, Max watched Jade

slam into one of the guards who seemed impervious to bullets, and not just because he had a bulletproof vest on. His reflexes were incredibly fast. Still, the guy seemed just as terrified of the Kra-ell as the others and turned to flee with a speed that reinforced Max's impression that he wasn't human. But even a Doomer couldn't outrun a pureblooded Kra-ell animated by bloodlust.

She tackled him to the ground, but instead of sinking her fangs into his neck, she used her bare hand to punch him. That wouldn't hold him down for long, not unless she cut out his heart or chopped off his head, but they didn't have time for that.

Oops, Max had forgotten how strong Jade was and how vicious. With a bone-crushing punch, her fist went through the Doomer's chest, and when Jade pulled out her hand, she was holding his heart, dropping the bloody mass on the ground.

Max was a hardened warrior, but he'd never seen such savagery, and as his stomach heaved, he gulped air to keep it from emptying on the ground. Drova, however, didn't have the benefit of his battle experience and puked her guts out.

"Weakness will get you killed, girl!" Jade barked. "Get moving!"

On the other side of the courtyard, Mehira threw a knife at a soldier who was advancing at her with unnatural speed. He hissed but kept running with his fangs bared and his eyes flashing, only to get tackled by Anton, who grabbed him by the neck and twisted. A sickening snap followed as the Doomer collapsed.

Max was impressed. The Kra-ell had no compunctions about using lethal force, and these Doomers wouldn't regenerate. They were gone, and good riddance.

The moment of quiet that followed was interrupted by Jade's voice in his earpiece. "Drova, that's your chance!"

The girl inhaled shakily before cupping her hands around her mouth. "Stop fighting!" she yelled in Farsi, one of the phrases she'd been taught, projecting from her diaphragm as best she could. "Drop your weapons and lie face down on the ground."

Only those close enough to hear her paused, confusion and then frustration on their faces before they obeyed her command.

The rest were too far away to hear the command over the thunder of battle. Drova's voice alone wasn't enough. The miniature loudspeaker was supposed to have amplified her command so it would carry across the courtyard, and without it, half the soldiers didn't register her words at all.

Max made a mental note to find and collect this proprietary piece of equipment before they left the compound. It should not fall into the Doomers' hands, as it might reveal the clan's involvement. Nor should it find its way to the regime's labs, where it could be reverse engineered.

Max grunted and fired a short burst from his custom-made clan-issued weapon, aiming high to force a small group of Iranian soldiers back behind a stack of metal crates. "I'm going to flank them," he said into his mic.

Jade's response was a clipped affirmation. She and her warriors were pinned down near a toppled guard tower, forging a path through the ones who didn't hear Drova's command.

Ahead, a guard charged Ell-rom, an animalistic snarl twisting his lips. Ell-rom raised his handgun but didn't shoot.

Something flickered in his eyes, and Max held his breath, hoping for a demonstration of Ell-rom's death ray, but Dima launched a savage kick from the side, sending the guard sprawling.

The guy didn't get up, and Max was willing to bet that he was dead. That kick must have shattered his ribcage and smashed the organs it was supposed to protect.

The Kra-ell warriors were unstoppable. Gunshots popped in a staccato rhythm, but most of the bullets missed their targets, ricocheting off concrete or tearing through the many crates that were stacked in the yard. One by one, the Doomers and human guards fell, the Doomers taking just a little longer to die. Mehira slashed the throat of a

Doomer, going all the way and severing his head off his neck while Asuka and Dima cornered another. He tried vaulting over a stack of broken pallets, only for Dima to tackle him mid-leap. The savage sounds that followed revealed that it was a short fight.

These Kra-ell were lethal, and Max was glad they were on the same team. The only way an immortal could fight them was from inside an exoskeleton war suit like the Guardians had deployed when liberating Igor's compound.

The outcome of that battle would have been much different without those suits.

Several soldiers were holding positions on upper floors and shooting at his team, and he tried to take them out, but they were coordinating their forays at the windows, making it harder to expect where they would appear. Yet the two Max was certain he nailed seemed to chill the shooters' enthusiasm to expose themselves to further risk, and the fire from above mostly died down.

It was taking too long. They had to push forward and be done before reinforcements arrived.

"Everyone, hold your fire so Drova can be heard," Max barked into the comm.

Drova didn't wait for him to repeat his request. "On the ground! Don't move!" she projected with all the might her voice could muster.

The gunfire stopped.

The few soldiers Max could see froze, wide-eyed, sank to their knees, and lay flat, pressing their faces to the grimy pavement.

Others who were too far away or hadn't heard her over the racket from their rifles still took potshots from cover.

It took a few more moments for Jade's Kra-ell squad to eliminate those stragglers as well, and the frantic battle tapered off, leaving the courtyard scattered with unmoving bodies—some dead and some pinned to the ground by Drova's command.

Chest heaving, Max scanned for potential shooters. Sporadic muzzle flashes popped from a far corner, but Jade's team had it handled. Once they dealt with them, an eerie quiet settled over the courtyard, broken only by the moans of the wounded and the hiss of small fires sparked by bullet impacts.

Max nodded and jogged toward a group of humans splayed out on the ground, courtesy of Drova's compulsion, choosing the one whose uniform identified him as an officer. He crouched beside the man, who was on his belly with fingers laced over his head. Max gripped him by the hair and twisted his head so he was forced to look up.

Their eyes locked. "Where are the prisoners kept?" Max asked in Farsi while delving into the soldier's head.

Max didn't need the human to verbalize a response since he was already seeing the path in the man's head, but the soldier answered nonetheless, practically suffocating on his own fear. "E-East Wing," he rasped, blinking rapidly. "Third floor." He swallowed convulsively.

Max caught a flash from the man's memories—long, ugly corridors, steel doors, and a single face that the solider thought of as The Doctor. The soldier's fear of that man overshadowed everything else.

"East Wing's third floor," Max said, standing up quickly. "Drova, Jade, Anton, and Dima. You are with me." Max clicked the comm again. "Yamanu, how are you doing?"

"Just another day at the office, my friend." The calm reply put Max's anxiety about Yamanu's condition at ease.

"OK. We are headed to the third floor of the East Wing. That's where the prisoners are kept. If you are up to it, make sure no hostiles remain to come at our backs and join us. We might run into more Doomers inside."

"We'll see you inside shortly, Max."

"What about me and Jasmine?" Ell-rom asked. "Jasmine wants to be there when we liberate her mother."

Max was well aware of that, but for now, the two with no combat experience were a liability. He preferred that they wait until the yard and surrounding area were secured and then join Yamanu's team when they came in to meet them.

"You will come up with Yamanu. We will clear the way for you so it is safe to do so."

50

KYRA

Kyra drifted in and out of darkness. She felt no sense of time for a while, only a half-aware haze that swirled through her mind and trapped her in a slow, heavy daze. The bite of metal around her wrists and ankles remained constant, though the dull ache reminded her that this wasn't a dream.

It was a nightmare.

No matter how often she blinked, she couldn't peel away the floating spots or the thick fog of sedatives. She wasn't sure how long she'd been under. Minutes? Hours?

Possibly more than a day.

Thoughts floated up in no particular order of the cruel smile on the doctor's too-handsome face, the echoes of a far-off scream, the memory of fear as she'd crouched in the corridor, waiting for him and his entourage to depart, her scarf being ripped away.

She shuddered involuntarily, the chain rattling in response. If he'd come back to see her, she had no recollection of it. The cell's stale air pressed down on her, still reeking of cleaning solution, old sweat, and a faint whiff of burnt metal from the overhead lamp.

Who cleaned these cells?

She had never been allowed in, and neither were the other staff members. Who brought in food? Did they starve the prisoners?

Oh, that's right. The soldiers did that. They brought in the food and took the prisoners to the bathroom and back. Kyra had already investigated all that when she'd planned to switch places with Twelve.

Her mind wasn't working properly, like right now it was registering the sounds of gunfire. They didn't do target practice inside the compound. So, what was the deal with those sounds?

Was she imagining them?

The sharp crack of shots sounded authentic, but the stone walls and the thick door muffled it.

She strained to lift her head, blinking rapidly. If this was a hallucination, it was a damn good one. Still, she kept listening, and then it started again—a rattling burst followed by men shouting and then more gunfire.

One part of her believed she was imagining it

or perhaps remembering old battles, but the sounds were too consistent and insistent to originate in her compromised mind.

A scream, sounding closer this time. Another wail answered, more distant but no less agonized. Kyra swallowed what little saliva she could muster.

They hadn't given her anything to drink or eat since she'd been captured. Perhaps it hadn't been that long ago, or maybe she was just too drugged to remember.

Her throat felt dry and scratchy.

Could it be her people?

Had Soran and Zara gathered enough fighters to attempt a rescue? Surely, they weren't stupid enough to attempt this with the small force at their command.

She'd never wanted them to risk this and told them so. She refused to let them sacrifice themselves for her. But maybe they had ignored her wishes and decided she was worth saving.

She had to help them.

She'd escaped similar confinement before and could do it again if only she could clear her foggy mind.

Pain was the answer.

Pain could cut through the fog, and she might gather enough strength to break the chains.

Kyra grunted with effort and lifted her head a few inches from the mattress. Her vision swam, the drugs hammering at her skull and stealing her strength just as effectively as the restraints.

"Come on," she muttered to herself, throat convulsing. "Move." The words came out hoarse, cracking mid-syllable. She tried flexing her biceps, forcing the chain to yield.

Nothing.

The steel cut into her skin, and the bed frame rattled but refused to budge.

Another round of gunfire echoed, this time closer. She heard frantic footsteps overhead—boots clattering on the floor above. Her senses were all scrambled. She tried to count how many different footsteps there were, but everything blurred.

Her team didn't have enough manpower to wage a loud, drawn-out assault in broad daylight, or was it night? She wasn't even sure of that.

Had they secured cooperation with another resistance cell?

No, there hadn't been enough time to organize that. Her sense of time might be all screwed up, but she couldn't have been in this cell for more than a day or even a few hours. They would have been forced to take her to the bathroom, and she would have remembered that.

Unless there was a chamber pot in the cell.

She sniffed the air, but other than the stale smell of moldy walls, nothing would indicate a pot with anything in it.

Kyra exhaled shakily.

"Soran... Zara...Hamid," she whispered.

She wanted to believe those dear faces would come barreling through the door, cutting down any guard standing in their way and freeing her. But it was nearly suicidal for a unit of Kurdish fighters to storm a secure compound that housed several enhanced soldiers.

Just listening to the commotion released a fresh wave of adrenaline that burned through the sedative and gave her a bit of clarity. She groaned and pulled, but the rattling clank of the cuffs reminded her that even if she mustered some supernatural strength, these new chains were designed for someone as strong as her.

The doctor had learned from his past mistakes.

A thunderous boom rattled the overhead light. Maybe a grenade or a heavy blast. The building itself seemed to quiver, and dust drifted from the ceiling.

Kyra sucked in a breath, tasting grit on her tongue.

Shots rang out again, a flurry of them, followed by shrill shouts in multiple languages. She couldn't parse them, but the raw panic carried through. She pressed the back of her head against the flat cushion, imagining the courtyard in chaos.

A strange knot twisted in her chest, a tangled mix of guilt and longing. If it truly was her people, how many would die trying to rescue her? The thought made her stomach twist so violently that she feared she would vomit.

She closed her eyes, tears gathering under her lids.

She was so tired. So unbelievably tired.

A strangled cry penetrated the thick walls—someone near her cell—the scuff of footsteps, then a low moan. Kyra's eyes snapped open, adrenaline surging. If a fight was that close, maybe the front lines of the incursion had pushed deeper into the building. She jerked at her wrist cuffs again, ignoring the tearing pain.

There was no give. Gritting her teeth, she tried thrashing her legs, but the chain at her ankles was no kinder.

"Damn it," she hissed, frustration and desperation eating away at what was left of her sanity.

Gunfire flared anew, stuttering so close now that she felt the floor vibrating. Another explosion rocked the corridor, sending a muted tremor through the bed frame. Her breath caught. Something large had definitely blown up. Possibly a door or a security barrier.

She fought not to black out again.

A guard barked an order, and a distinct pop of rifles answered, forcing a hush. Kyra prayed to whatever deity that would listen that the rebels had made it inside, that the enhanced soldiers were dead, and for the door to her cell to burst open, followed by the familiar faces of her friends.

She almost chuckled at how her imagination ran wild.

Noise crackled in the hallway—the shuffle of boots, clipped curses.

Her lungs itched with the need to call out, but she didn't know who was out there. If it was the doctor or his men, a shout might sign her death warrant. If it was her allies, a cry for help might bring them right to her.

Another sharp rattle of gunfire overhead. Then, a thunderous silence. She froze, ears straining for the slightest hint of voices, footsteps, or anything. The silence pressed on her eardrums, so absolute it made her breathing sound deafening. That hush was worse than the noise. Because she had no idea what it meant. Had the rebels won? Or were they all dead?

Her eyes drifted shut, forced by exhaustion. Her body trembled, each spasm making the cuffs dig deeper into her wrists. She recognized a slow trickle of warmth from the raw chafing, but pain hardly registered. How many had already fallen if it was indeed her friends battling out there? How many more would die if reinforcements arrived? She willed them to hold on, to prevail with fewer casualties than she dared guess. The idea that her team might be lying in pools of blood was too horrific to consider.

"Just stay alive," she murmured. "Please."

Her head swam, the world tilting. For a

moment, she wanted to surrender to that blackness so she wouldn't have to face the truth if it was dire. Instead, she clenched her fists and held on, clinging to consciousness like a drowning woman holding on to driftwood.

Gunshots echoed once more, faint but definitely close. A final flash of adrenaline surged through her, stopping her from sinking under. She listened desperately, waiting for familiar voices or footsteps that might burst through the door.

None came. Yet.

51

MAX

The East Wing's entrance loomed, its steel doors hanging askew from an earlier explosion. Max pressed forward, keeping his weapon trained on the shadowy corridor beyond. Behind him, Drova's breathing came in short, controlled bursts—the girl was barely holding it together.

"Remember," Jade said into the comm, "We can't leave anyone alive to report back about us."

Anton and Dima fanned out to either side, their movements fluid and predatory. The Kra-ell hybrids might not have formal military training, but their instincts were razor-sharp.

The corridor stretched ahead, fluorescent lights flickering. Max's enhanced hearing picked up the shuffle of boots from multiple directions—too many to pinpoint. The acrid smell of gunpowder still hung in the air from the earlier fighting, mixed with something else.

Fear.

The entire building reeked of it.

"The stairs leading up should be around the next corner," Max said as he carefully moved forward.

The images from the soldier's memory were still vivid in his head, making the place look oddly familiar. He knew where each door was located and what was behind it. This floor was mainly used by the serving staff, but that didn't mean that soldiers weren't waiting for them with guns ready, hiding behind corners and doors to supply closets.

The other thing that remained stuck in Max's mind from that short peek was the face of the doctor. The soldier was even more afraid of him than his higher-ups in the Revolutionary Guard. And now, that face was burned into Max's memory.

Next to him, he heard Drova's heavy breathing, and he glanced at her to see if she was okay. The girl was barely seventeen, a fledgling warrior with a compulsion power that could freeze everyone within earshot, but she was still a kid.

She'd proven her worth in the courtyard and before that during the Beverly Hills mission, but her eyes revealed the aftershocks of what she'd witnessed.

A session or two with Vanessa might be in order.

Max took the lead, raised his weapon, and moved forward with Jade by his side and Anton and Dima slithering along behind them like a pair of coiled cobras while keeping Drova protected between them.

The corridor was only partially lit by intermittent overhead fixtures, some flickering, some shattered. Every few yards, bullet holes marred the walls, and the sour tang of spent rounds hung thickly in the air. The place was in disrepair, and it wasn't just because of the current battle. It was years of neglect.

They slipped around a corner where two uniformed men crouched behind an overturned desk, the stench of fear radiating from them. The muzzle of a rifle peeked above the desk edge, trembling. Max signaled to Drova with a curt jerk of his chin. She understood instantly. These were humans, and her compulsion was sure to work on them.

A sharp crack tore the air, and Drova cried out, staggering sideways. A streak of bright red blossomed along her shoulder, near her collarbone.

"Drova!" Jade lunged, grabbing her daughter before she hit the ground.

A roar like thunder reverberated through Max's skull as Jade's sidearm joined his, unleashing a volley of gunfire into the men behind the desk.

One soldier toppled backward with a strangled cry, the other slumped sideways, dead eyes still wide in shock. Blood pooled beneath the makeshift barricade. Their weapons clanked uselessly to the floor.

For a second, everything went eerily silent. Drova crumpled against her mother, breathing raggedly, one hand pressed to the wound at her shoulder. Jade's face twisted with fury as she knelt, examining the injury. The bullet must have torn through the muscle, maybe grazed bone. Drova's dark eyes welled with tears, but she didn't utter a sound.

She tried to stand, but Jade clutched her protectively.

"Don't move," Jade growled. Her free hand pressed onto Drova's shoulder, stanching the blood. Beneath Jade's fierce persona was a surge of maternal worry that practically radiated from her every movement. "I need to dress your wound."

Given how fierce the Kra-ell were, it was easy to forget that they didn't heal as fast as immortals and that Drova would need a few days for her injury to recover.

They'd just lost their compeller.

Drova couldn't project a command if she could barely breathe.

Max cursed silently.

Without her, they'd have to rely on brute force, which, thankfully, Dima and Anton had in spades.

The Kra-ell hybrids were a force to be reckoned with in close combat.

As a dozen uniformed figures materialized behind them, rifles spitting bullets, the two Kra-ell hybrids responded with lethal efficiency, moving like specters, darting side to side, returning fire, and cutting them down.

Shots rang out, muzzle flashes igniting the gloom. A bullet ricocheted, sending fragments of concrete into Max's face. He swore, leveling his own gun at a guard charging in front. Three short bursts from his semiautomatic weapon, and the guard collapsed, chest bloody and eyes blank.

One of the guard's companions sprinted forward, howling in either rage or terror. Anton swiveled with inhuman speed, caught him by the throat, and snapped his neck in a single motion. The limp body hit the ground with a sickening thud.

All at once, silence settled again. The bodies lay sprawled in disordered tangles, warm blood creeping across the tiled floor. Max's ears rang from the gunfire despite the sound being somewhat muted by his earpieces.

His gaze darted to Jade and Drova, the latter looking as pale as a ghost while her mother dressed her wound.

That she hadn't fainted from the pain was impressive.

"Stay with her," he told Jade. "We've gotta move."

Jade's jaw tightened, but she nodded. "The bullet's gone through—she'll heal, but it'll take time." She glanced at Drova's face, brushing the girl's sweaty hair aside. "You'll be fine."

Max nodded, checked his ammo, and notified Yamanu of the situation and Jade's location. "Anton, Dima, you're with me."

The Kra-ell were splattered with gore from the men they'd killed, and their fangs were on full display. As hybrids, they didn't look as alien as the purebloods, but right now, no one would have mistaken them for humans.

Together, the three of them advanced through the corridor, leaving Jade to guard Drova and their backs.

It was eerily quiet with no shots being fired, but Max had no doubt that he was about to encounter more soldiers and probably Doomers.

Yamanu's team would join them shortly, and together they would eliminate the last of the resistance.

The hallway veered to the left, and at the far end, a closed steel door barred the way.

"They must be holed up on the higher floors," Max muttered. "We need to go through this door to get to the stairs that lead to the third floor."

Anton, taller than Dima by a couple of inches, pressed his ear to the steel door. "I hear footsteps on the other side," he said, voice low. "Maybe five or six." His eyes flickered red for a moment, betraying his Kra-ell heritage. "We can breach fast as soon as the door is down."

After setting up the C4 explosives, Max joined the hybrids behind a corner and pressed the trigger. The door was blasted along with its frame.

Anton crouched, muscles coiled like a spring. They exchanged a silent count to three, and both charged through the blasted opening.

Flashes of muzzle fire greeted them. Bullets clanged on the twisted steel and ricocheted off the floor. One clipped Dima's shoulder, but the Kra-ell barely flinched. In a single motion, Dima flung himself past Max and Anton, crashing into the group of guards. Anton followed, a living avalanche. Max took advantage of the confusion, stepping through with his weapon raised, picking off a guard trying to line up a shot at Dima's back.

The chaos—screams, grunts, the wet sounds of fists on flesh, rifles clattering—was brief. Dima and Anton were an unstoppable force, like lions among sheep.

The last breathing guard tried to flee, stumbling over the corpse of a comrade, but before Max could raise his gun, Anton stepped in, hooked an arm around the man's waist, lifted then slammed him to the floor, headfirst—there was no room for mercy.

They couldn't leave witnesses, or the Brotherhood would learn who'd launched this attack, and worse, learn of the existence of the Kra-ell. They would eventually learn of the additional alien race present on Earth, but the longer it took, the better it was for the clan.

The Kra-ell were their secret weapon.

Dima panted, a shallow wound seeping from his arm, while Anton scanned ahead, not a single scratch visible on him.

Yamanu's voice came through the comms. "We are coming in behind you. All is secured outside. I instructed the pilots to be ready to pick us up directly from the courtyard. I'm bringing the rest of the team with me."

"We are waiting for you," Max said.

When the rest of the team cleared the blasted door, Anton frowned, looking alarmed. "Where is Mehira?"

Yamanu lifted a hand to calm him down. "Guarding the building's entrance so no one will sneak in behind us."

Anton nodded.

As they ascended the winding concrete steps, Drova had to lean on Jade for support, but Yamanu looked fully recovered.

The higher they went, the more potent the reek of fear became.

At the second-floor landing, they were surprised to find bodies—probably guards who'd been using the window to shoot down at the courtyard and got hit by Max's team's return fire.

The entire building was a war zone.

"Keep your eyes open," Max warned. "If any of them are Doomers, they might be already regenerating. They are immortal, and they heal as fast as we do."

"We know," Anton said in heavily accented English.

Dima nodded, lips curled back to expose his elongated canines. "They smell different."

That was good to know. Max wasn't aware that Doomers smelled differently than other immortals, but now was not the time to inquire in what way. If he had to guess, though, it would be that they reeked because they didn't shower as often as they should.

On the next landing, a battered metal sign read *Third Floor*.

Max felt a thread of ice trickle through his veins. He recalled the soldier's memory of the broad corridor and the rows of locked cells.

This was where they were keeping Kyra.

52

MAX

The third floor was untouched, except for old bullet holes in the walls that had been covered with the same ugly greenish-yellowish oil-based paint that covered the walls of the other floors. And standing in the corridor, framed by the harsh overhead fluorescent light, was the man from the memory Max had picked from the soldier's mind, but he wasn't a man. The so-called doctor was an immortal, and given the fancy uniform and the two bodyguards flanking him, he was a high-ranking Doomer.

Kian would love to get his hands on this one.

Tall, impeccably dressed in a dark uniform that looked like it had been custom-tailored for him, he wore a haughty expression with a slight sneer twisting his mouth. While his bodyguards' eyes were blazing and their fangs were in full view, all the doctor projected was bored arrogance.

Why was he so cocky?

Multiple footsteps from the two flanking corridors provided the answer.

Two groups of four Doomers, each with soldiers behind them, were advancing to join the doctor and his bodyguards.

The doctor thought that he had them outnumbered, which was why he seemed so relaxed and assured. That, or he was a sociopath who felt nothing at all.

Yamanu's team split into two groups, each facing a corridor, which left the doctor and his goons for Max, Anton and Dima.

"Ell-rom," Max said calmly without taking his eyes off the doctor, "leave this one untouched. He's mine."

To Ell-rom's credit, he played along. "As you wish, Max."

"So," the doctor said, voice contemptuous, full of bravado Max suspected was not all really there. "The betrayer's whelps have come to play." His accent was thick, but his words were clear enough. His gaze flicked to the hybrids and then to the purebloods, lingering on their fangs. A glimmer of fascination mixed with further worry crossed his features. "And who are these? Have the betrayer's daughters stooped to breeding with monkeys?"

It had been meant as a provocation, but Max didn't know to what end, so he lifted his hand, stopping the hybrids from pouncing. Perhaps the doctor was counting on the enraged hybrids to lose control and do something stupid, like pounce on the immortals with their fangs bared.

Right now, it was a standoff, all weapons raised.

The Doomers and humans flanking them couldn't fire because they were as likely to hit each other as they were to hit Yamanu and his team, and they were clearly waiting for a signal from the doctor.

"I'm not about to engage in a game of insults with you," Max said.

The doctor's smirk widened, revealing elongated canines. "Annani's spawn are as pathetic as the humans they coddle. I'll enjoy dissecting your friends' corpses for whatever secrets they hide."

Max recognized the moment the two Doomers flanking the doctor tensed, probably responding to some secret signal he'd given.

"Tell your dogs to stand down." Max fixed his gaze on the doctor. "Let's do this the old-fashioned way," he said, forcing the words out in the Doomers' language. "One on one. Fangs and claws."

A heartbeat passed, the doctor's eyes narrowing in amusement. "You want to fight me?" he translated with mild surprise. Then he let out a mocking laugh. "It would be so much more pleasurable to rip out your throat with my fangs." He turned to his bodyguards, issuing a curt command. "Kill the monkeys."

He and Max locked eyes. For a moment, they

both seemed to exhale. Then, as if on cue, they charged at each other, their weapons flung aside mid-step, clattering on the floor.

Max was dimly aware that everyone engaged in hand-to-hand combat at the same time. He had a split second to mentally smile at the surprise waiting for the Doomers.

Max collided with the doctor, grappling in a flurry of fists and elbows. The doctor's strength was staggering, even for an immortal, and it occurred to Max that he might be on drugs.

Max let out a grunt, hooking an arm behind the man's shoulder and driving him backward. They slammed into the wall. The doctor hissed, delivering a savage knee strike to Max's ribs. Pain flared, and Max stumbled but didn't let go.

A savage flurry of punches erupted between them—too close to dodge effectively, each blow connecting with flesh. Max tasted blood. The doctor's nails raked across his cheek, leaving burning scratches. But decades of Guardian training and countless battles had hardened Max, and he let his instincts and training take over. He shifted his stance, hooking a foot behind the doctor's calf to unbalance him, then hammered an elbow into the male's temple.

They went down in a heap, rolling across the old linoleum floor that was slick as if it had been recently mopped.

As the doctor tried to latch on to Max's throat

with his fangs, Max jerked sideways, the male's breath hot and rancid on his neck. He braced a knee on the doctor's hip, prying them apart. The doctor bared his teeth in frustration, eyes blazing with malice.

Dimly, Max heard crashes and snarls from all sides. Next to him, Anton and Dima were tangling with the other two Doomers in a furious exchange of fists, kicks, and savage roars. A gunshot rang out, echoing. Then, a wet gurgle. Max didn't have time to look.

"Die!" the doctor snarled, hooking a hand around Max's throat. His monstrous strength pressed down, squeezing the air from Max's lungs. Darkness crept at the edges of his vision. Summoning the last of his will, Max twisted sideways, ignoring the burn in his shoulders.

He let the doctor think he'd pinned him down, and then he struck. He freed one arm just enough to grab the back of the doctor's head, forcing him closer, and sank his own elongated fangs into the doctor's exposed jugular. A hiss tore from the doctor's throat as venom flooded into him.

He should have gone lax the moment the venom entered his system, but the drugs he was on must have weakened or delayed the venom's effect, and he thrashed violently.

Max held on, biting harder until thick, bitter blood filled his mouth. His stomach lurched at the taste, but he clenched his jaw, injecting more venom with every heartbeat. The doctor's fingernails raked Max's shoulder, but he latched on, unrelenting. Gradually though, the struggles weakened. The doctor's heart hammered erratically, then faltered.

With a final spasm, he went limp.

Face still buried in the man's neck, Max listened carefully for the heartbeat of his opponent. As much as he wanted the lowlife dead, he was able to restrain himself and modulate the venom to induce stasis. The prospect of reviving the doctor to interrogate him was all the motivation he needed not to succumb to the desire to finish him off right there and then.

When it was over, the tang of blood made his stomach turn, and as he retracted his fangs, Max shoved the doctor's dead weight aside and rolled to his knees, chest heaving.

Across the corridor, Dima and Anton were crouching over the bodies of the two Doomers, one with a snapped spine, the other nearly decapitated by a Kra-ell blade. Blood glistened in savage pools around them.

The situation was similar in the other two corridors as well. Human and Doomer bodies in various shapes of ruin were everywhere.

One body lay crumpled on the floor with no marks of violence, and Max knew this was Ellrom's doing.

Quickly scanning his team, Max was glad that no one seemed seriously hurt.

Jade and her Kra-ell were covered in blood and gore, and the hybrids were bruised and cut, but none of them seemed to mind. Other than Drova who looked in pain, the others were still riding high on the adrenaline rush.

Yamanu was fully recovered, Drova's shoulder was bandaged, and Ell-rom and Jasmine were unhurt.

"That was intense," Yamanu quipped in his calm voice, as if he was reporting on a movie scene rather than on a gory killing field where a battle for life and death had just taken place.

Anton glanced down at Max. "You good?"

Max coughed, spat out the doctor's blood from his mouth, and nodded. "The taste is horrible, but I'll live." He wiped his lips with the back of his hand, tasting copper and venom in equal measure.

"Who wants to wrap this one in a red ribbon and bring him as a present to Kian?" Looking up at Yamanu, Max pointed at the Doomer.

Yamanu lifted his hands in the air. "He's all yours. Kian wanted the leader of this place to interrogate, but I have a feeling that we've just bagged someone far higher up than that. Kian will be thrilled."

Ell-rom eyed the bloody scene. "What do we do with all this carnage?"

Yamanu placed a hand on Ell-rom's shoulder.

"After we free the prisoners and confirm no one is left alive, we'll set up incendiary explosives. That should take care of all the evidence."

Max slowed his breathing, ignoring the fire in his ribs from the hits he'd taken. Their mission was still incomplete, but they were getting there. If they managed to get out of there with Kyra alive and before reinforcements arrived, he would count it as a great success despite all the fuckups.

53

KYRA

Kyra must have fallen asleep again—the kind of drugged, half-there sleep that offered no dreams or rest. She was dimly aware of the cold clamminess on her cheeks, the too-thin mattress beneath her back, the dull ache in her muscles from not being able to move more than an inch or two, and the heavy rattle of chains every time she tried.

The gunshots she'd heard earlier had stopped, but a different kind of noise had pulled her from her restless sleep. It wasn't right in front of her cell door, but close enough for her to hear the sounds of footsteps that were definitely in the same corridor.

There was a cluster of them. The sound of muffled shouts came from too far away for her to decipher what was being said. Then, a clatter of something hitting the floor. Something big. She could hear tense voices echoing down the hallway, and the hair on her arms prickled with foreboding.

She realized with a start that her pendant was gone. They had taken away the amber stone that had guided her for so long, and now she was blind without it. The people outside could be her friends coming to rescue her, or it could be even worse monsters than the doctor, and she had no way of knowing.

Kyra wanted to cry out in helpless anger but clamped her teeth shut. No sense in attracting attention. If it was the doctor or someone even worse, she didn't want them to remember that she was there until she recovered at least a sliver of her strength.

Her mind was a little clearer, and it occurred to her the drugs were slowly loosening their grip on her, and no one had come to administer more.

Perhaps those were the people outside?

But then, why the commotion?

She heard someone utter a vile Farsi curse, then another voice lashed out in a foreign language that she recognized from her earlier disastrous infiltration. The enhanced soldiers and the doctor spoke it.

The words echoed off the walls, and she could only catch snippets of sound, but the cadence and aggression suggested fear.

Suddenly, footsteps pounded right outside her cell.

Kyra went rigid, expecting the door to burst open, but nothing happened, and she exhaled shakily. They weren't coming for her.

Then came a voice—the doctor's—clear and ringing with arrogance. "The betrayer's whelps have come to play," he said in accented English. "And who are these two? Have the betrayer's daughters stooped to breeding with monkeys?"

What was he talking about? Who was the betrayer whose daughters were breeding with monkeys? Did he mean ugly men? Or was it some kind of a racial slur?

There was a mocking quality in the doctor's tone, as though whoever he was addressing was beneath him. *The betrayer's whelps.* Maybe he was referring to some old grudge or vendetta. He sounded angry but also wary. Almost as if he felt threatened.

The blood in Kyra's veins pulsed faster.

"I'm not about to engage in a game of insults with you." The answer was delivered in what was clearly American English. The man's voice was smooth, calm, and strangely familiar, even though she was sure she had never met him.

Something about his inflection and the timbre of his words awakened an ache deep in her chest.

Kyra closed her eyes, the lack of visual input sharpening her hearing. The thick door muffled the sounds, but she could pick out the anger that laced the doctor's voice, while the American sounded almost bored with the hostility. The rest of the words became a jumble of half-caught phrases.

"Annani's spawn are as pathetic as the humans they coddle. I'll enjoy dissecting your friends' corpses for whatever secrets they hide."

"Tell your dogs to..."

"Fangs and claws."

"You want to fight me?" A pause. "It would be... to kill you with..."

"Kill the monkeys."

Kyra tensed. Someone barked something in that foreign dialect again, and then the corridor erupted with the sounds of struggle—the distinctive crash of bodies hitting walls, the grunt of someone absorbing a heavy blow, and the sharp scrape of boots pivoting on the floor. Then came gasps and strangled curses in English.

By the commotion, the number of people engaged in combat outside her door was significant. The doctor's voice rose, though she couldn't discern the words, and another man—maybe the same American or a companion—let out a hiss of pain or exertion. A loud metallic clang reverberated as if a piece of equipment or a weapon had dropped. She pictured them grappling, maybe fists flying or knives clashing.

Kyra jerked at her shackles, and the heavy cuff

around her right wrist tore into already raw skin, sending rivulets of warmth trickling over her palm. She bit back a cry, cursing herself for doing something so stupid. Pain flared, sharpening her senses, but even with adrenaline pumping through her, she was pinned like an animal in a trap.

A muffled shout—a shot—someone's strangled exclamation—then silence.

Kyra's pulse thundered in her skull. *Did the doctor kill them?*

She imagined the doctor's twisted sneer or that unnamed American lying in a pool of blood. She had no reason to care about the stranger with the smooth voice, and yet her chest tightened at the thought.

If he was on a mission to take down the vile doctor, maybe he was also her chance of survival. But if the American died, she'd be left at the mercy of a monster that had none.

Another wave of terror and despair gripped her, intensifying the ache in her battered body.

The corridor beyond remained silent. Not even the faint shuffle of bodies being dragged or voices calling for reinforcements.

She hated that kind of hush. It felt like a coffin's lid had just slammed shut.

Her head lolled to the side involuntarily as a wave of lightheadedness caught her. The dryness in her throat became unbearable, and she coughed, tasting blood. She must've bitten her lip earlier.

The man's voice echoed in her thoughts, smooth, confident, with a touch of humor in it despite the tense situation. It stirred up fragments of a murky past. She must have spent some time in America to speak English as well as she did. Perhaps that voice reminded her of someone she used to know there.

The memory teased at her like a half-forgotten melody, bringing a pang of longing so sharp it almost drew tears.

The overhead lamp flickered out, momentarily plunging the room into near darkness. In that brief instant, she heard a faint scratching, like something scraping the door. Her heart leaped. She tried to listen more carefully, but the lamp buzzed back to life, and everything fell silent once more.

Did I imagine it?

She stared at the metal door, half expecting it to open. But it didn't. No shadows moved under the narrow space at the bottom. Just an impenetrable barrier. If the fight had concluded, whoever won apparently had no interest in the prisoners and had left.

Exhaustion battered her, or maybe it was the crushing sense of disappointment that was making her breathing grow ragged. Tremors wracked her arms, either from muscle fatigue or the last vestiges of adrenaline. Tears pricked the corners of her eyes. She had always prided herself on being strong—a survivor. But there was no surviving this.

She was caged, drugged, and powerless, and no one was coming for her.

54

MAX

Max inhaled slowly, steadying his breathing in the aftermath of the battle. His pulse was still pounding from the intensity of the fight, and he was nauseous from the disgusting taste of the Doomer's blood in his mouth.

"Dima, Mehira, Rutza." Jade motioned for them to come forward. "Make sure that no one else is hiding on this floor." She turned to the other two. "Drag all these bodies to a pile somewhere out of the way. There is no need for the freed prisoners to see the carnage."

She looked at the doctor's nearly lifeless body. "What should I do with him?"

"Put him next to the wall over there." Yamanu pointed. "He's not going anywhere." He turned to Max. "Let's check all the cells. Kyra should be in one of them."

With Yamanu, Jasmine and, of course, Ell-rom in tow, they headed toward the row of cells.

"We are all clear here," Jade said in his comm. "The floor is secure and ready for the prisoners to be brought out. My team and I are back to looking acceptable, except for the blood on our uniforms."

Yamanu grinned. "Don't worry about it. I will shroud everyone to look human and hide the bodies, including the blood and gore. There is no reason to distress the prisoners further, or to make them worry about someone getting caught again and having their memories scanned for information on who freed them."

Observing the keypads and scanners at the cells' doors, Max turned around and found what he was looking for in the doctor's pocket.

He returned to his waiting party. "All right, let's get Kyra."

"What do you want to do with the rest of the prisoners?" Jasmine asked anxiously. "Shouldn't we take them as well?"

"We will set them free," Max said. "We are only taking Kyra, but we are leaving no one behind."

Max placed the keycard against the reader, and the locking mechanism opened smoothly. An older man in a rumpled suit stood in the far corner of the cell, trying to melt into the wall. His eyes darted frantically from Max to Yamanu.

"*Azadi...?*" the man whispered in Farsi, voice cracking.

Max recognized the word for freedom. "You're safe," he said gently, stepping forward with his hands raised to show no threat. "The soldiers are gone." He reached into the man's mind and planted a visual of the rebels coming to free him.

The man's eyes unfocused briefly, and a ripple of calm spread across his features as Max impressed in his mind the notion of safety and freedom.

The man sagged in relief. "Thank you."

Ell-rom came closer, steadying the man's elbow to prevent him from collapsing.

With a nod from Yamanu, he led the guy out of the corridor and away from the gore, then transferred him into Jade's team's care.

The second cell's lock opened as readily and smoothly. The occupant, a young man barely out of his teens, was hiding under the bed.

They repeated the routine from the first cell, and soon, they were on to the next.

Max was almost as impatient and anxious to find Kyra as Jasmine was, and he explained it by his need to bring her to safety and get out of enemy territory.

Jasmine approached the next door. "Three is a lucky number, right?" She peeked through the window. "It's a woman." Her voice cracked.

Max's gut clenched in anticipation as the lock slid open.

A whimper sounded from inside the cell, the sound cutting through Max like a knife.

Dark hair was spread across the dingy pillow, and her face was gaunt, but he knew her instantly.

Kyra.

Even without having met her, he knew. A flood of recognition and an inexplicable pull hit him hard in the chest.

"Dear Fates..." he whispered, swallowing. "What did they do to you?"

Yamanu moved forward and then motioned for Ell-rom to come closer. "We need to snap these cuffs without hurting her."

Max didn't answer, stepping closer.

Kyra appeared barely conscious, lips parted as if she was trying to breathe through a parched throat. Her cheeks were sunken, and fresh bruises colored her wrists where the metal cuffs bit into tender flesh.

"Kyra," Max said softly, crouching next to her and reaching out with trembling fingers to brush the hair away from her face. A raw wave of protectiveness overtook him. He'd never felt anything quite like it, a fierce, almost possessive need to ensure no more harm could come to her. "We are getting you out."

She stirred, blinking up with bleary eyes, pupils dilated from drugs. "Who?" she croaked.

"Don't try to speak." Max leaned in, ignoring the dryness in his own mouth. "You are free."

"Not yet," Yamanu said. "But if you move aside, she will be."

Reluctantly, Max straightened to allow access.

Ell-rom and Yamanu sprang into action. Their formidable combined strength was barely enough to snap the steel links of the chains, which fell away with a harsh clang.

They could now move Kyra's limbs, but the cuffs were harder to snap.

Yamanu decided to take Kyra as she was. "We'll have the tools and the time to deal with the cuffs on the flight."

A soft whimper from behind him drew Max's attention away from Kyra to her daughter.

Jasmine stood in the doorway, her hand pressed to her mouth and her eyes leaking tears.

Max wished he hadn't let the doctor fall into stasis so mercifully. He would have relished the opportunity to wake him up and inflict hell upon him endlessly.

A faint moan escaped Kyra's lips. Then, with what seemed like a monumental effort, she lifted her trembling arms toward Max, voice cracking, "Y-you... came for me...?"

He was confused, but he leaned down and took her into his arms. "I came for you, Kyra. You're safe now."

Footsteps approached from behind, and then Jasmine uttered a choked sob. "So, it's true."

Max had a good idea why Jasmine was

sounding so shocked. Kyra looked the same age as her daughter. She was immortal.

Kyra's gaze flicked to Jasmine, eyes widening with a strangled gasp, and then her arms spasmed, and she abruptly went limp in Max's arms.

"What happened?" Jasmine sounded panicked.

"She just fainted," Max said, lowering Kyra gently back on the bed. "Seeing you must have been too much of a shock." His eyes darted around the room, searching for a blanket he could cover Kyra with, but there was nothing, and her skin was ice cold. The only thing she had on was a dirty shift and he suspected she had nothing under that.

He took off his tactical vest and then removed the thick sweater he was wearing underneath, leaving just a white T-shirt. Gently, he pulled the sweater over Kyra's head and then guided her arms into the sleeves. The sweater reached her knees, but he had nothing else to cover her legs with.

He was about to lift Kyra into his arms when Ell-rom reached for her. "I'll carry her."

A wave of frustration mingled with longing coursed through Max. He wanted to hold Kyra, cradle her battered body in his arms, and offer reassurance, but he had no right to her, and Ell-rom was just taking care of his mate's mother.

Arguing about who was going to take Kyra to the helicopters was ridiculous.

Jasmine, tears glistening in her eyes, brushed

her mother's hair from her brow. "Dear Mother of All Life, thank you for keeping her alive."

As Ell-rom carried Kyra out of the cell, a stab of jealousy—or something akin to it—twisted in Max's chest, but he beat it down and then strangled it for good measure. Now was not the time for weird, protective instincts to come out and cloud his judgment.

55

JASMINE

Jasmine glanced at Ell-rom, who was walking just behind her, his hand resting on the handgun holstered at his side. He detested the violence even more than she did, and she wished she could whisk him away from it all.

Heck, she wished she'd had the foresight to insist that he stay in the village, but he wouldn't have agreed, and she needed to be here when they found her mother.

So far, the two prisoners they'd freed were men, and she prayed that the next door would be her mother's.

When they reached the third door, Jasmine moved up anxiously to be the one looking through the barred peep-glass at the top of it even before they got it open. "It's a woman," she whispered hoarsely.

When Max opened the door, Jasmine lost her

nerve and did not dare enter the room for fear the woman was not her mother. The disappointment might undo her. But then she heard Max say her mother's name and still couldn't move a muscle.

Would Kyra recognize her?

Did she even want her abandoned daughter to find her?

Would she be disappointed in her like her father always was?

Ell-rom re-emerged from the room, placing a reassuring hand on the small of her back. His calming presence and touch finally got her moving into the cell, where Max was kneeling next to the bed.

Was it even a real bed?

It looked more like a torture device, and the chains lying in pieces on the floor weren't there for decorative purposes.

Ell-rom and Yamanu had freed her mother from the chains that had shackled her to the bed, but Max was still blocking her from view.

But then Max shifted.

A slim woman wearing a thin, stained shift lay motionless on the bed, her long dark hair spilled across a pillow that was the thickness of a pancake, the strands matted with dried sweat.

Jasmine's pulse quickened.

The woman turned and lifted her trembling arms toward Max. "Y-you... came for me...?"

It was her mother, exactly as she remembered

her from her childhood. Well, no, not exactly. She was leaner now, more muscled, but still young. She hadn't aged at all.

"I came for you, Kyra," Max said softly. "You're safe now."

A ragged sob escaped Jasmine's throat. "So, it's true." She couldn't manage more than that, pressing a hand to her mouth to stifle a cry.

Her mother's ageless beauty had been frozen in time.

Jasmine's eyes flooded with tears, burning hot. She couldn't tell if they sprang from relief, shock, or the heartbreak of seeing her mother in such a state. She inched closer.

Max was murmuring something soothing, wiping hair away from Kyra's face.

Kyra's lashes fluttered, her lips parted in a silent gasp. Her gaze, dazed and half-lucid, skimmed over Max with a flicker of trust in her eyes—an instinct that seemed to tell her that she was safe with him. Then her focus wavered, drifting past him. Slowly, as if through fog, Kyra locked on to Jasmine's face.

Jasmine's whole body stilled under that faintly familiar gaze. A hundred emotions collided in her chest, jamming into a single heartbeat.

She wanted to gather her mother in her arms and never let go.

But before she could do more, Kyra's features crumpled with a wild, desperate confusion, and then, like a candle snuffed out, she passed out—head lolling sideways, body going limp in Max's arms.

A strangled sob escaped Jasmine's throat. "What happened?"

"She just fainted," Max said. "Seeing you must have been too much of a shock."

Ell-rom placed a supportive hand on her shoulder.

Jasmine could only nod, words failing her.

With gentle care, Max let go of Kyra and unclipped something from his tactical vest, setting it aside. Then he pulled his sweater over his head, leaving only his T-shirt. He carefully clothed Kyra, like one would a fragile flower, with the sweater. Jasmine's chest constricted at the gentle gesture.

And to think she'd thought he was callous when he'd been so unfriendly to her on the cruise, when he could manage such tenderness for a woman he'd never met, especially after the bloody battle he'd fought.

He tugged the sweater down to cover Kyra's thighs. It was big enough to swallow most of her, even though she was nearly as tall as Jasmine.

She turned to Ell-rom. "Can you please carry my mother?"

"Of course." Ell-rom stepped forward, but it took Max a long moment to move aside and allow him access.

As Max put his tactical vest back on, Ell-rom

gently slid his arms around Kyra and lifted her off the bed. Her head rolled to rest against his shoulder.

Jasmine brushed her fingertips over Kyra's brow, swallowing back tears. "I can't believe she's real and that we actually found her."

As Ell-rom carried her mother out of the cell, Max and Yamanu followed them out into the corridor.

Max handed the keycard to Yamanu. "We need to pick up the pace." He glanced at his watch. "We barely have any time left."

Jasmine turned. "We can't just leave them here to fend for themselves. We need to help these people." She gestured to the corridor. "The older guy from the first cell could barely walk. Others might be in worse shape than that. There could be women in here."

A muscle in Yamanu's cheek twitched. "This isn't what we came here for, Jasmine," he said as calmly and gently as he could. "We have your mother—that was our mission. We don't have the time or resources to do anything else. Reinforcements are probably already on the way, and we can't risk being here when they arrive."

"We could take them with us," Jasmine said.

He looked puzzled. "And what? Leave them in Turkey? I said we'd bust them out of their cells. They'll have to figure out the rest. If we stay too long, we might lose everything. You understand that, right? We can't save everyone."

56

MAX

Jasmine glared at Yamanu. "Fine. But we should contact the rebels and tell them to come for their people."

It wasn't a bad idea, but it also wasn't something they could do. Perhaps Turner had contacts who knew someone in the Kurdish resistance.

Yamanu relented. "I'll see what I can do. But first, we are getting out of here."

They continued down each cell, time becoming critically short.

Ell-rom shifted Kyra's weight in his arms, and the sudden movement must have jolted her because she moaned. Max was immediately there, nearly pushing Jasmine aside, and then Kyra's eyes opened, but her pupils were so dilated that Max could barely see the whites.

Kyra's lips parted. A shallow, raspy breath. She

tried to raise an arm but only managed a weak twitch of the hand.

"What is it?" Jasmine asked.

"Twelve," Kyra murmured, and then, with a surprising surge of strength, she twisted in Ell-rom's arms, and her eyes focused on Max. "Twelve—get the woman in cell twelve." The words tore out of her in a desperate rasp but in perfect, nearly accent-free English. "Take her."

"I will," Max promised.

Now that he knew there was another female prisoner, there was no way he was leaving her in this place, especially if she was in the same state as Kyra.

It complicated things, but his conscience wouldn't let him leave a woman behind.

Kyra's mouth opened again, but no sound emerged, and her eyes rolled, consciousness flickering out like a candle. She slumped, limp again in Ell-rom's arms.

"You will have to carry her to the helicopter," Max told Ell-rom.

"I'm well aware of that. She weighs very little."

Max wondered if she'd lost weight in captivity, and his anger rose at the way she'd been treated by the so-called doctor. He was looking forward to interrogating the bastard where he could return the favor a thousand times over.

The satisfying music of doors being swung open continued, and when Max turned to look at the next prisoner liberated, he was surprised when, a moment later, one of the Kra-ell who was helping them to expedite the process emerged with a half-conscious young woman in his arms. The captive sagged against Anton's hold.

Just like Kyra, the woman was wearing a thin shift that used to be white but had turned a dingy gray from overuse. She was pale, her skin covered in goosebumps from the cold, but he'd already given his sweater to Kyra, and he had nothing else he could offer the woman.

"Why is she so heavily drugged?" he asked no one in particular, but the Kra-ell must have thought that he was asking him and shrugged.

"How should I know?" Anton said. "What do you want me to do with her?"

Was this the woman in cell twelve that Kyra had asked him to take?

Max released a resigned breath. "We're taking her with us. Which cell number did you free this one from?" he asked, just to be sure.

"Six," Anton said.

Damn. So now they were taking three females with them. Kyra was coming back with them to the village or the keep, but they had no reason to take the other females all the way to California.

"You will have to carry her to the helicopter. We'll figure out the rest once we're airborne."

Anton's brows rose, but before he could

answer, Yamanu emerged with another limp young woman in his arms.

Max sighed. "Please tell me that you got her from cell number twelve."

Yamanu frowned, looked back the way he came from, and then shook his head. "All the cells in that part of the corridor are single numbers."

Damn.

What had they been doing in this place? Trafficking?

That actually made perfect sense. It explained why the Doomers had bothered with this outpost in the middle of nowhere.

But why here?

"I think we should heed Jasmine's request. Kyra gained consciousness momentarily and emphatically had me promise that we would liberate the woman in cell number twelve as well, and I promised her I would. I think we should take all the females we find in these cells with us."

Yamanu nodded. "Of course. We can't leave them to fend for themselves." He looked down at the young woman in his arms. "They are so severely drugged that they are barely conscious. I've already told the pilots to be ready to pick us up from the courtyard."

Anton looked at the girl and shook his head. "What if we run out of space in the helicopters?"

Max wasn't going to leave any women behind. "We have enough room. These girls don't weigh much. In the meantime, put her down next to the wall." He turned to Yamanu. "We should also alert the pilots for the extra cargo."

Yamanu set the girl down next to the others and moved aside to contact the pilots.

Max flagged Rishba over. "We need to find some blankets to cover the prisoners with. They will freeze outside."

"I will look," she said and then headed to search.

The next two to emerge from that side of the corridor were thankfully men, and their rescuers pointed them in the direction of the stairs.

A few moments later, the Kra-ell female returned with a stack of thin gray blankets and, without waiting for directions from him, wrapped each of the young women sitting on the floor with a blanket.

Jasmine took one to cover Kyra's legs, tucking the blanket all around her.

"Let's go to cell number twelve." He motioned for Anton to come with him.

He followed the numbers until he reached the right door and peeked inside through the small window to verify Kyra's information.

The woman inside was in a similar situation to how they had found Kyra, chained to a bed.

Max opened the door and strode inside.

Anton followed him. "It stinks in here."

He wasn't wrong, and Max grimaced at the stench of old blood, sweat, and fear.

The single fluorescent light revealed a metal-framed bed, identical to the one Kyra had been strapped to, and a woman, whose arms and legs were chained the same way Kyra's had been. Her dark hair spilled over the pillow in a disheveled mess, and her face was turned away from the door despite all the commotion outside.

Panic gripped Max. Were they too late? Was the woman dead?

He stepped closer, and then he heard it.

The faint sound of her heart beating.

The woman was alive.

She was either drugged out of her mind or had suffered so much that she'd turned apathetic and stopped reacting to anything.

He intended to say something, to reassure her, but he only knew a few words in Farsi, and he had a feeling that this time his tone of voice would not be enough.

Anton walked over to the bed and gripped the thick chain. Muscles bunched beneath his uniform as he threw his full Kra-ell strength into a savage pull. Metal screamed against metal, and with a sharp crack that echoed through the cell, one of the links twisted and snapped apart.

The woman remained partially turned away as if nothing had happened.

Maybe she couldn't move?

What if her muscles had seized up from being

forced to lie in the same position for Fates knew how long?

Anton let the broken chain drop to the floor and started on another one. "Except for Kyra, the other women weren't bound. The men weren't either."

Something about this prisoner was different, important enough to keep her under extra restraint, just like Kyra.

Max slid a hand over the heavy padlock chaining the occupant's left wrist and shot a quick questioning glance at Anton.

"I've got it." The Kra-ell walked over, and Max moved aside to give him room to work.

Curiosity getting the better of him, Max walked around the bed so he could take a look at the woman's face, and then froze, feeling his blood turn to ice.

He would have recognized her anywhere, even thin and abused, he knew that face so well.

"Fenella?"

Her lashes parted, revealing familiar dark eyes that seemed to widen in the same moment they locked on to his. Pain, confusion, and a flicker of terror waged across her expression.

She sucked in a breath. "Max?" She stared in disbelief. "Am I dead?"

COMING UP NEXT
The Children of the Gods Book 93
DARK REBEL'S RECKONING

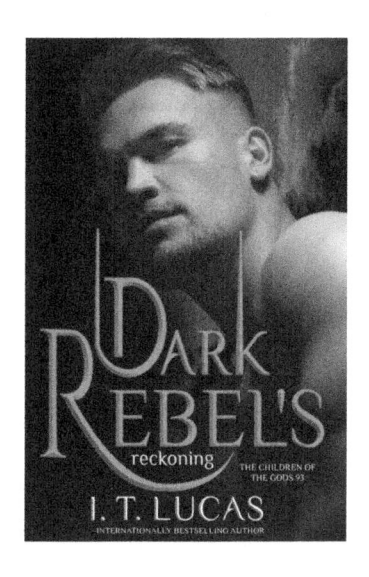

Torn between intense emotions, fragile alliances, and buried secrets poised to upend her future, Kyra is driven to uncover the truth behind the darkness she once believed she'd left behind.

JOIN THE VIP CLUB
To find out what's included in your free membership, flip to the last page.

NOTE

Dear reader,

I hope my stories have added a little joy to your day. If you have a moment to add some to mine, you can help spread the word about the Children Of The Gods series by telling your friends and penning a review. Your recommendations are the most powerful way to inspire new readers to explore the series.

Thank you,

Isabell

Also by I. T. Lucas

THE CHILDREN OF THE GODS ORIGINS
1: GODDESS'S CHOICE
2: GODDESS'S HOPE

THE CHILDREN OF THE GODS
DARK STRANGER
1: DARK STRANGER THE DREAM
2: DARK STRANGER REVEALED
3: DARK STRANGER IMMORTAL

DARK ENEMY
4: DARK ENEMY TAKEN
5: DARK ENEMY CAPTIVE
6: DARK ENEMY REDEEMED

KRI & MICHAEL'S STORY
6.5: MY DARK AMAZON

DARK WARRIOR
7: DARK WARRIOR MINE
8: DARK WARRIOR'S PROMISE
9: DARK WARRIOR'S DESTINY
10: DARK WARRIOR'S LEGACY

DARK GUARDIAN
11: DARK GUARDIAN FOUND
12: DARK GUARDIAN CRAVED

13: Dark Guardian's Mate

Dark Angel
14: Dark Angel's Obsession
15: Dark Angel's Seduction
16: Dark Angel's Surrender

Dark Operative
17: Dark Operative: A Shadow of Death
18: Dark Operative: A Glimmer of Hope
19: Dark Operative: The Dawn of Love

Dark Survivor
20: Dark Survivor Awakened
21: Dark Survivor Echoes of Love
22: Dark Survivor Reunited

Dark Widow
23: Dark Widow's Secret
24: Dark Widow's Curse
25: Dark Widow's Blessing

Dark Dream
26: Dark Dream's Temptation
27: Dark Dream's Unraveling
28: Dark Dream's Trap

Dark Prince
29: Dark Prince's Enigma
30: Dark Prince's Dilemma

31: Dark Prince's Agenda

Dark Queen
32: Dark Queen's Quest
33: Dark Queen's Knight
34: Dark Queen's Army

Dark Spy
35: Dark Spy Conscripted
36: Dark Spy's Mission
37: Dark Spy's Resolution

Dark Overlord
38: Dark Overlord New Horizon
39: Dark Overlord's Wife
40: Dark Overlord's Clan

Dark Choices
41: Dark Choices The Quandary
42: Dark Choices Paradigm Shift
43: Dark Choices The Accord

Dark Secrets
44: Dark Secrets Resurgence
45: Dark Secrets Unveiled
46: Dark Secrets Absolved

Dark Haven
47: Dark Haven Illusion
48: Dark Haven Unmasked

49: Dark Haven Found

Dark Power
50: Dark Power Untamed
51: Dark Power Unleashed
52: Dark Power Convergence

Dark Memories
53: Dark Memories Submerged
54: Dark Memories Emerge
55: Dark Memories Restored

Dark Hunter
56: Dark Hunter's Query
57: Dark Hunter's Prey
58: Dark Hunter's Boon

Dark God
59: Dark God's Avatar
60: Dark God's Reviviscence
61: Dark God Destinies Converge

Dark Whispers
62: Dark Whispers From The Past
63: Dark Whispers From Afar
64: Dark Whispers From Beyond

Dark Gambit
65: Dark Gambit The Pawn
66: Dark Gambit The Play

67: Dark Gambit Reliance

Dark Alliance
68: Dark Alliance Kindred Souls
69: Dark Alliance Turbulent Waters
70: Dark Alliance Perfect Storm

Dark Healing
71: Dark Healing Blind Justice
72: Dark Healing Blind Trust
73: Dark healing Blind Curve

Dark Encounters
74: Dark Encounters of the Close Kind
75: Dark Encounters of the Unexpected Kind
76: Dark Encounters of the Fated Kind

Dark Voyage
77: Dark Voyage Matters of the Heart
78: <u>Dark Voyage Matters of the Mind</u>
<u>79: Dark Voyage Matters of the Soul</u>

Dark Horizon
80: Dark Horizon New Dawn
81: Dark Horizon Eclipse of the Heart
82: Dark Horizon The Witching Hour

Dark Witch
83: Dark Witch: Entangled Fates
84: Dark Witch: Twin Destinies

85: Dark Witch: Resurrection

Dark Awakening
86: Dark Awakening: New World
87: Dark Awakening Hidden Currents
88: Dark Awakening Echoes of Destiny

Dark Princess
89: Dark Princess: Shadows
90: Dark Princess Emerging
91: Dark Princess Ascending

Dark Rebel
92: Dark Rebel's Mystery
93: Dark Rebel's Reckoning

PERFECT MATCH

Vampire's Consort
King's Chosen
Captain's Conquest
The Thief Who Loved Me
My Merman Prince
The Dragon King
My Werewolf Romeo
The Channeler's Companion
The Valkyrie & The Witch
Adina and the Magic Lamp

TRANSLATIONS

DIE ERBEN DER GÖTTER
Dark Stranger
1- Dark Stranger Der Traum
2- Dark Stranger Die Offenbarung
3- Dark Stranger Unsterblich

Dark Enemy
4- Dark Enemy Entführt
5- Dark Enemy Gefangen
6- Dark Enemy Erlöst

Dark Warrior
7- Dark Warrior Meine Sehnsucht
8- Dark Warrior – Dein Versprechen
9- Dark Warrior - Unser Schicksal
10- Dark Warrior-Unser Vermächtnis

LOS HIJOS DE LOS DIOSES

EL OSCURO DESCONOCIDO
1: EL OSCURO DESCONOCIDO EL SUEÑO
2: EL OSCURO DESCONOCIDO REVELADO

3: EL OSCURO DESCONOCIDO INMORTAL
EL OSCURO ENEMIGO
4- EL OSCURO ENEMIGO CAPTURADO
5 - EL OSCURO ENEMIGO CAUTIVO
6- EL OSCURO ENEMIGO REDIMIDO

LES ENFANTS DES DIEUX
DARK STRANGER
1- Dark Stranger Le rêve
2- Dark Stranger La révélation
3- Dark Stranger L'immortelle

The Children of the Gods Series Sets

Books 1-3: Dark Stranger trilogy—Includes a bonus short story: **The Fates Take a Vacation**
Books 4-6: Dark Enemy Trilogy —Includes a bonus short story—**The Fates' Post-Wedding Celebration**

Books 7-10: Dark Warrior Tetralogy
Books 11-13: Dark Guardian Trilogy
Books 14-16: Dark Angel Trilogy
Books 17-19: Dark Operative Trilogy
Books 20-22: Dark Survivor Trilogy
Books 23-25: Dark Widow Trilogy

Books 26-28: Dark Dream Trilogy
Books 29-31: Dark Prince Trilogy
Books 32-34: Dark Queen Trilogy
Books 35-37: Dark Spy Trilogy
Books 38-40: Dark Overlord Trilogy
Books 41-43: Dark Choices Trilogy
Books 44-46: Dark Secrets Trilogy
Books 47-49: Dark Haven Trilogy
Books 50-52: Dark Power Trilogy
Books 53-55: Dark Memories Trilogy
Books 56-58: Dark Hunter Trilogy
Books 59-61: Dark God Trilogy
Books 62-64: Dark Whispers Trilogy
Books 65-67: Dark Gambit Trilogy
Books 68-70: Dark Alliance Trilogy
Books 71-73: Dark Healing Trilogy
Books 74-76: Dark Encounters Trilogy
Books 77-79: Dark Voyage Trilogy
Books 80-81: Dark Horizon Trilogy

MEGA SETS

The Children of the Gods: Books 1-6
INCLUDES CHARACTER LISTS
The Children of the Gods: Books 6.5-10

Perfect Match Bundle 1

CHECK OUT THE SPECIALS ON

ITLUCAS.COM
(https://itlucas.com/specials)

FOR EXCLUSIVE PEEKS AT UPCOMING RELEASES &
A FREE I. T. LUCAS COMPANION BOOK

JOIN MY *VIP CLUB* AND GAIN ACCESS TO THE VIP PORTAL AT ITLUCAS.COM

TO JOIN, GO TO:
http://eepurl.com/blMTpD

Find out more details about what's included with your free membership on the book's last page.

TRY THE CHILDREN OF THE GODS SERIES ON
AUDIBLE

2 FREE audiobooks with your new Audible subscription!

FOR EXCLUSIVE PEEKS AT UPCOMING RELEASES &
A FREE I. T. LUCAS COMPANION BOOK

Join my *VIP Club* and gain access to the VIP portal at itlucas.com
To Join, go to:
http://eepurl.com/blMTpD

INCLUDED IN YOUR FREE MEMBERSHIP:

YOUR VIP PORTAL

- Read preview chapters of upcoming releases.
- Listen to Goddess's Choice narration by Charles Lawrence
- Exclusive content offered only to my VIPs.

FREE I.T. LUCAS COMPANION INCLUDES:

- Goddess's Choice Part 1
- Perfect Match: Vampire's Consort (A standalone Novella)
- Interview Q & A
- Character Charts

If you're already a subscriber and you are not getting my emails, your provider is sending them to your junk folder, and you are missing out on important updates. To fix that, add isabell@itlucas.com to your email contacts or your email VIP list.

**Check out the specials at
https://www.itlucas.com/specials**

Made in the USA
Middletown, DE
23 April 2025